ASSAULT AND BATTING

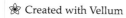

ASSAULT AND BATTING

A TAYLOR QUINN QUILT SHOP MYSTERY

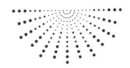

TESS ROTHERY

ALSO BY TESS ROTHERY

The Taylor Quinn Quilt Shop Mysteries

Assault and Batting

Bound and Deceased

Cups and Killers

Dutch Hex

Emperor's New Quilt

Fruit Basket Upset

Good Bones

CHAPTER ONE

*A*t 11:15 in the morning the chimes over the door to Flour Sax Quilt Shop jingled a welcome. The sound was a part of Taylor Quinn's biological clock. On hearing it, she stood straighter, smiled broader, and her brain was filled with quilting knowledge. Taylor had grown up here with quilt fabric in her blood, and seven years away had done nothing to change that.

Grandma Quinny, Taylor's paternal grandmother, sauntered through the door, her sunglasses on the end of her nose. Her flowing, chiffon kimono complimented her full, motherly figure. Her hair color had softened through the years as the gray slowly took over, one of those subtle changes Taylor wouldn't have noticed if she hadn't been gone so long. Grandma Quinny's cheeks were full and rosy and the smile she offered Taylor was one of love and sympathy. "Taylor, dear, it's good you've opened the shop again." She set her purse on the counter.

Taylor hadn't been sure about opening up this morning. Her mother's funeral had been two days before, and she and her sister, Belle, were still existing in a fog of flower arrangements and potluck leftovers.

"I was afraid you wouldn't be in this morning. I don't think the girl can handle this place on her own."

The Girl. Grandma Quinny did call Belle that a lot. Taylor couldn't remember why she used to think it was cute.

"Belle needs to focus on school." Taylor had sent her off this morning, hoping it was the right thing to do. Routine was supposed to be good after a crisis.

"Belle?" There was a sincere lack of recognition on Grandma's face, as the light dawned slowly. "You have her working here now? Your mom never did. I was thinking of that Roxy." Grandma leaned in and lowered her voice. "I think she might use drugs."

"Roxy doesn't use drugs." Roxy had been the right-hand man at Flour Sax for at least ten years. She was a little rough around the edges, but as clean and sober as they come.

Grandma lifted an eyebrow.

"Belle and I have a lot to figure out still. I'm not sure what Mom had Belle do around here, but I always worked in the store when I was her age." Taylor folded a paper label around a roll of pastel vintage print cotton, a fat quarter she had just cut from the end of a discontinued bolt. It wasn't urgent work, but it felt practical.

Grandma Quinny's sunglass lenses had slowly faded to clear glass while they were talking. She furrowed her brows and looked around the store. "You'll have your work cut out for you, won't you?"

Taylor rocked her head side to side, a sort of acknowledgment that said nothing. The not-so-veiled criticism of the family shop didn't bother her. Since the call ten days ago that her mom had drowned on a weekend away with her girlfriends, Taylor hadn't felt much of anything.

"Is the house in as bad a way as the shop?" Grandma Quinny's eyes were glued to a dark spot on a ceiling panel.

"The house is fine, and if it's not, I'll take care of it."

"What do you mean you'll take care of it?" Grandma Quinny turned her focused gaze to Taylor. "You haven't done anything foolish, have you?"

"I've come home, Grandma. I need to take care of Belle."

Grandma Quinny frowned, the smile-lines that framed her mouth made the frown so much sadder. "She's already sixteen, isn't she? She'll be heading to college soon."

"In the meantime, she can't live by herself, can she?"

A hacking cough from the back of the shop reminded Taylor that Belle didn't live by herself. Their mom's dad, Grandpa Ernie, wasn't up to running the store, but he was the other adult in the house.

Grandma turned and waved. "Hi, Ernie." Her voice carried well, but Grandpa didn't respond. "Come over for dinner on Friday. The cousins want to see you. It's been two years since you've all been together. You know that, right? Not since baby Hattie was born."

They had all just been together at the funeral, but Taylor could see why it didn't count. That hadn't been a social event. "I'm sorry, Grandma. What time do you want us to come over?"

Grandma Quinny lifted an eyebrow.

"And…would it be okay if we brought Grandpa Ernie? I'd hate for him to be lonely."

Grandma Quinny held her chin up for a moment, then shook her head. "Ernie is always welcome, but darling you are going to have to do something for him. Your mom, rest her soul, wouldn't hear me when I spoke to her about it. He needs more care than she can—than you," she corrected herself, "can give him. It's the dementia."

"I know." Taylor felt her throat closing. She hadn't known about Grandpa Ernie's memory loss before her mom had died, but the last few days something had seemed off with the old guy. He used to be the rock of the family, the man in their lives after her dad had passed away when Taylor was a kid. "I don't want to rush any decisions, for Belle's sake."

"She's not going to make it easy for you, that one." Grandma Quinny looked her granddaughter up and down, clearly assessing what Taylor was made of. "Come by at five thirty on Friday. It's a little early but that's probably better for Ernie."

Taylor leaned over the counter and kissed her soft, warm cheek. "Thanks Grandma. Love you."

Grandma Quinny gave her a squeeze. "I love you too, dear. And we're here for you, whatever you need."

Grandma Quinny swept out of her daughter-in-law's store. Taylor knew she meant well, but after the devastating news of their loss, when her baby sister needed someone to look after her, Grandma Quinny had not called to offer help.

Flour Sax, the little shop Taylor had just inherited in Comfort, Oregon, sat on the corner of Main Street and Love, in a row of tourist friendly stores that included three other quilt shops.

One hundred seventy years ago, pioneer families had gathered on the banks of a little creek in the fertile valley and found it a comfort after the dangerous wagon trip they had just survived. The rolling hills were fertile, like the homes they had left in Missouri, but it was blessedly free from the heat, humidity, and mosquitos.

Comfort Flour Mill popped up almost immediately, providing jobs and prosperity to the town for over a hundred years, but when the railroad closed the Comfort spur in the sixties, the mill followed suit shortly after.

The town seemed to fall apart quickly as families drained out looking for work, but as Yamhill county embraced wine culture, new tourist businesses followed. Flour Sax Quilt Shop was the first, named in honor of the flour and feed sack fabric that had served housewives of the Depression era, as well as the flour mill that had served the town for so long.

Taylor's grandfather had been a tailor, scraping a living together by making bespoke suits for wealthy business owners from around the region, and for politicians who worked in the state capital, just a bit less than an hour away. Her grandma Delma had added quilting cotton and notions to the shop a little bit at a time through the years. One day her section of their shop was the only part making a profit, and Flour Sax Quilt Shop was born.

Three other quilt shops soon followed, along with an antique mall that took up one whole side of Main Street. Residents of Comfort who had survived the lean times were eager to enjoy the tourist money grapes brought to the region.

The house Taylor had just moved back to was a small Craftsman style home in the older part of town, just a couple of blocks down from the shop on Love Street. Farther down Love Street was the Arts and Crafts College where she received her bachelor's in fiber arts.

Comfort College of Art and Craft was a good little school, and part of why the town had leaned in heavily on the quilt shops.

It was a suitably snooty school as well. The kind of place that lent a little panache to the small pioneer community. Comfort might be off the beaten path, but quilters and artists found it worth the drive.

A rattling, comfortable, familiar voice rose from the back of the shop. "You're going to have to do something about that Belle." Grandpa Ernie sat in a threadbare corduroy recliner in his corner of the store nursing black coffee out of an old thermos. The same chair and thermos he had used back when this had been his tailoring shop. "She says she went to school yesterday, but that fellow in the office called again and said she didn't."

That fellow was the vice-principal and Taylor had talked to him twice already since coming home.

The shop was quiet, so Taylor joined Grandpa Ernie. "She's having a really hard time." She sat down on the arm of the old chair and patted her grandpa's shoulder. "I'm going to take her out to dinner tonight. Just the two of us. I think we need some girl time."

He nodded and chewed on his mustache. "What am I supposed to eat?"

"There's soup leftover." Taylor hadn't planned on taking

Belle out, but Grandpa wanted an answer, and she was the kind of girl who answered a problem head on. Her mom dies leaving an underage orphan? She quits her job managing a Joann's Fabrics, sells her condo in Portland, and moves home to raise her sister and run Flour Sax Quilt Shop. Said little sister is acting out due to shock, grief, hormones, and God knows what else? She takes her out to dinner to give Grandpa Ernie a respite.

Taylor's education was in fiber arts and business management. Not teen psychology. But her old friend Maddie Carpenter did have a degree in child and adolescent psychology and was practicing just down the street. Over dinner she'd see if she could convince Belle to make an appointment with Maddie.

Taylor let her hand rest on her grandpa's shoulder. He had been a sport when his wife had overtaken his business many years ago. He liked strong women who ran stuff. Maybe it was because he was a mild man himself and it let him off the hook. Or maybe because strong women who run stuff are pretty awesome. Either way, after her dad had died fighting fires when Taylor was eleven, Grandpa had become the man in her life. A stand-in dad through those rough teen years.

He had been a father figure for her sister too—adopted by her mom on the first anniversary of her dad's death.

Belle had been good for them. They'd needed a reason to be joyful after their loss. Her mom, Grandpa Ernie, and she had managed to come back to life after Belle came to the family.

Until the last year or two she had been their golden headed girl, rosy of cheek and disposition. A bright spot in a world that could get awfully dark.

Now she dyed her hair black and used more eyeliner every morning than Taylor had used in all her life. And that was before they suddenly lost their mom.

Taylor sighed and straightened up. "At least she comes home after school."

"She's not going to school." Grandpa Ernie reiterated his point with a gruff cough.

"At least she comes home. This has been a hard week, Grandpa, but we'll get it together."

He gazed across the displays of gentle fabrics with familiar, comforting patterns. Laura Quinn's death had been one loss too many for Grandpa. First, the son-in-law who was like a son to him, then his parents, one directly after the other. Then his wife. Now his daughter.

Taylor leaned over and kissed the top of his head. A gentle man and a gentleman. Grandpa Ernie hadn't deserved this new loss.

It was far from the end of the school day, but the back door of the shop opened, and her beautiful baby sister slumped in. Belle was hiding behind a shag of hair, and under shapeless black clothes. She wore her old Doc Martens and had a bull ring in her nose, which was new today.

Taylor didn't comment on it. "Hey, Belle, are you thirsty?"

Grandpa Ernie's little area of the shop was by the back door, tucked behind a classroom space. His chair sat comfortably next to a minifridge that was chock full of generic brand soft drinks.

Belle shook her head. She loitered, her gaze on the door to the upstairs apartment.

Taylor went to her and wrapped her in a wordless hug.

Belle inhaled sharply, pushed Taylor away, and went straight back out the door she had just come in by.

It didn't matter that Belle pushed her away every time she did that. Taylor wasn't going to stop. Taylor was absolutely going to err on the side of too many hugs.

"I told you she wasn't in school today." Grandpa Ernie grumped.

BELLE DIDN'T COME BACK to the shop that afternoon. Taylor called her cell, but she didn't answer. Taylor called the home phone, possibly the last one in town, but there was no answer there either.

She'd like to think there wasn't much trouble to get into in Comfort, Oregon, population a couple thousand, but her mother had drowned on sleepy little South Yamhill River. Just about anything could happen, anywhere, to anyone.

The more Taylor tried not to think of Belle throwing herself into the spring-fast water of Bible Creek, just outside of town, the more that was all she could see. She called both numbers more times than was reasonable, then locked up the store. She wouldn't feel right till she could see Belle with her own eyes.

"Closing up early? You kids don't have the kind of work ethic we had. I sat in this shop all day and night making suits for men. And why don't men wear suits anymore? Because you girls turned all the shops into quilt shops. Makes no sense." Grandpa Ernie was muttering, but Taylor could hear.

"Just...closing for a break. I need to talk to Belle for a moment."

"Good luck. She's probably off with that boyfriend of hers. He's no good, that's what I say."

Taylor froze. She swallowed and tried to pull herself together. She wasn't ready to deal with risky behaviors with boys. "Where do they go when they, um, sneak around?"

"Sneak? Who knows? But all those kids go to the diner. Me and Boggy used to go there every afternoon at two, but all those dumb kids go now, and they talk too loud. And sometimes they sit in the back booth and kiss."

"And Jess doesn't send them back to school?" Jess Reuben ran the diner at the end of the Main Street with an iron fist. At least she had when Taylor was a a teen hanging out with a noisy crowd.

Grandpa Ernie harrumphed.

Taylor hustled to the diner.

Belle was tucked into the corner of a back booth with a boy Taylor thought she recognized as Cooper, or maybe Conner,

Dorney. He was clean cut and wore a crisp button-down cambric shirt. Taylor slid into the brown vinyl booth with them.

Belle turned red.

"Hi, Ms. Quinn," Cooper or Conner said.

"Is school out already?" Something about the way those words sounded embarrassed Taylor. Had she suddenly aged two decades?

"Yeah," the boy said. "It gets out at 2:55."

"Ah, um. Yeah. Great." Taylor scratched her ear. She was pretty sure it had only been 1:30 when Belle had swung by earlier. "So, um, anyway, here." She dragged her wallet out and passed it to Belle. "For snacks. Or whatever. I'll be at the shop."

"Okay." Belle looked at the wallet, then at Taylor, with a sly little smile.

"Bye, Ms. Quinn." The boy gave her a kind, sort of condescending, smile.

Taylor hustled back to Flour Sax, embarrassed but glad, but also concerned. Boys like that, the ones with the extra good manners and the pretty smiles, those were the ones you had to worry about. And Taylor hadn't remembered to invite Belle out to dinner.

Six o' clock came slowly. Grandpa had napped, snoring softly in his chair while Taylor faced displays, tidied shelves, and ran the sweeper over their dusty rose indoor/outdoor carpet. When the clock finally released her from working hours, she closed, nudged Grandpa Ernie awake, and took him back home.

Taylor hadn't heard from Belle since her embarrassing visit to the diner. She didn't like to think Belle was avoiding her, but everyone grieves in their own way. They needed their dinner out alone where they could bond and discuss the school attendance thing.

She gave Belle till seven-thirty before she allowed herself to panic. She knew seven-thirty wasn't late but the spontaneous plans she'd made felt urgent.

When Belle hadn't come home by eight, Taylor found her

mom's old cell phone and scrolled through the numbers. She still needed to transfer the contacts to her own phone, but that seemed so…permanent.

There were two numbers for Dorney. Taylor went with the first one.

"Hello?" The voice that answered sounded like it had just woken up.

"Hi, this is Taylor Quinn, I'm looking for my sister Belle."

The person on the other end yawned. "Sorry, we were having family movie night and I fell asleep. I don't know how the kids can watch these shows, so boring."

"Ahh…um…I'm just wondering, have you seen Belle?" Taylor paced her living room, counting the steps in her head to slow her racing brain.

"Belle, your sister wants you." There was a murmur of conversation on the other end.

"Sorry about that." The voice was clearer, more awake now. "I guess she's staying the night here."

"Oh, you guess that, do you?" Taylor's heart felt like it had exploded. Who was this woman and why did she think it was okay for Belle to sleep over with that Conner or Cooper or whoever he was? "Belle's coming home right now, and if you don't send her, I'll come get her."

The voice chuckled again, but it sounded forced. "Calm down. Maybe you didn't know, she stays over all the time. Your mom didn't mind."

"I'm not my mom."

"No, you're not Belle's mom." The voice suddenly went stern. "And I don't think it's real bright of you to start acting like you are."

"Who am I speaking to?" Taylor turned on her retail management voice. She knew how to deal with difficult people. She just needed to settle in and do it. t

"Sissy Dorney. Surely you knew that, since you called." Sissy paused, then started again with a softer, more sympathetic voice.

"You're under a lot of stress right now, but that is no reason to upset the kids. Disruption to your sister's normal life won't be good for her." There was an emphasis on the word sister that stuck out. As though being sisters meant Taylor had no right to set boundaries.

"And her normal life is staying nights with her boyfriend? You think that's okay for a high schooler?"

"Her boyfriend?" Sissy laughed. "Cooper and Belle aren't dating. They're just best friends."

"Sure, I'll believe that when I see it with my own eyes."

"Oh yeah?" Sissy was on the defense again. "My son has been dating Dayton Reuben for over two years."

Taylor paused. In this world Dayton could be a boy or a girl. If a girl, then Cooper was most likely a two-timer. If a boy, then obviously it was no big deal for Belle to stay over.

"I don't know who that is." That seemed like a safe answer.

"Dayton is the love of my son's life and Cooper would never…"

There was a riot of voices on her end of the phone. Something banged and then a door slammed.

"Never mind. Belle's on her way home. Cooper's bringing her, but listen, you can't just show up out of the blue and start bossing teenage girls around. It's not how this works."

Taylor wanted to hang up on this woman. Sissy Dorney was only a few years older than her. Sissy's parents owned the auto body shop down the road. Her aunt sold jewelry in the antique mall across from Flour Sax Quilt Shop. Sissy had dated one of her professors at the crafts college, but then eloped with a truck driver. The truck driver ran the family auto body shop now.

Sissy had been an anonymous voice, but when she said her name, the flood of information rolled over Taylor.

This town was small.

Everyone knew everything.

Just not what their own sisters were doing in their spare time.

It only took fifteen minutes for Cooper and Belle to show up.

They walked in like it was their house and settled into the slip-covered couch.

"We need to talk," Cooper said in his smooth, so polite voice.

"I agree." Taylor stood in front of the TV arms crossed.

"My mom loved Dayton, but we broke up over spring break." Cooper held Belle's hand in both of his. "Dayton goes to church with us. I haven't told Mom that we broke up. She'll flip her lid."

"If Belle stays nights at your house, I'm going to flip my lid."

He gave Belle's hand what he thought was a subtle squeeze and dropped it. "I just wanted to be honest with you. If you decide to tell Mom, I understand." He stood up and offered his hand to Taylor.

"I'm not doing your dirty work for you, kid." Taylor shook his hand. He gave hers a squeeze too. "Be honest with your mom and be honorable with my sister."

Taylor didn't know how to describe the sound Belle made from the couch, but if you could verbalize an eye roll, she did.

"Head home." Taylor walked to the front door and opened it. "Belle and I need to talk."

When the door was securely shut behind him, Belle spoke up. "I'm not sleeping with Cooper. He's my best friend and has been since we were six. He thinks he's in love with me, but he's wrong. The important thing for you to remember is even if I was, it's none of your business." Despite the bravado, her big blue eyes seemed childlike.

Taylor chewed her bottom lip. "There's only one thing I really want to know right now."

Belle stiffened.

"Is Dayton a girl or a boy?"

Belle's lips curved into a knowing, sneaky smile.

They stared at each other, neither giving in.

"The restaurant at Berry Noir Vineyards doesn't close till eleven. Let's go get some dinner."

Belle made a face that indicated she was both bemused and

knew the real definition of the word bemused, but she followed Taylor out to their mom's ten year old Audi.

BERRY NOIR WAS a small family run vineyard five miles East of town. Their restaurant was nicer than the local diner, and the atmosphere more conducive to heart to heart talks.

And yet Belle sat across the small square table in the atmospherically lit dining room grim-faced as though Taylor was attempting to drop her off at prison for the weekend.

Taylor ordered a plate of mushroom and spinach ravioli, waited through the silence and then ordered the same thing for Belle.

"Grandpa Ernie is worried." The kitchen at Berry Noir wasn't fast, so they had a long time to talk before the waiter returned. "And so am I."

Belle's mouth pursed, a moody version of the duck face that had been popular when Taylor was her age.

"Do you want to take some time off from school? Everyone will understand."

"No one understands." Her words were muffled, and her eyes downcast.

"I do, anyway. We're in this together."

Belle looked up at her, one eye narrowed suspiciously. "Are we?"

"I'm here, aren't I?" Taylor attempted a warm smile. It was a challenge as this new version of her sister frankly terrified her.

"I suppose you think I'll say, 'You're not my mom'."

"I don't expect anything." Taylor wondered if Belle could tell she was lying. She had totally figured that would be Belle's next line.

Belle unfolded her napkin and then folded it again, but smaller. "My mom wasn't your mom."

"Belle…"

"I'm not talking about my birth mom. I'm talking about *Mom*. She was a different woman raising me. For like twelve years she was a married woman, a woman with a kid. That was you. When your dad died, she changed. She got me, and that changed her too. I was only five years old when you left for college. All of a sudden she was just this lady—a single mom all alone with a really young kid."

"But that's what's so wonderful about you. Mom wasn't alone."

Belle scrunched her mouth. "We were both alone. She was in the shop every day and I was upstairs in the apartment with Gramps."

"Yeah...but I mean, she was a single mom for me too. From when I was eleven until I was seventeen. That's a lot of growing up."

"You all had me though, like a pet or something, to play with. What did I have? After you left, just...Gramps."

A shiver of defensiveness ran up Taylor's spine. Grandpa Ernie was awesome. Or, had been awesome. He had aged a lot in the last year. Either way, when Belle had been upstairs chilling with Grandpa Ernie, he had still been fun.

"It's okay to tell me this. I need to know what it was like for you." Taylor tried hard to remember anything from her psychology elective in high school. Allowing Belle to talk without judgement was the best she could come up with.

"When you went to college you just...left."

"I mean..." Taylor smiled naturally this time. "I was just at the other end of Love Street at the Comfort College of Art and Craft. It's not like I wasn't around."

"But you weren't around. We went to your gallery shows, and I saw you at the shop sometimes, if you were working, but you never came home. Not for lunch, not for a weekend, not even for Christmas."

Taylor cringed, remembering the holidays with her college boyfriend and his family. "I came home in the summer...."

"No. You didn't. You stayed on campus."

"But I worked at the shop."

"But you took classes and stayed on campus. Working in the shop during the summer wasn't the same. Then you moved to Portland for grad school and work and stuff and we really never saw you again."

"Oh, come on..." Taylor sipped her water, trying hard to change her attitude. "I'm sorry. You're right. I didn't come home enough."

"Never on my birthday."

"I'm sorry."

Belle continued, her voice tired and young. "Never on Christmas, Thanksgiving or Easter."

"We were never much of a holiday family after Dad died." Taylor glanced around for the waiter, dying for an interruption. He was headed their way, laden with their plates.

"I wouldn't know the difference. I wasn't around before he died."

"I'm sorry."

The waiter joined them, asked something about cheese, and left them to flounder.

"You went to your grandparents for your last birthday." Belle stared at her plate like she didn't recognize it.

"I wanted you to come." Taylor also wanted to dive into the food to escape her guilt.

Belle was good at this. She made it sound like Taylor had abandoned her mom and sister.

But that wasn't the way it had felt. She'd just taken the opportunities as they came. Jobs, houses, trips with friends. Each decision had made sense in the moment. Even going to her grandparents for her birthday dinner instead of seeing her mom and Belle first. "They're your grandparents too." Taylor stabbed a little square of pasta.

"No, they aren't. Don't you understand that? I never met

your dad. He wasn't my dad. His parents don't want me." Belle also stabbed a ravioli. Then she ate it, slowly.

Taylor exhaled, glad for the break.

It didn't last long enough.

"Do you know what happens when I run into them in town?"

Taylor ate another ravioli, not wanting to hear what Belle had to say about their other grandparents.

"They don't even say hi."

"Oh, Belle…" Taylor reached for her hand, but Belle gripped her napkin.

"They shop at Bible Creek Quilt and Gift. They never come into Flour Sax."

"I'll talk to them. I'll make this right." Taylor's fork hovered over her plate. The coldness between Grandma and Grandpa Quinny and Belle had been obvious from the start, but that was sort of who they were. They weren't baby people. They warmed up to kids, bigger kids. They went to sports games, but Belle hadn't played sports. They had big open hearts for teenagers and young adults.

"They aren't wrong…Todd wasn't my dad." Belle stared at Taylor with a challenge in her eyes.

Todd Quinn had been Laura's only husband, her true love. Laura and Taylor had told Belle stories of him, his bravery in the face of danger, his funny falsetto singing voice. They had kept his memory fresh by sharing him with her. He was gone, but he was Belle's dad too. That's how Taylor and her mom had seen it.

He would have loved her.

"Belle…"

Taylor's dinner stared at her, daring her to remember her appetite, but it was gone. She missed her dad every day. Every single day for the last eighteen years. It hurt to hear Belle talk like this, but she wouldn't show it. Taylor was the adult. Taylor was in Comfort, for Belle and not for herself. "Why don't we go away? Roxy can run the store while we're gone. Let's stay a week at the time share. We can go all the way up to Long Beach, or even Blaine. Let's just get as far away as possible."

Belle locked eyes with Taylor, and though there was just that hint of drama in her face that made Taylor doubt her sincerity, her eyes sparkled like they might be full of tears. Taylor would do anything for this kid.

"We can't leave Gramps that long anymore. Didn't you know that? Mom hadn't gone away for even one night in more than three years."

"I'm sorry." Taylor held her fork in a white knuckled fist. Her mother hadn't told her how badly Grandpa Ernie had deteriorated.

"Anyway, I have a paper due on Monday. I can't leave right now."

"But, um, you're not going to classes."

"I only skip the stupid ones." Belle squared her shoulders and stuck her jaw out. "I don't have a car, so I have to walk and bike everywhere. Why would I need gym class? And seriously, Taylor, why on earth would a Quinn girl need home ec?" She almost laughed.

"It is absurd, but you don't want to flunk the stupid classes, do you?"

Belle snorted. "No one will give me F's right now. My mom just died." She seemed to notice her ravioli again, and after a moment, she dug in as though no one had fed her all week. Considering what they'd gone through together, Taylor suspected it was true. Taylor certainly hadn't thought to cook family dinners for her and Grandpa Ernie.

CHAPTER TWO

The weak spring sun cast its gentle light through the east window. No one had turned on the kitchen light, so Taylor didn't either. She sat at the well-worn pine table nursing a cup of coffee. Grandpa Ernie had seemed fine at breakfast, lucid, with it. Belle had been efficient but quiet. Taylor, herself, was in a fog. It had been three days since the funeral, and the flowers on the kitchen counter had begun to drop their petals.

The excitement of putting her condo on the market, throwing all of her stuff in a van, and coming home had buoyed her up through the immediate loss, but now that all of that was over, the adrenaline rush from being needed had passed.

Her stuff was in the shed behind her house. Her house? No. This was Belle's house. She would need it more than Taylor did. Taylor let her spoon sit in the bowl of oatmeal as it cooled. This house was so empty without her mom.

Taylor expected to hear her voice, to feel her warm hand on her shoulder as she passed—giving gentle touches throughout the day was her little habit.

She hadn't come home enough, but she hadn't known she needed to. Her mom had only been forty-nine. Exactly twenty years older than Taylor. How could she have known they didn't still have a million years together? It had never occurred to her that she could lose both of her parents.

Taylor watched Belle scrub out the pot she'd made their oatmeal in.

Grandpa Ernie was in his room getting dressed. She could hear his grunts and heavy sighs all the way in the kitchen. This was a small house, but it was still funny to hear him getting dressed.

Taylor had been younger than Belle when her dad died. She'd been awful to live with for a full year, acting out, running to Grandma Quinny's house, talking back. She hadn't recovered till they got Belle.

Did that mean Taylor needed to adopt a baby to fix all of this? Someone for Belle and her to dote on, to give them a reason to keep going?

She sincerely hoped not. Having a moody teen and a baby at the same time was too much to imagine.

Grandpa Ernie shuffled into the kitchen. "What's for breakfast?" He had just finished his oatmeal. Taylor looked at her own bowl.

"Better have some toast with your vitamins." Belle didn't try to convince him he'd already eaten.

He put two slices of raisin bread in the toaster.

Belle gave him a handful of pills from a plastic week long pill container. "There you go. Coffee's hot too."

He took his pills, one little swallow at a time, but not with water. When they were all gone, he looked at his hand, just to make sure, and then poured himself a mug of coffee.

He joined Taylor at the table. The toast popped, but he ignored it.

"Eat that oatmeal, young lady." His gruff voice was serious, his bushy eyebrows drawn together. "You're wasting away. Men aren't lookin' to marry sickly girls."

Taylor put a spoonful of oatmeal in her mouth.

Belle wrinkled her nose at her sister. "Love you, Gramps." She kissed the top of his head, grabbed her sherpa jacket, and left out the kitchen door.

Belle had handled him so well.

Was that her morning job? Surely not. The store didn't open till eleven, and her mom wouldn't have made the baby take care of Grandpa Ernie.

But if she had, then no wonder Belle resented Taylor now. Belle was capable, responsible, thoughtful even. She didn't need Taylor there to take care of them. All they needed Taylor for was to run Flour Sax, like her mom.

"We'd better head to the store." Grandpa Ernie stood.

"No rush, Grandpa. It's only seven-thirty."

"Lots of work to do before it opens. You got stock coming in today at nine, and you have to film, don't you? You always film at eight-thirty unless there's stock, so you have to go in now and film."

"Film?"

"Your show. You always film at eight-thirty, but you have stock coming at nine so you have to do it earlier. For heaven's sake, Laura, you'd forget your own name if it wasn't embroidered on your shirt."

Laura. Her mom.

What would Belle do? Roll with it? That seemed weird. "I'm, um, taking the day off."

He shook his head. "I told you, you'd never stick with this." He took a long drink of his coffee, then looked at Taylor with a new light in his eyes. "Internet shows. What was your mother thinking?"

And like that, he seemed to remember who he was talking to.

"Grandpa, did Mom have a YouTube show?"

"A boob tube show's more like it. Who wants to watch your mom cut fabric up? And it was never on TV, so I don't know what she thought she was doing."

"She never told me…." Taylor pulled her phone to her and

searched for Laura Quinn and Flour Sax on YouTube. The show popped right up. She found a channel with a year's worth of daily ten minute videos filmed in their little shop. Taylor started to watch one, but when her mother's voice came through the little phone speaker, it hurt. She tapped pause quickly. "Thanks Grandpa," Taylor said it quietly, not really for him to hear.

"You're welcome. And don't be lazy. Just because your store doesn't open till eleven doesn't mean there's not work to do."

"Yessir." Taylor left her phone open to the show but got up and filled her coffee. She wanted to watch the videos, but she also didn't want to watch them. Not quite yet.

TAYLOR WAS at the shop in time to get the new stock. Tulip Festival was opening soon, and they had a big order ready for the tourist season. She worked in quiet till she couldn't take it anymore. Her mom had always played music. Every store played music. Clearly, she was off her game.

But Taylor didn't want music.

Flour Sax's speaker system was remarkably up to date for a shop that catered to those who loved pre-war printed cotton and hand stitching. Taylor plugged her phone into an aux cord and found the show on YouTube. Laura Quinn's voice descended from the carefully placed speakers like a ghost, or an angel, filling the room. Her heart leapt to her throat. She spun, looking for her mom, though she knew it was just the phone, just the speakers. It wasn't really her. She quickly unplugged it and sat down.

The video had paused on a shot of her mom smiling behind the worktable, a delicious spread of candy colored story book prints spilled before her. Had she gotten sponsorships for this? She ought to have. Taylor couldn't bring herself to press play again.

Had her mom really not told her about the YouTube show, or

had Taylor been so caught up in her own life that she hadn't remembered?

She smiled at her mom. Laura Quinn had always been beautiful and bright. She couldn't just turn her off, so she set her laptop in the corner by a display of quilting notions and set her mom's show to play continuously.

Through the day customers stopped to watch it and murmur to themselves. It was good for them, healing, to get to see her. Taylor knew because they all said so as she rang them up. It would likely be good for her too.

Belle, however, was nowhere to be seen all day.

Taylor didn't get out of the shop till eight. Tulip festival season was the start of their tourist season, and the shop was a disaster. When she finally got home, Belle wasn't there either, but her backpack was.

Taylor's new found and deeply felt sense of mama bear protectiveness told her it was not only right, but good and kind to dig through the bag.

Belle's huge black canvas backpack was heavy and likely to give her lifelong chiropractic bills. As Taylor unzipped it, she realized she'd have to connect better with Belle's teachers, make sure she had lunch money, and find out how to see her grades. That was her job now.

The bag was packed tightly, so it wasn't easy to rifle through. Taylor tugged folders up one at a time, glanced in, then maneuvered them back down. A dozen or so crumpled papers were shoved in the bag like packing material. She grabbed a handful and smoothed them out. Nothing but class notes, in careful handwriting, with lovely doodles in the margins.

Taylor folded one and stuffed it in her pocket for later. Belle had always had a gift for art. Taylor rocked back on her heels. The last time she and her mom had talked about Belle's future had been when she quit ballet at the beginning of middle school. They'd both been disappointed. Taylor hadn't been to a recital in a few years, but Belle had been such a cute little dancer.

There were no notes from friends in the bag, not hidden in notebooks or in the pockets. Probably because everyone had phones and sent texts or snaps or whatever. Taylor swallowed hard, thinking about the kinds of things teens sent each other on their phones, and wondered if she had a strong enough stomach to check.

There were two cards in envelopes, though. One of them was from a teacher, Mrs. Vincent, expressing sympathy. Mrs. Vincent had been the fine arts teacher for at least thirty years. The other card was from her mom's old friend Colleen Kirby. A tremor of grief passed over Taylor. Colleen had been on the weekend away with her mom.

Her hands shook as she slid the card out of the envelope. Nobody hurt as badly as family did. Grandpa Ernie, her, Belle. They were the ones this was really hard on, but her mom's friends Colleen, Amara, and Melinda had been with her when she died, and it had to be awful for them too.

A folded piece of paper was tucked inside the generic sympathy card. One more step before she had to face someone else's grief. She unfolded it slowly, holding her breath.

Baby Girl,

Laura was the best friend I ever had in all my life. She did an act of kindness for me 16 years ago that was more than any friend could ask. When I was sick, alone, and pregnant, she came to me, and helped me, and took you home so you could have a better life than I could give you.

While you were growing up, I was able to get off the streets, get a job, get a home, find love, and start a family. All things I never thought I could do before Laura allowed me to start my life over.

I owe her everything, and so I owe you, our baby girl, everything as well. I know we don't know each other well, but I have never stopped loving you or praying for you. My home is open to you forever and always. I don't know what your grandfather has planned for your last years of high school, but I would be honored if you chose to move here with me, Dave, and your little brothers. Please consider it and please know I love you with my whole heart.

Sincerely, Colleen

TAYLOR STARED and didn't breathe and didn't hear the front door open.

She didn't see or hear or understand anything until Belle's little white hand grabbed the card from hers and she hissed, "How dare you?"

Her feet thundered up the stairs to her room. Her door slammed. And Taylor stared into the distance.

It wasn't a shock that Belle had a birth mom.

It wasn't a shock that Colleen Kirby had lived a hard life.

Taylor knew all of that.

And if Taylor thought hard enough, the fact that Colleen was Belle's birth mom wasn't a surprise, either.

That she dared—*dared*—to take Belle away?

That was unforgivable.

And yet, the most natural thing in the world.

Why would Belle want to stay here with Taylor, when she could live in the mansion with Colleen and her software engineer husband in Portland?

Belle's footsteps echoed overhead.

Grandpa Ernie coughed from his bedroom, then adjusted the volume on his TV.

Taylor wasn't all alone yet.

They still had each other.

She sat up, stretching her back, and breathing deeply.

In this house, Taylor was the adult, and Belle needed her. If this card had been painful for Taylor to read, it must have been misery for Belle.

Taylor took one more deep breath, pressed her hands to the floor and stood. She needed to see her sister.

When she got to Belle's room, the door was ajar. She knocked lightly. "Can we talk?"

Belle pulled the door open.

"I'm sorry." Taylor figured if she started pretty much all of their conversations with that, she couldn't lose.

Black lines of melted eyeliner and mascara traced down Belle's face.

"I didn't know." Taylor sat on the edge of Belle's bed.

Belle held out a very thin flat iPhone. "Colleen and Dave sent me this for Christmas." She waved her hand at a MacBook on her desk. "That was the year before."

"Did you know?" Taylor asked.

"I wondered." Belle's words were calm but did nothing to stop the flow of tears. "Mom didn't want Colleen to come on the weekend trip. They fought about it—Mom and Amara, I mean. I could hear them all the way up here. All of them knew. All of Mom's girls."

"I guess they would, huh?"

Belle dragged the back of her hand across her cheek. "It's my fault."

"No."

"I hated the yelling, so I went downstairs and reminded Mom how nice Colleen had always been and told her she should let her come. Amara just said 'See?' and then Mom gave in."

"It's still not your fault. Mom fell. She hit her head…" Taylor was trying to describe how her mom had drowned after one too many margaritas with the girls, but she couldn't get it out. The words stuck in her throat.

Belle stared at a spot on the floor. "Colleen wanted me back."

"Who wouldn't?" Taylor, after all, fiercely wanted her to stay.

"I think she killed Mom so she could get me back." Belle's words were hoarse and came out slowly.

What a nightmare of a burden for a child to carry. Taylor cursed Colleen for sending that card. How dare she do that to her baby sister? "Belle…it was just an accident. A tragic accident."

Belle exhaled. "That's what the police said, but I overheard Amara and Melinda at the funeral. They thought they were

26

alone, but I was around the corner. They were talking about that night and how mom and Colleen had argued."

"No..." Taylor's stomach turned. "No. If that were true the police would have arrested her already."

Belle wrapped the sleeves of her thin black sweatshirt around her fingers. "That's what Melinda said too. The police would have figured it out if something bad had happened."

"Did they say what Mom and Colleen were fighting about?"

Belle shook her head. "But I can guess." She peeled back one of her sleeves and stared at the black smear of mascara on the back of her hand.

"Belle, can I give you a hug?"

Belle shuffled slowly toward her sister.

When she was close enough, Taylor wrapped her in her arms, and held her for exactly a long as Belle allowed, and not one second more.

CHAPTER THREE

*A*fter school on Monday, Taylor and Belle sat in Maddie Carpenter's little counseling room. Their stiff, awkward, posture were exactly the same—two copies of their mother.

Maddie sat across from them on a roomy, sage green velvet armchair. Her legs, in a pair of vivid paisley leggings, were crossed and she had a yellow legal pad on her knee.

"This is a safe space to say whatever you need," Maddie said. "The only time I could, or would, ever share what is said is if I found evidence of abuse or of self-harm that endangered your life. I hope you understand. I only want to help."

Taylor exhaled.

Belle gritted her teeth.

"It's okay." Taylor patted Belle's knee. "Maddie is good. She's safe."

"Ok." Belle hadn't shifted from her touch. "Mom was murdered. It was my fault, and I have to fix it."

Each word was a little punch in Taylor's stomach. She knew Belle was going to talk about this, but she hadn't expected it to be the first thing out of her mouth.

Maddie rested her pen on her notepad, tilted her head thoughtfully, and spoke without a hint of patronization. "You are not responsible for the actions of anyone but yourself. Every individual has the same opportunity to make their own decisions. I know we're having our first conversation together, but I'd like to give you an assignment, and a quiet place to do it in. Would that be all right?"

Belle was looking at her feet and didn't say anything. Her body had sagged, matching the slouchy knitted cardigan she wore that had been their mom's in the '90s. The momentary adrenaline rush of admitting her greatest fear had been deflated by the common sense of Maddie's words.

"There's a big comfy chair in the waiting area. I have a pen and paper for you. Can you go snuggle up in there and write fifty things you love about your mom?"

Belle looked up, her face contorted in confusion.

"I know it doesn't sound like it's related to what you just said, but I promise, it is. Are you willing to do that while I talk to your sister a little bit?" Maddie ripped the top page from her legal pad, folded it and placed it onto her side table. Then she held out the pad and pen to Belle.

Belle accepted it.

Taylor walked with her to the waiting room. "I'm sure we won't be long."

"I don't need much time. I could list a thousand things to love about Mom in thirty seconds."

"I know." Taylor kissed Belle's temple and rejoined Maddie.

"She is 100% right." Maddie folded her hands and rested them on her knees. Her professional calm was unnerving. This woman, this expert, had replaced the giddy girl Taylor remembered from their childhood.

Taylor flinched. "Excuse me?" Her sister was by no means responsible for their mother's death, and she would excommunicate anyone who claimed it was so.

"Belle is riddled with grief, confusion, and guilt. Obviously she isn't responsible for her mother's death." Maddie waved one hand to dismiss the mere thought. "It was an accident, pure and simple. Her mom slipped, hit her head, and drowned. But at her age and emotional development, Belle's brain just won't accept that."

"Yeah, I know." A sigh of relief escaped Taylor. She hadn't realized how on the edge she had been until Maddie echoed what she already believed.

"Belle needs two things right now, more than anything else. First, she needs an active project to give her a reason to wake up every morning."

The hint that suicide was even possible hit her like a sneaker wave.

"And second, she needs to know, to truly know, that this wasn't her fault. You could tell her. Her grandparents could tell her. Her friends could tell her. I could, cops could. Whoever. But what we know about adolescent brain development is that Belle will not believe it until she tells herself it is true."

"Um...." Taylor was still struggling to find her way out from under Maddie's casual suggestion of suicide. Whatever project she was imagining was as far away as the shoreline.

"The only way Belle will ever tell herself she isn't at fault, is if she learns for herself exactly what happened."

Taylor shook her head, like you do when your ears are full of water. "What on earth are you talking about?"

"Belle needs to play detective. She needs a list of witnesses to interview. She needs to go to the scene and see it for herself. If she can hear it, see it, touch it...then it will be concrete, and she will believe."

Taylor exhaled in a short, sharp breath. Maybe this play-pretend worked with Maddie's young clients, but Belle was basically grown. She'd never buy it. Besides, just because they looked for witnesses didn't mean they'd find any. If they tried this, they might just end up worse off than they already were. "But what if..."

Maddie nodded as though to acknowledge that Taylor had spoken. "You probably think this was your fault too, but haven't acknowledged it yet." She looked her up and down. "How I wish I had been your counselor when you lost your dad."

Taylor hadn't had a counselor. There hadn't been any child psychologists in Comfort, Oregon back then, and her mom hadn't had time to drive her to the city.

Taylor closed her eyes and tipped her head, resting it on the back of the chair. Would she have wanted a counselor back then? If so, would she also have wanted to play detective?

"Belle is a lot older than you were when your dad passed. What she's going through right now is actually more similar to what you're going through this time. It's her second loss."

"How so?" Taylor didn't open her eyes.

"Adoption was a gain for you and your mom. It was healing and wonderful. Your home was an ideal place for Belle, I don't deny that. But as she grew and learned about how your family was created, she's had to process the loss that comes with knowing she was released for adoption. No matter how right the reasons were, it's still a loss for both her and her biological family."

"Ah." The words were logical but impossible for Taylor to understand. The Quinn family was ideal, in almost every way, and even if it hadn't been perfect, it had been full of love.

"It takes a lot longer to come up with a list of fifty than it sounds like it will, so we'll need to let Belle back in shortly. Before we do, would you allow her to try this?"

Taylor lifted her head, opened her eyes, and took a deep breath. She didn't have any better ideas. "Only if I get to be a part of it too."

"We can make that work." A flicker of humor danced in Maddie's eyes. The old friend from childhood showing through. "After all, we've done this before." She let herself dimple into a smile, then smoothed her face back into a look of care and gentle interest.

They had done this before, but it had hardly been the same.

Belle had managed to list thirty-two things to love about her mom and was struggling for a thirty-third when they let her back in. She declined the offer to share her list.

Her assignment from Maddie was to work on the list whenever she felt despair.

Their assignment—for the three of them—was to head out to South Yamhill River to visit the B&B where Laura Quinn and her friends had been staying when she drowned.

Her job, that Taylor had given herself, was to call Colleen Kirby and give her a piece of her mind. No way was Colleen stealing Belle.

"WHAT DOES DESPAIR FEEL LIKE?"

Belle and Taylor were in Flour Sax the next day after school. Grandpa Ernie was snoring softly in his chair. Their mom's voice was murmuring from the little corner of the shop where her YouTube videos played on a loop. Taylor knew she was gone, but there was sweet comfort hearing her from the around the corner as though she were telling a friend how intimate knowledge of the color wheel would elevate her quilting.

Taylor hadn't sat and watched it yet herself. She just couldn't. But the voice in the distance was lovely.

Belle sat on a stool at the cutting table while Taylor dusted shelves. Rain poured outside like someone had turned on the shower of the gods. It was a dark, bleak spring day and no sales would come of it.

"It feels like a sadness that shouldn't go away," Taylor offered.

"Sure," Belle said. "But physically...what does it physically feel like?"

"Oh...um...." Creative writing had not been her favorite subject. Unless you count ad copy. "Maybe like...um...like a pressure? On your chest?" Taylor stopped and considered how she felt at this exact moment. "More like pressure sort of all over…hard to move."

"Yeah. And maybe like a rush of fear in your heart? With lots of shaking?" Belle asked.

Taylor hooked the step stool with the toe of her foot and dragged it over to the next row of shelves. She remembered that feeling, curled up in her bed, heart racing, head pounding… "Yeah," she said. "Like that. And a headache too."

Belle was doodling on the edges of the legal pad that Maddie had given her. "How can I make a list when I feel like that?"

Taylor ran the faux feather duster over the thin edge of the laminate wood shelf that showed in front of the bolts of polka dotted quilting cotton. "I don't know. We go to see Maddie again in two days. Let's ask her."

"Do you think it's okay if I work on the list now? I don't feel great, but I don't think I'd call it despair."

"I say you should do it." Taylor stood on her tip toes to reach the top of the shelves where the dust of thousands of yards of cotton fiber gathered continuously. Her eyes could use a wiping right now. She hadn't thought about the nights of panic after dad died in years. Her mom had gone somewhere, and Taylor was staying with Grandma and Grandpa Quinn. They hadn't had the funeral yet. Taylor had been very well-behaved when everyone was around, but every night she felt like she'd never make it till the next morning.

The door jingled. "Good afternoon!" Taylor turned on the stool, to offer her customer a very forced smile.

A well-bundled woman slipped off her plastic rain jacket, trying not to drip on their carpets, then hung it on a rack next to the door.

She turned, fluffing her head of brilliant and unnatural red hair. "I'm so glad I find you both here."

Colleen Kirby. In the flesh.

Taylor gripped the shelf so as not to fall. Or maybe to keep from throwing herself at Colleen in a rage.

Belle stared at her, color draining from her face.

"Does the shop still close at six on weeknights?" Colleen asked.

It was 5:45.

"Yes," Taylor croaked.

"Good. I'd like to take you both out for dinner tonight so we can talk."

Her bright smile faded to a look of fear as she watched Belle. Her eyebrows drew together as though begging.

Belle sat up and composed her features, though her face remained colorless and her words were soft. "What about Gramps?"

"We can bring him something back. I'd...I'd like us ladies to have some time alone."

"We're practically alone now. Gramps is napping." The grip Belle had on her pencil made Taylor fear she'd snap it.

"That's okay too." Colleen moved toward the display where Laura's videos were playing. "Oh..." She paused in front of it, engrossed.

"You and I can have dinner." Taylor stepped down to the solid floor. "Belle can stay with Grandpa."

"I'd really rather..."

"I think it's better this time." Taylor gave Colleen her warmest professional smile, though she didn't plan on giving her a second dinner.

Colleen hadn't looked away from the video. "Okay." She settled into one of the slipper chairs they had strewn across the store, the one with random French-like words in turquoise script across a creamy linen background. She watched Laura's show while they closed up shop. Belle and Grandpa Ernie went out back, through the rain, to their little house two blocks down the road.

Colleen and Taylor swathed themselves in rain jackets and hurried to Reuben's Diner.

They ordered quickly. The home style food was nothing to write home about, but the soup was hot and the bread was soft.

"Has Belle talked to you about our situation?" Colleen's voice was low, as though she didn't want to be overheard, but the only other customers were a booth full of students from the college.

"She showed me your letter." This was a boldfaced lie, but Taylor felt like she was hardly the boldest of the two.

Colleen sipped a spoonful of minestrone. "Your mom and I had talked about it—about telling Belle about me. Did you and your mom discuss it at all?"

"No." Taylor spun her spoon in her bowl of cheesy broccoli. Adrenaline held her gut in a steel grip.

Colleen licked her lips and inhaled slowly as though centering herself. "I had wanted, hoped, for an open adoption where I could be involved in Belle's life once I was on my feet again. Somehow it always seemed too disruptive, so we didn't try. But your mom sent pictures…"

"She sent them to all of her friends, at back to school, Christmas and Easter."

"Oh." Colleen's eyes dropped to her soup.

"Belle only has one year left of high school. It would be terrible to make her leave her friends right after she lost her mother." Taylor sounded like Cooper's mom, but in this case, she was right. You just don't disrupt the life of a grieving child.

Colleen bit her lip. "We can afford so many opportunities for her."

Taylor straightened up and jutted her chin out like a caricature of an enraged child.

"Just, I mean, opportunities that could help her get into a good college…"

"By all means, help her financially." Taylor reached for her water cup but just held it, the icy, damp glass cooling her fingers, maybe even cooling her temper a little.

"It's not money. She can have that whether she lives with me or not, but we have opportunities that don't exist here." Colleen turned to look out the window at the long block of buildings full of antiques.

"I'm her legal guardian till she turns eighteen in a year and a half." Taylor slid her thumb up and down the glass letting the slipper cool surface soothe her.

"You'll have so much to do with the shop, and taking care of your grandfather, and…your life back in the city."

"I'll have the same things to do that Mom had."

"I know."

"You have your other kids. You'll be too busy with them."

"No! Not at all!" Colleen brightened up. "It will be good for Belle to be part of a family, to have siblings. I'm a stay at home mom." She blushed, clearly proud of how her life had turned out since the adoption.

"I'm her family."

"Oh! Yes, I know, but she didn't grow up with you around."

"She's sixteen. She didn't grow up with *you* around." Her words tasted bitter but true.

"Taylor, surely we can come to some kind of arrangement. Maybe Belle could stay with you during the summer."

Taylor let go of the glass. "This is Belle's home. She's not going anywhere. You don't have a legal or moral claim to her. I wish you'd just leave us alone."

Colleen sighed heavily, her eyes big, sympathetic…but then they shifted. There was steel behind those large blue eyes.

"I know that Laura recommended Belle stay with you in her will, but it doesn't really matter. I gave Laura legal guardianship over Belle as an infant because I wasn't capable and I didn't want the state to take her. I never petitioned to have it ended because I knew it would hurt Belle to lose her….her mother. But it was never a full adoption. It felt more like a handshake agreement."

Taylor stared at her.

"I'm sorry your mother never explained this to you. I was her best friend, Taylor. She would do anything for me and did. When I was at my worst, at the very bottom of who I could be as a person, sick with addiction, I got pregnant with Belle, and your mom keep my baby safe while I got better. And I'm better now. Much, much better."

She didn't sound better to Taylor. She sounded like the kind of woman who would kill her best friend to steal a baby.

The room started to spin, and Taylor realized she had been holding her breath. As she exhaled, things came back into focus. Colleen didn't look insane. She looked sad.

Colleen reached across the table. "I've been better for a very long time. But now my baby is hurting, and I want to make her better. You've got to understand."

"Please don't take my sister from me." The voice that escaped Taylor sounded like a child. Like the kid who had lost her daddy. And her heart was exploding like it had those nights at her grandparent's house.

This was what despair felt like.

Colleen paid for the meal and then walked her home, her arm hooked through Taylor's, keeping her upright.

Taylor honestly didn't know if she could have made it on her own.

Jess Reuben would have had to call an ambulance and Serge, their volunteer paramedic, would have had to come for her in his converted Honda Odyssey, the one that looked like a hearse.

They didn't talk while they walked except for Colleen to say, "You were right. It's too soon to talk about this with Belle. Let's not mention anything to her yet."

CHAPTER FOUR

*T*aylor didn't know how Colleen got home that night, or where she was staying. She collapsed on the couch, while Belle hid in her room, and Grandpa Ernie watched Mayberry on cable.

She longed for her mother to solve this problem for her, the way she'd been able to do when she was little, but her mother not being here anymore *was* the problem.

Taylor fiddled with her phone. Her mother had left a little bit of herself behind. If she was brave, she could watch her now.

Slowly, as though she was giving herself plenty of time to change her mind, Taylor opened her YouTube app, searched for Flour Sax, and picked a video at random.

The volume was low, Grandpa Ernie would never hear it over his show, but her mom's laughter seemed to ring out.

She pulled the well-worn, log cabin quilt off the back of the sofa and tucked it around her knees.

In the video, her mom was demonstrating how to fold fabric so you could cut one long strip from it to create bias tape. She did it so quickly, the folding and the cutting was so smooth. It was a matter of seconds and then she was ironing it with a fun little iron they sold in the shop. "Heat and pressure. Heat and pressure. Gentle, but firm. Like parenting a teenager." She looked down at the slim little iron in her hand. "Not that I'd use a hot iron on my daughter, but sometimes…" Her laughter seemed to bubble up from deep within, the joy of parenting being too much for her.

Taylor paused the video on a particularly pretty shot of her mom smiling down at the fabric she was bending to her will, that she was improving with her knowledge.

Heat and pressure.

That's what it took to turn that thin strip of fabric into the piece that held the whole quilt together.

She and Belle had plenty of that right now. But she manage to hold her family together?

THE NEXT MORNING Taylor called the school to let them know she was keeping Belle home for two weeks. She explained that she'd need Belle's work so she could keep up, and that Belle was under the care of Dr. Maddie Carpenter. The school secretary was very understanding.

Then Taylor called Maddie and asked her to meet them at the shop at nine a.m. They had to make a plan and make it fast.

Maybe Colleen *had* killed her mother to get Belle back. If so, she wasn't going to get away with it.

Maddie, Belle, and Taylor gathered around the cutting table with cups of tea Taylor made in Grandpa Ernie's little sitting area. He sat in his chair, watching the morning news on a small black and white TV.

It took them about twenty minutes to catch Maddie up on all the details.

"Let's not assume murder." Maddie's calm professional voice matched the creamy linen suit she wore. Cool, almost casual, but buttoned up. "Let's go into this investigation with the idea that we want to know exactly what happened, whatever that is."

"But doesn't it help to have a premise to start with?" Belle was practically bouncing in her seat.

Maddie had been right. A project would be good for Belle.

"We don't need a premise. After all, we know where, when, and have a pretty good idea of how. We just need to be able to understand why."

"Our starting premise is that Colleen had been putting pressure on Mom to give me back." Belle dropped her voice a few notes and increased the vocal fry. This was serious talk. "So, Mom invited the girls for a getaway to come up with a plan to prevent it."

Taylor was still shaken that there had not been a full adoption. Legal guardianship was so flimsy, so temporary. She was impressed that Belle hadn't flipped out on hearing that news.

"But didn't you say Mom didn't want Colleen to come?" Taylor reminded Belle of the fight she'd intervened in.

Belle thought for a moment. "Yes, but maybe that's because she wanted alone time with Melinda and Amara to explain everything and get them on board. Maybe she didn't want Colleen there messing it up."

"Did your mom take these kinds of girls trips often?" This question was for Belle. Taylor should have been able to answer it, but she didn't know, or wouldn't have if Belle hadn't told her already.

"No. This was the first one in ages." Belle tapped the toe of her Van's clad foot on the rung of the stool.

"How did she seem?"

"She was really excited. She'd gone shopping for cute clothes and had a cooler full of fancy food and drinks. She loved margaritas, but never had them." Belle sounded wistful.

Taylor felt the same. Nothing would have been more healing than a day in town with her mom, shopping till dark. Maybe it was because she was from a small community, maybe it was something else, but when hard times hit, nothing was as good as heading to town for a serious shopping spree.

"Not much of a drinker?" Maddie asked.

"Just wine tastings, mostly." Taylor pulled herself back to the moment. Now was not the time to try and figure out where she could get her own linen suit, no matter how ragged her jeans and Flour Sax sweatshirt made her feel.

"Yeah, no places for a good margarita around here. It was like a treat." Belle added.

"They were staying off the Belleview-Hopewell road, right? They hadn't gone far." Maddie asked. Taylor was impressed by her memory.

"That's right. She was worried about Gramps and and wanted to be nearby in case of emergency. I told her Cooper's parents were close and had promised to keep an eye on us, but she still worried."

"It's natural. Leaving you with an aging grandparent would be hard on her. She was used to being the one who took care of everyone." Maddie nodded, acknowledging Belle and giving her positive support. "What would you girls like to do first?"

"We should go to the B&B," Belle said.

Taylor shivered. Like Belle, a part of her needed to step onto that dock her mom had fallen from, and to see the last things her mom had seen.

"And we need to talk to the other ladies, don't you think?" Belle asked Taylor.

"How about this, could you girls invite all of them back there?"

Belle nodded. "Very good. How's tomorrow?"

"I expect they work during the week." Taylor patted Belle's hand.

Belle shifted from her sister's touch.

"It wouldn't hurt to ask. Everyone has to eat dinner." Maddie smiled and nodded. "It doesn't make sense for me to come along, so I'd like to do some background research for you, if you'd like the help. What do you want to know that I could look up?"

"Is it...legal? Could Colleen just revoke the guardianship and take Belle away?" Taylor swallowed, hard.

Belle's face drained of color. "Yeah...that. Could you find out?"

Maddie nodded, but in a way that made the sisters think she already knew. "I'll see what I can learn." There was a hint of sadness, maybe even apology, in Maddie's answer. After all, she was a child psychologist. This kind of custody issue must have come up before.

AMARA AND MELINDA were happy to meet with them for dinner, but they didn't want to go anywhere near South Yamhill River. Taylor could hardly blame them, but Belle wasn't happy.

They settled on a family dinner at the Quinn house. Taylor was more than a little concerned about how the presence of Grandpa Ernie would affect their openness to talk about that night. To use up some of her nervous energy, she worked herself to the bone cleaning after a long day at the store. She also made pot roast, her one fail-safe meal. That, with Yorkshire puddings and a salad, never failed to impress, mostly because roast is always good and who makes Yorkshire puddings anymore? It was a bit heavy for what had turned out to be a shining example of a wine country spring day, but no matter.

The table was laid with a linen cutwork tablecloth her grandma Delma had received as a wedding present, and the daisy patterned china her parents had received. It was overly formal, but Grandpa Ernie had insisted. After all, these ladies were company.

Taylor's mother and Amara Schilling had been best friends since preschool, which had really just been daycare at Amara's house. Colleen didn't go that far back, but for most of their child-hood, she had always been around. A friend in Sunday School, grade school, karate after school. Whatever her mom and Amara had done, Colleen had done too, except the preschool. Melinda Powell had moved to town when she was a second grader and had instantly been welcomed to the cozy little threesome that was Laura Quinn, Amara Schilling, and Colleen Kirby. The four of them had the type of undying friendship that people make movies about, though this one felt more like a soap opera.

"So…what you're saying is everyone was really excited about finally going away together." The conversation had been very surface since the ladies arrived, and Taylor, seated across the formal table from Amara, was struggling to get a foothold.

"It had just been so long." Amara cut a forkful of the crusty Yorkshire pudding.

"Why do you kids drink so darn much?" Grandpa Ernie huffed into his mustache. "Not like there's a war on. What do you have to forget?"

Amara's eyebrows popped up.

Melinda's mouth opened in a little circle.

"Oh, it's been war forever, Gramps." Belle passed him the plate of roast. "Have a little more. I don't think we'll ever get out of Afghanistan. We've been at war my whole life."

"Not a real war." Grandpa Ernie wasn't mollified by the roast, though he did add a little more to his plate. "Not like Korea."

"It's a pity Colleen couldn't be here." Amara sipped her wine, despite Grandpa's look of disapproval.

Melinda sighed. "She must just be sick over all of this. If I had been fighting with Laura like that, there's no way I could live with myself right now." Melinda stuck two fingers in the collar of her cashmere mock-turtle neck and tugged.

"No, I couldn't either." Amara swirled the wine in her glass like it was something more expensive than the house wine from Berry Noir.

"Did you ever figure out what they were arguing about?" Melinda asked Amara.

"I tried to get Colleen to tell me, but she wouldn't. From

44

what I could hear, it was about some girl they both knew, but then, we'd have to know her too, wouldn't we?" Amara sipped the water, her look apologetic.

"What about the...girl?" Belle did a good job of sounding interested but not morbid, and definitely not terrified.

Taylor's throat seemed to close up. The only "girl" she could think of that Colleen and her mom would be fighting over had to be Belle.

"I just heard snatches of the argument. Colleen said something about wanting to see her or wanting to have her here." Amara explained.

Taylor dropped her fork. "Sorry," she murmured as she picked it up with a shaking hand.

"But your mom replied she didn't really like her..." Amara pushed the sleeves of her satin bomber jacket. "Is it warm in here?"

Belle's face crumpled in confusion, but she pulled it straight again, quickly. Her eyes were still grieved, but that was to be expected.

"I know the fight kind of dragged on, but that door was solid wood. I just couldn't figure out who they were talking about." Melinda looked to Amara for confirmation.

"Probably Brandy East, since her sister, Andrea, owns the bed and breakfast. Your mom never like Brandy, but I always thought she was fun." Amara exhaled slowly, then took off her jacket and draped it over the back of her chair. "It is warm, isn't it?"

"Yes, sorry." Taylor pushed her chair back and went to open the window. She needed to turn her face away for a minute. Obviously her mom wouldn't have said she didn't like Belle. Then again, Belle was going through a difficult phase. It could be very hard to like emo teens.

"Why would they be fighting over her after all these years?" Melinda asked.

Taylor returned to her seat, cooler and calmer. She knew of

Brandy and Andrea. Brandy worked at the antique mall, but lived in Willamina. Their nephew, Hudson, had been a few years behind Taylor in school. He was…very good looking.

Belle was focused on eating. Taylor would have given her left arm to have never had these women over. Mothers needed to let off steam sometimes. It didn't change their love, but the idea that her mom was saying things about Belle not being likable, and now Belle having to hear about it, was hard to stomach.

But maybe the ladies were right. Her mom had to have been talking about someone else. A friend. Maybe even Colleen. That made more sense. Colleen wanted to be in Belle's life. Taylor's mom had said she had never liked "her" but the "her" in question might have referred to Colleen. She desperately wanted their guests to leave so she could tell Belle this theory.

"Did you remember Gina Croyden?" Melinda asked. "She looked familiar, but I didn't remember who she was till the next morning."

"Wasn't she a couple of years younger than us? She did look familiar. I talked with her mom the next morning. Sweet lady." Amara was nibbling her salad. Like the rest of the ladies, her appetite seemed to have died.

"How awful for them to have this happen on their little mother-daughter get away," Melinda sighed.

"Who knows how many nights they had planned to stay, but they left when we did the next morning. Couldn't seem to get away fast enough." Amara set her fork down, maybe giving up on food for the night.

"We should have invited Gina up for drinks, then maybe Colleen and Laura wouldn't have felt comfortable enough to fight." Melinda set her fork down as well.

"So, you all knew the other guests?" Taylor asked, wondering if the others could have had something to do with her mom's death.

"Knew of, anyway. Gina went to school here, but was enough

46

younger that we didn't really know her. She was there with her mother Nancy. You know, Nancy was a real comfort." Amara sipped her water. "Nothing like a mother's touch in a time of crisis."

Belle stared at Amara, but Taylor wasn't shocked by the insensitivity of the comment. Amara was a lawyer and not necessarily clued in to the feelings of those around her.

Melinda wasn't much better—an accountant. Taylor had always thought of her mom and Colleen as being the balancing forces, the relationship types that had kept the friends close through the years.

"I wonder...." Melinda tapped the tips of her fork against her lip. "Wasn't Gina good friends with Shara? I wonder if Gina reminded them of Shara, and that's who they were fighting about."

Amara brightened at the thought. "Your mom has had trouble with Shara since sixth grade, when she and Shara sang the same song at a talent show."

"Since when does Mom sing?" Belle asked. Their mom was great at many things, but her tuneless singing was a bit of a joke with the family.

"She was a kid. Have some grace." Amara smiled. "Sixth grade talent show was supposed to be fun. Shara made it a competition."

"Still that doesn't seem like something to fight about all these years later." Taylor pushed her plate away. Most of her food was untouched. Shara Schonely owned Dutch Hex, one of the four quilt shops in their town. Dutch Hex was a blatant rip off of Flour Sax and the relationship between her mom and Shara had always been a tough one.

"Everyone knows Shara and Laura hated each other. But Colleen always wanted everyone to be friends. Maybe it's nothing. It was just an idea." Melinda held up her hands in surrender.

"I don't see how that would be something they would fight

about though." Belle was staring down Amara, practically begging for answers with her eyes.

"You know how things go when you're arguing, right? Especially reminiscing. And your mom...she really hated Shara. She never hated a soul, except that girl." Amara's eyes were narrowed as she thought about it. "So out of character."

"When Shara opened Dutch Hex, I thought Laura was going to completely lose it," Melinda said.

"What a name." Amara shook her head. "Could it be more obvious she wanted to be the edgy version of Flour Sax?"

"Who needs an edgy quilt shop?" Grandpa Ernie grumbled. He seemed to be following the conversation better than Taylor was. "I think she sells drugs."

"What?" Taylor stared at her grandpa.

"Have you seen her fabrics? Terrible. All dark, dark stuff and the prints..."

"I thought it was a focus on Amish style...Dutch Hex referring to those good luck designs on the sides of barns." Taylor tried to bring a moment of order to the chaotic conversation.

"Amish use a lot of dark colors," Grandpa Ernie insisted.

"I wouldn't be surprised." Belle sipped her ice water like she was dropping some news. "Kids around here don't do meth. And pot's legal, so they're into mushrooms and other psychedelics. They've got to get them somewhere."

The room went silent as the women in their late forties stared at the teen with her dark eyeliner, shaggy black hair, and ripped and torn clothes.

"I don't do any of that stuff." Belle held her head up high. "Makes me a rebel."

"Straight edge punk." Melinda smiled approvingly. "Like your Auntie Mel. I remember those days."

Belle flicked her long black bangs out of her eyes with a puff of breath. "Someone has to drive the getaway car, and that someone had better be sober."

Taylor's head sort of floated above her for a moment. Just

another reminder from her dearly beloved that grief was only one facet of the completely horrifying job that was raising a teenager. She would definitely need to talk to Maddie about some of this.

Nonetheless, Belle's revelations seemed to have opened the well, and the ladies were talking again.

"I would swear on my life your mom wasn't drunk that night. Not when she left her room. We'd had a big dinner and she only had two margaritas. Now, she did make them strong, I won't deny that, but we had eaten like beasts. There was no way she passed out," Amara said.

"What was the weather like that night?" Taylor needed a better picture of the situation. If it had been stormy, her mom might have been blown into the river.

"Dry and sunny during the day. It was damp the next morning, but I don't think it would have been that night. Not enough for her to literally slip on the dock." Melinda offered the weather report.

"But she didn't have to be totally drunk to fall, either. She had those sandals with the little heels, and the dock was old, not perfectly smooth. The boards were well spaced out. She could have been just light-headed enough to not be able to balance herself if her heel caught."

"I told her not to pack those shoes," Amara said. "It was too cold and there weren't going to be any men to impress."

Men?

Taylor stared at Amara. Her mom had been single for so long that it hadn't occurred to her she might have been looking for a man.

"I know it sounds morbid," Belle looked up at Amara, using her big blue eyes like a Precious Moments illustration, "but I really do want to go there. I feel like I need to see it. Force myself to believe this is real." Belle hadn't deigned to take part in either of the school plays since she'd been in high school, but she was playing this part well.

"Oh, honey…" Amara's hand hovered over the table as though she wanted to reach for her but was scared. "You don't want to do that."

"Girl can do whatever she wants," Grandpa Ernie said. "All you do is talk, talk, talk, and drink. If you didn't do so much talking and drinking my daughter would still be alive." He slumped in his chair.

Amara and Melinda exchanged looks. Their plates were almost empty. Taylor had dessert in the kitchen, but she felt like they had all had enough.

Taylor stood. "Thank you for coming. I know…it's not easy to talk about. Not for me, anyway."

Amara looked at her, almost surprised. "I hadn't been thinking." She stood and reached across the table. "This must be just awful for you too. It's nice that you have, oh, I'm sorry, what was his name…Clint? No, I know, Clay. Nice that you have Clay at a time like this."

Taylor swallowed.

Melinda stood as well. "Thank you for inviting us, Taylor. Let's not be strangers, okay? Your mom wouldn't have wanted that."

Belle walked them out.

Taylor fell back into her hard, wooden dining chair.

She agreed. It would have been nice to have Clay. Very nice.

Grandpa Ernie took himself to his room.

Belle joined her for cleaning up the dishes.

"That fight…"

"She didn't mean you." Taylor put her hand on Belle's shoulder. "When Mom said she had never liked her, she did not mean you. You know that, right?"

Belle snorted. "Duh, obviously she didn't. The question is, did she mean Colleen or were she and Colleen fighting over someone else?"

"We could ask Colleen…" Taylor didn't like the idea even as she said it.

"I should probably talk to her without you. Sorry." Belle stood straight her eyes fixed on a spot somewhere in front of her. "The thing about Colleen…" Belle ripped a piece of foil to put over the pot roast platter. "Before Mom died, I liked her. It would be nice to think she didn't do this."

"It would be very nice." Taylor took the platter from her sister and stuck it in the fridge. "It would be very, very nice to think she didn't murder Mom." She gritted her teeth. For Belle's psychological health, it would be nice. For her pending custody battle, not so much.

CHAPTER FIVE

*R*oxy, the sweet and salty lady in her mid-forties with a wide, bright grin and a slight limp, had the opening shift at Flour Sax the next day. She said she liked Grandpa Ernie's company, so Taylor left the two of them at the store and took Belle with her to South Yamhill River. They needed to see the scene of the crime. On the way, they picked up Maddie. She claimed she had no news about the custody situation, but Taylor wondered. It didn't seem like it would be that hard to figure out.

Taylor glanced at Maddie as she buckled up in the backseat of their mom's old Audi. She was realizing that she wasn't ready to know the answer to the custody dilemma, but Maddie had already known that. Maddie was a very good counselor, Taylor suspected.

The bed and breakfast Laura Quinn and her friends had stayed at was delightfully traditional. The two-story Queen Anne with the associated fish scale siding in the dormers, and the porch with fancy scroll work and turned posts, sat on a couple of acres of river front. Baby blue, yellow, and white paint clearly aligned it with the Scandinavian heritage Taylor usually associated with Junction City, a bit south of the location. The lawn was lush this spring, but the landscaping looked half-hearted. A few shrubs not yet in bloom. No early spring flowers. Almost like it knew this wasn't the right time to show off.

South Yamhill was a small, smooth, slow flowing river. A peaceful place for a canoe ride, or for kids to learn to paddle a kayak. It was hardly a destination getaway, but for her mom, who was afraid of leaving Grandpa Ernie for too long, it must have felt perfect.

Taylor parked in the big empty gravel parking area, and they made their way toward the house in silence. Andrea Millson, the owner might have heard something, might know something they didn't, but there was no answer to her knock, and the curtains were drawn in all the windows.

Belle had gone straight to the water, but Maddie had followed Taylor.

"How are you doing?" Maddie asked, her head tilted slightly.

"Ok." It came out more slowly than expected.

"You look a little green. Do you want to sit?"

The front porch had an old pew and a swing, both covered in a sun-faded plaid canvas that used to match the house.

"No. We'd better not leave Belle alone." Taylor felt like running back to the car. Instead, she took several slow, careful steps off the front porch, and then allowed herself to hurry around the side of the building to find Belle.

Belle had stopped halfway down the lawn and was holding her hand over her eyes like a visor. Her black sweater stood out against the cool, soft colors of very early spring.

It was a misty day, fresh, with a cool morning breeze, but the sun was beginning to break out in small bright streaks.

Belle moved finally, walking toward a little wood patio that flanked the riverside. A small dock, about twelve feet long, extended from it to the water. Taylor followed her.

The earthy, wet air of the riverbank smelled wholesome, like childhood. Taylor was glad that was the last thing her mom had known. This peaceful, good place.

"There isn't any crime tape," Belle said, almost under her breath.

They all knew why. Officially, it had been an accident.

"It's a pretty old deck." Taylor's eyes were glued to the weathered wood and the gaps between boards. "Did you see Mom's new shoes? Think she could have gotten tripped up out here?"

Belle squinted at the wooden planks. "Probably. They were funny, old fashioned looking things. Kitten heels. Short, but pointy."

The three of them walked to the edge of the dock. Taylor looked upriver, Belle looked down, and Maddie watched Belle.

"Not a lot of rocks." Belle slipped her foot out of her canvas loafer and dipped her toe in the water. "She'd have had to fall just right."

"Or just wrong." There were three large granite stones at the edge of the water. They looked to be ornamental, since this wasn't a granite kind of area. "Those must have been it, huh?"

"But how did she drown?" Belle shoved her hands in the pockets of her high-waisted mom jeans.

"There's enough water." Taylor reached for Belle, as though she didn't want her to fall too, but she let her hand hover next to her, not touching. "If she was knocked unconscious, face down, it wouldn't take much water."

Belle was dragging her toe back and forth in the greenish water, her eyes on the rocks.

Taylor turned to the house. Two stories of windows faced the river. The ground floor was under the shade of an upstairs deck, but it seemed like her mom's friends should have been able to see her, maybe even hear her fall. "No, it was dark," Taylor said it out loud, a non-sequitur, but Belle and Maddie followed her thought.

"And there aren't any lights beyond the backdoor patio." Belle pointed at the outdoor lamps that flanked the paver patio that was under the deck. "They might have seen her as she walked this way, but not once she got down here."

The lawn between the patio and the river was long. At least two thousand feet. Most of the acreage at this bed and breakfast was out there in the back. You could see the water from the house, but not after dark.

"So, it was possible." Taylor knelt and touched the boards. "With those shoes on, and even a little bit tipsy, she could have tripped."

There was a crack in one board. A thin gash of fresh wood in the otherwise aged silver cedar. "Right here," Taylor whispered.

Belle crouched beside her. "That must be where her shoe got stuck."

They stared at it together. Evidence of the accident. Evidence that Belle wasn't responsible for anything.

"And then she fell," Maddie offered, one hand on her shoulder.

"Or she was pushed," Belle said. "Both Melinda and Amara said Colleen went out too. Maybe Mom's shoe got stuck when Colleen pushed her."

"Oh, Belle…" Maddie didn't seem to be a dedicated detective. This little cracked board seemed to satisfy her curiosity.

But it didn't satisfy Taylor, because if Colleen wasn't the one who pushed her mom into the water that night, then she might be able to push Belle out of their house.

Taylor sat crosslegged on the dock. "While I'm sure the police have talked to everyone, I'd like to talk to the lady that owns this place." She dug around in Google till she found the website for the Riverside Getaway. Owner, Andrea Millson.

Taylor tapped the phone icon and, to her surprise, Andrea answered right away. "Are there any vacancies?" Taylor asked as soon as the lady who answered was done with the commercial welcome.

"We have quite a few spring dates available."

It was only Tuesday. Wednesday and Thursday wouldn't be too busy at the shop. Roxy could handle it. "I'd like a double occupancy room for tomorrow night for my sister and me."

"Ah! That should be two rooms then. We don't have twin bed rooms here, but I tell you what, I'll give you a two for one deal. We've had a…well, we've had some cancelations."

Taylor gave her name and phone number.

"Quinn?" Andrea said in hushed tones.

"Yes. Laura Quinn is my mother. My sister and I need closure."

Andrea cleared her throat. "I'm not so sure…"

"We are. Please let us come."

Belle stared at Taylor, but Maddie was watching the road. A pickup truck had pulled into the parking area.

"All right. You can come."

"Make it three rooms." Maddie interjected.

"Is there a third room available?"

"Yes, Miss Quinn. Whatever you need."

"Thanks."

Andrea didn't ask for a credit card over the phone. Taylor was glad since she wasn't sure she had one she could use. She needed to run to the bank in Willamina and find out what her mom's finances were like. It was on the to do list, but so many things were.

The door to the pickup slammed shut and a tall, broad shouldered man sauntered down their direction.

When he was in hollering distance, Taylor waved.

He waved back and joined them on the dock.

"Can I help you all?" Hudson East, the very handsome nephew.

Taylor stood. "No, we were just…. Had you heard about Mom?"

"Yeah. I'm sorry." He offered her his hand, and when Taylor

took it, he enveloped hers in two muscled and rough hands. "Are you all right?"

"No." She looked away from his rugged face with the dimpled chin.

Belle stared at him. He was a far cry from the peach fuzz of her friend Cooper. She seemed impressed.

Hudson had been a freshman in high school when Taylor was a senior, but he was still far too old for her teenage sister. "My aunt saw you and called me."

Taylor looked back at the house, shivering. Had Andrea been watching us?

"She's been staying with my grandma the last few days, but saw some activity via the security camera feed. She just wanted me to check it out."

"I totally understand."

"So...all's good?" He stuffed his hands in his pockets and scanned the property.

"We were just leaving. Your aunt gave us a few bedrooms for tomorrow night. We, um, want to say goodbye."

He nodded, and they all walked back to their cars. "I'll see you then."

"Oh?" Taylor asked.

"Aunt Andrea's not up to staying here yet, so breakfast will be on me." He grinned. "Hope you like bacon and sausage and eggs. I do a mean fry up."

Belle blushed and fluttered her eyelashes.

Taylor wouldn't have wanted to admit it, but she did too.

Roxy was willing to open and close on Wednesday and Thursday. Willing, eager, and supportive seemed to be her wheelhouse. Taylor gave her Saturday off to compensate, but knew full well it wasn't enough. She would have to figure out some way to make sure Roxy knew how much her years of loyalty and hard work meant to her.

Taylor explained the plan as she and Belle packed their bags. "Why is it you don't work at the shop?" Taylor tried not to sound judgmental.

Belle looked over at Grandpa Ernie who was adjusting framed pictures in the hallway outside her door.

Taylor understood the simple gesture. Grandpa was Belle's after school job.

But she hadn't remembered he might need someone here with him while they were gone overnight. "Crap."

"It's fine." Belle unzipped the bag she had just finished. "You and Maddie go. I'll stay here." She sighed. It was clearly not fine.

"Maybe Maddie will stay with Grandpa Ernie."

"I'm not a child," He interjected. "And I will be just fine while you girls go off to drink and talk."

"We won't be drinking."

"Good. Your sister's not old enough." He shuffled back downstairs, tipping framed pictures as he went. Taylor suspected he liked their company better than being alone, but still wished he wouldn't use the stairs quite so often. He wasn't as steady on his feet as she would have liked.

"Maybe it would be better if you and Maddie went." Maddie was, after all, the professional. Better her and Belle for the weekend, than Belle and Taylor who felt completely out of her depth.

Belle brushed her bangs out of her eyes. "Really? Do you mean it?"

Taylor swallowed. She was already sorry for suggesting it, but what option did she have? "I mean it. Let me give her a call." She had to leave a message and made it brief.

Belle finished packing while Taylor made dinner.

An hour later Maddie called back, and they sorted out the details. She promised she'd keep Belle from doing anything stupid *in re* handsome Hudson, but she wouldn't swear the same thing for herself. That was another hint of the goofy Maddie

Taylor used to know. It was like finally seeing an old friend again. Taylor reminded her of Mr. Dr. Maddie who would be waiting loyally for her at home. Maddie laughed.

THE NEXT MORNING, Maddie picked up Belle and they drove the winding country roads to the little bed and breakfast on the river.

"Well, Grandpa, I guess we'd better get to the shop."

"Good girl," he said. "Work first and you'll never want."

Taylor sighed. He'd had a lot of work first through the years, and yet, right now, he wanted for a lot, including his daughter, his wife, and his short-term memory.

Roxy jumped with a start when Taylor hollered a hello from the back door. "Did something happen? Is everything all right?"

"It's fine, it's fine. Just a small change in schedule and, since I was home still, I figured I might as well work."

They had a tiny smattering of midweek customers. Only three in fact, including Taylor's Aunt Carrie with her newest kid in a stroller. She didn't buy anything but did hint around trying to find out if Laura had always been a drunk.

It was a bright, rain free day and the tulips were all in bloom, but they had no customers. Taylor knew she'd have to formulate a marketing plan. See what kind of co-op deal she could run with the three other quilt stores, just as soon as she'd shored up her sister during her time of trial. In the meantime, the empty store was wearing her down. "Grandpa, I know you won't like this, but I think I'm heading out early. I still haven't taken care of Mom's business at the bank,"

He grunted and stood up from his chair. "Then let's get going."

"You don't have to come."

"You think that bank in Willamina is just going to hand you all Laura's money?"

"Not exactly, but the will…"

He barked a short laugh again. "We'll see what they think about the will. You never can tell with these financial institutions."

Taylor smiled and helped him into the rusty tweed suit jacket he never left home without. "I'd rather have your company anyway."

THE BANK in Willamina was a local branch of the Old Mill Credit Union, a tiny little low slung building from the seventies with heavy cedar shingles hanging low over the dark windows. Three tellers stood waiting for customers, and an elderly lady with a bright pink walker stood at a side desk filling out small check-sized papers. Taylor didn't know the teller who they talked to, or the higher-up who had to come when Taylor realized she had forgotten a copy of the death certificate.

Grandpa Ernie, however, was a cosigner on the account, so they were able to ascertain that Laura Quinn had over three-hundred-thousand dollars in her business savings, not including the account for regular shop expenses.

Taylor stared at the statement in shock. Flour Sax was just a little fabric store in a tiny little town off the beaten path. Taylor had grown up with free lunches and hand-me-down clothes, even when her dad was still living.

"How?" Taylor couldn't make more than one word come out.

Grandpa Ernie pointed to the deposits on the statement. "Her boob tube show. Now will you start filming again?"

Taylor needed to sit down.

But she didn't. She stood strong and pretended she was perfectly happy that their family fortune now rested in her ability to be charming on the internet.

"You'd better get home and figure out what your mom was doing, because she was doing it real good."

"When you come back with your death certificate, we'll get

this all sorted out. We can make an appointment, if you'd like." The higher up who'd been called to their aid wore a name tag that said "John". He was another of the broad shouldered handsome types like Hudson. Grandsons of the loggers the area used to be thick with. A kind smile and soft eyes gave him a different, easy going look though. Taylor liked it. Why had she not noticed the wealth of manly men in this area when she lived here?

Taylor took a long deep breath. "Thank you. I'll get this sorted out as quickly as I can." She glanced at John's hands. No ring or tan line where a ring used to be.

On the drive home Grandpa Ernie broke into a tsk-tsk. "Clay won't like it when he hears you're looking at rich men's wedding fingers."

"Rich men?"

"Bankers. They've always got money."

That part hadn't even occurred to her. Taylor was not sorry that John, the one to talk to for business and investment banking might be rich. "Clay dumped me, Grandpa."

"Oh? Never did like him. Mealy-mouthed."

"You're probably right." Taylor, however, had liked him very much, and for quite a few years. She still couldn't believe it was over. It had been less than two weeks since his ultimatum, and it seemed impossible, the sweet, goofy guy she had been with for so long, would break up with her just because she needed to move home to take care of Belle. He had always been a good guy. A nice guy.

When they got home, she hunted high and low for her mom's death certificate. When she had literally run out of places to check, she called the funeral home and left a message. The funeral director was almost as old as Grandpa Ernie, but he'd know what she needed to do.

Then Taylor called Belle, just to check in. No answer there, so she called Maddie, but she only reached the very professional and caring sounding voicemail.

Taylor hoped that Maddie and Belle were having a very

healthy counselor-client-detective time. As she made a simple dinner of macaroni and ham slices for herself and Grandpa Ernie, she tried to squash her envy. She could not be jealous of every person who got to hang out with Belle. It wasn't healthy.

She also considered not opening the store the next morning. She certainly didn't need the money, but she supposed Roxy did, and her needs mattered too.

CHAPTER SIX

aylor was washing up dinner dishes when Grandma Quinny called. "You forgot us."

Grandma was right. In the middle of her play-detective plans for Belle, Taylor had completely forgotten the dinner party Grandma Quinny was throwing. "Oh Grandma, I'm so sorry. I didn't mean to." She dropped a slippery pot in the soapy sink.

"It's only seven. You could still come by for dessert. We're serving your favorite, strawberry scones."

Grandma Quinny's strawberry scones with freshly whipped cream were a definite draw. "Belle's not here tonight."

"That's fine, love. The cousins all want to see you."

Taylor gritted her teeth. Was it impossible to make her grandma see her and Belle as a package deal?

"Grandpa Ernie's having a bit of a lie down."

"And that's all right as well. If he's sleeping, he'll be fine for an hour or two. Come see your cousins." Grandma Quinny was almost begging.

"Give me five minutes to make myself presentable."

It took a little longer than five minutes to sort out her hair and face and find something nice to replace the clothes she had gotten wet while washing up.

Grandma and Grandpa Quinn farmed their strawberries off Bible Creek Road, not far from the creek itself. Vine maples, sword fern, birch, and red alder framed the curving road. The sun was just starting to set, and the dusty orange tint above the tree line warmed her heart. There were brief moments when it was so nice to be home, and she almost forgot why she was here.

Grandma and Grandpa's house had been built in the '90s, not long after Taylor was born. It had all the dormers and decorations the bed and breakfast had, but none of the charm that only comes with age. They grew strawberries on their five acres every spring, and the rest of the time they played chicken farmer. It wasn't much by way of a money-making industry, but it was the kind of retirement you'd expect from a reformed yuppy and his college professor wife. Grandma Quinny had taught what few business classes Comfort College of Art and Craft had once offered. She was a smart, funny teacher, but tough.

On long summer evenings their property was usually crawling with grandkids. There was a dozen of them—make that a baker's dozen with Aunt Carrie's newest. But the gentle rolling hillside was quiet tonight. Early April was a little chilly for the adults to sit out and, anyway, there were only two other cars in the long driveway when Taylor arrived.

Taylor let herself in and followed the sounds of chattering voices to the kitchen. Grandma Quinn and Aunt Susan were plating dessert while Grandpa, Uncle Sean, and her cousins Ellery and Reid played pinochle.

"Oh good. You made it. We had about given up." Aunt Susan passed her a plate. "It's too late to join the game."

"That's all right." Taylor sat with the card sharks at the table.

Grandpa Quinn took his pinochle seriously and only gave her a quick, grim smile as a greeting.

"He's losing." Reid was red-faced and excited. He was not one of the big burly sons of loggers this region seemed to be full of. Like Clay, who Taylor had left in Portland, he was one of the thin shouldered computer types who gets away with murder because he can fix your internet when it goes down.

Ellery was right in the middle of the mess of cousins, just starting college. Last Taylor had heard, she was thinking of going into medicine. "Do you need coffee?" Ellery tilted her head as she spoke, like she was assessing Taylor's health.

"Better not, it's late."

"Tea then. Mama, can you get Taylor some tea? She looks like she could use it."

Taylor wasn't feeling a million bucks, but she thought she was hiding it better than that.

Aunt Susan went to the sink to fill the kettle.

Reid grumbled under his breath as Ellery played a card.

"It's been a long time since I've played this." Taylor tried to remember the rules as Grandpa Quinny laid some cards down, but they eluded her.

"Never mind the game, bring your scones in here, we need to talk." Grandma Quinn carried a plate into the formal front room.

Taylor followed her.

She supposed all of her many cousins and aunts and uncles might have been here earlier, but this was a far cry from the big family reunion she'd been promised. And their private chat was certainly not the same as a long visit with her cousins who were dying to see her. Taylor had definitely been played by a master.

"Sit down, love."

Taylor sat on the edge of the fancy couch that they were never allowed to sit on as kids, concerned she might drop whipping cream on the silk damask upholstery.

"Relax. I scotch guarded it just last week." Grandma Quinny smiled, but not with her eyes. Today she was dressed in what seemed like a country grandma costume. She wore a soft lemon flannel and gently used denim slacks with wide cuffs. Her immaculate yellow suede Keds matched the shirt. But she still had a hand full of large gemstone rings, yellow, clear, and sapphire. Also perfectly matching her blouse.

Taylor couldn't relax in the formal space. "I'm sorry I forgot to come."

"It's to be expected. Susan said I should have texted you a reminder earlier in the day."

Taylor shrugged. "It's hardly your fault."

Grandma Quinny picked up a red leather-like binder from the side table and opened it on her lap. "I have heard a rumor that you are selling your home in town."

Taylor nodded.

"Your town house condominium in Portland?"

"Yes. I couldn't possibly manage it as a rental from here. I knew I'd have my hands full with Belle and the shop."

Grandma Quinn exhaled with disapproval. "I was afraid that was the case. But just as I was most worried, I remembered something I had for you that might help."

Taylor frowned in confusion. "Help how?"

"If you had enough money you could pull it from the market, no?"

"You mean enough to pay to keep it empty?"

"Yes, exactly. Property is a wise investment and I hate seeing you lose yours." Grandma Quinny slipped a page from a plastic sleeve and passed it to Taylor. "Firefighting is a very dangerous job."

"Yes…" Taylor stared at the page. The non-sequitur had thrown her.

"Your mother and father had you so early in their marriage, and your father's job was very dangerous. I knew they were too young to think of it, so I took out a life insurance policy on him. For you."

The words on the page began to make more sense. Twenty-year term life policy. Thirty thousand dollars.

"You see, if the worst was going to happen, I wanted you to be able to have an education."

"But Grandma…."

"Yes, the worst did happen, but you had so many scholar-ships you didn't need this for school."

Taylor thought of the hefty grad school loan she still carried but didn't argue.

"I've been saving it for your wedding, but it seems like you could use it now, to save your home."

"I've already accepted an offer on it."

"You haven't finalized it, have you?" Grandma Quinny's face was one of calm assurance, like she knew what the answer would be. The only answer it could be. There hadn't been enough time to finalize a sale yet.

"No, that's still a few weeks away."

"Then change your mind." Grandma Quinny sat back, looking satisfied. "I'm glad you have time to save it."

"But I don't want to save it. It's not a great place. Bad loca-tion. Expensive HOA. It's better sold."

"Oh, darling, property in the city is always a good investment."

"But it's not in the city-city. It's all the way out in Gresham. My commute was a pain." Taylor worked hard to keep her voice from whining. If her mother had been alive, no one would press her about what kind of home she bought or sold. They never had before.

"Gresham has nice areas."

Grandma Quinn wasn't wrong. Gresham did have nice areas, but Taylor's condo wasn't in one of them.

"Please let me do this for you." Grandma Quinny merely smiled. She had the assurance of someone who knew she was only doing good.

"Grandma, you are so kind, and this is…" Taylor couldn't bring herself to say wonderful. The money, wherever she had it stashed, was kind of blood money. A payout because her dad was gone. "I made a solid profit on the condo. I bought low and sold high."

Grandma Quinny nodded in approval. "That's very smart."

"After the dust settles a little, I can buy something else....in town." Taylor was thinking about buying a newer home in Comfort, but Grandma didn't need to know that.

"I'm glad to hear you made a profit. When you're ready to reinvest, this life insurance money should help you buy something nice in the city."

"Or there's Belle's college to think of. Thirty-thousand dollars would be a wonderful help."

Grandma's face lit up. "Thirty-thousand was the payout seventeen years ago. It's substantially more than that now."

"It's very generous of you. It will be a big help for us."

"This money was for you, darling."

Taylor closed her eyes and counted to three. "Thank you. It will be nice not to co-sign loans for Belle."

Grandma Quinny's chin went up, and a half-smile appeared. "True. But don't make any rash decisions, please. We want to help you set yourself back up. The loss of your mother is dreadful, obviously, but we hate to see you lose the wonderful life you had created. Please don't do something you will eventually regret."

Taylor didn't have words for that. How, or why, would she ever regret Belle getting an education?

"There are so many decisions to make right now, it's kind of overwhelming." Though she didn't want Grandma Quinny dictating her financial decisions, she did need someone she could talk to. And Grandma was smart. Even better, she was wise.

"I'm sure it is. Do you have a good lawyer?"

"I have a lawyer, but I don't know if she's good. It's Mom's old friend Amara. She's got the will and we'll be going over it as soon as I make the time. I just...it doesn't really matter yet, does it? We all want what's best for Belle right now. That said, I'm lucky Grandpa Ernie is still a signer on the business accounts while I'm waiting to get things transferred to my name."

"Had your mother bought the shop from him?"

"No, after Grandma Delma passed, he gave it to her. He kind of lost heart."

"Indeed, he did. And I think that's about the same time his memory started to go."

"I wasn't around enough to notice. I feel awful about that."

"Well, don't. We didn't raise you to live in their shadows. You have your own light and need to do your own work in the world."

"I know you don't like it that I came back, but it's less than two years before Belle goes to college. It will be worth it. For her sake."

"I'm sure she's glad she doesn't have to move, but she's got many people to look after her. Who do you have? Clay? I don't see him around."

"No, he didn't want to move here." Taylor tried to figure out who Grandma Quinny thought was going to look after Belle. No one came to mind, unless Grandma Quinny knew all about Colleen.

"So, he's waiting for you in Portland?"

Taylor shook her head. She had sold her home out from under him. He was more than capable of making payments on the condo, but somehow, she hadn't liked the idea of moving away and leaving him there alone. He had been her partner for a long time, but part of her didn't trust him.

"Oh, darling, are you sure you made the right decision?"

Taylor straightened her sagging shoulders, her posture mimicking her grandmother's. "There was no choice. Belle is my sister and she needs me."

Grandma Quinny shut the binder with a snap, but her words were kind. "You have chosen a tough path, darling, but we are here for you, and that will never change."

Grandma Quinny set the book down, stood, and held out her hands for her granddaughter.

Taylor accepted her hug. She needed her hug. She desperately needed someone to lean on, if only for a moment.

THAT NIGHT TAYLOR laid in her mom's old bed—a surprisingly new mattress for a woman who didn't give herself a lot. The soft, well-worn, Dove in the Window quilt Grandma Delma had made for her eighth-grade graduation was pulled over her head. She was too warm, but she felt safe. Her mom smiled at her from the screen of her phone. All Taylor had to do was tap the arrow on the screen and her mother would be there, with her again, talking to her, giving her advice, helping her. Sure, it would be about quilting, and it wouldn't be personal, but that was better than nothing. When Grandma Delma had died, Taylor's mom hadn't had a series of videos to turn to in her loneliness.

Taylor closed her eyes and pressed her face into her pillow, feeling like a child who just wanted her mommy. But she quickly rolled over again, ready to see her.

She tapped the arrow , and her mother's warm, loving voice whispered to her. "You all watched me do that wrong. We could have edited it out, but if I had, I wouldn't have been able to show you the right way to fix it." The camera closed in on her hands as she took her seam ripper and placed it with the sharp pointy side on top of the seams and the little ball under it. With one swift motion she slid it across the stitching releasing the two fabrics from each other. "Smooth, isn't it? And simple. You aren't kids anymore, picking at stuff and making it worse. You are an expert now, a surgeon who can use their tools to heal." The camera showed the action of ripping the seam again but in slow motion. "Time spent learning how to heal properly is more valuable than time spent learning to match corners."

TAYLOR WOKE a pile of worry at five the next morning. She longed to get to the bed and breakfast to join Belle, but it was far too early. Instead of rushing in with the fools, she watched several YouTube videos about best practices in filming YouTube videos. It certainly didn't seem like rocket science.

She stared at herself in the camera of her MacBook. It wasn't a science, but it was an art, and right now she was a work in progress.

Around eight, Belle texted.

Bacon is good. Hot chef keeps talking about you. I kind of hate you for that. But I love you. When are you coming?

Taylor replied: *ASAP*. She ran downstairs to see if Grandpa Ernie seemed like he'd be okay at home for a while."

"Grandpa, I have to run out to the…" Taylor paused. Would he like this? Would he even understand? "To the river, want to come?"

He tilted his head, confused. "Did I take my pills?"

"Ah! Sorry!" Taylor popped some raisin bread in the toaster —it seemed like it had to be done that way, she didn't know why —then handed Grandpa Ernie his pills. He swallowed quickly but with care, then filled his coffee cup.

"Where's Delma?"

Delma.

Her grandmother.

Taylor patted his hand. "Sleeping."

He nodded and took his empty cup with him back to his room. Nope. He did not seem okay to be alone all day.

"Don't forget a jacket, Grandpa," Taylor called to him. "It can be cold out on the water."

Both her detective work and her innocent flirting would be hurt by this new addition to their party, but Grandpa Ernie might get hurt if she left him alone, and that wasn't worth it.

CHAPTER SEVEN

*B*elle, Maddie, and Hudson were lingering over breakfast when Taylor arrived with Grandpa Ernie.

Breakfast featured the largest plate full of bacon Taylor had ever seen, a matching plate of sausage patties, and a basket of muffins that had clearly come from Costco. It hardened her arteries just to see it, but the dining room smelled like heaven.

"Help yourself," Hudson said in response to her gaping maw. "I seem to have overestimated."

"Mornin' Gramps." Belle pushed a chair out for him. "You'll like that sausage."

"Got any coffee to go with it?" Grandpa picked up a mug and held it in Hudson's direction.

"Sure thing, Captain."

Grandpa smiled at the promotion in rank he had just been given and helped himself to sausage.

Taylor caught Maddie's eye. She just grinned.

"Have a good night's sleep?" Taylor asked.

"Beds were very nice." Maddie sipped her coffee. "Breakfast is also very nice. I have no complaints." Her warm smile was sincere.

Taylor's heart sparked in rejection. Had Maddie forgotten

they were here to learn how her mother had ended up dead? Surely Hudson's handsome face hadn't distracted her that badly. "That's nice." She pushed out the words.

Hudson's presence also meant the girls hadn't been able to interview the owner about the night in question. But maybe there had been some good heart-to-heart counseling instead. That might have made it worthwhile.

Hudson was quick with the coffee and brought some in for her as well.

"Hey Taylor, can I have a word?" His smile seemed innocent enough, but Taylor had that feeling you get when the teacher wants to talk in the hall.

"Sure."

He led her to the hall, which didn't make her feel any better.

"How well do you know Maddie?" His face reddened as he asked.

"She's happily married." Maddie was a beautiful woman, Taylor could see why he was interested, but she resented having to turn her attention to this.

He shook his head a little, and the corners of his mouth turned down.

"That's not what I mean." He exhaled sharply, like he was gathering strength. "Belle is a minor, and it's highly unusual for an adult to check into a hotel for the night with a minor. You understand, right?"

"Oh. Oh!" The light dawned slowly. "Oh gosh, I'm sorry they worried you like that. It was supposed to be all three of us, but we hadn't made plans for Grandpa Ernie."

"Yeah, I remember, but Maddie was the one who stayed, not you."

"He's not Maddie's grandpa."

"She's not Belle's sister." His brows were drawn together in what felt like more than concern.

Taylor had a feeling she was lucky he hadn't already called child protective services. "But she is Belle's counselor. Grief counselor." Taylor stood firm on the Persian rug that ran the length of the hall. She would put a stop to his worries with her no-nonsense attitude.

He leaned on the banister to the stairs, an attempt to look casual, though his face wasn't relaxed. "People do get into fields like child psychology so they can have access to vulnerable young people."

He was so off course it made her head spin. She was disgusted, downright angry, even. "You're slandering a good woman who just wants to help." She straightened up so she could get a little closer eye to eye with him. "And I don't appreciate it."

"I stayed in the room across from Belle last night and kept my door ajar. I didn't want to fall asleep, frankly. I put them in rooms on either end of the house too. I admit I dozed off, and I'm sorry I did. About two in the morning Belle left Maddie's room."

"How do you know she wasn't just leaving the bathroom?" Taylor crossed her arms and scowled at him.

"Because her room has a bathroom. I made sure she had as much privacy as we offer. This kind of thing is hard to talk about, I understand, but I'm really concerned for your sister."

Taylor couldn't see into the dining room, but she could hear Belle's laughter, possibly at something Grandpa Ernie had said. This was a sound Taylor hadn't heard since returning home.

"This is the last place Belle's mother stayed alive. Don't you think it's possible that last night she was scared or sad, and needed someone to talk to?"

"It's possible, but what I'm saying is also possible."

"No, it's not, but since Maddie seems to be someone you can't trust, we'll all leave."

"Please don't be hasty. I know you have something to do here. I'll entertain Maddie and Ernie if you'll take maybe twenty minutes to talk to Belle. I don't know how you'd get her to open up about something like that, but maybe you could."

"I'm surprised she didn't head to your bedroom last night." Taylor sneered as she said it. "Or didn't you notice the way she looked at you?"

He blushed darker red. He had noticed. "This kind of thing happens, and usually it's someone the teenager knows and trusts."

"Fine. You entertain the woman you suspect of being a child seducer and I'll go have a long talk with my grieving teenage sister about how maybe she shouldn't trust her psychologist after all. Happy?"

He raked his hand through his thick brown hair. "No. It doesn't make me happy. But I'm thankful you're willing to talk to her about it." He returned to the dining room and before Taylor could gather her wits, Belle came out.

"You want to talk?"

"Yeah...come outside with me."

"Okay."

Taylor took her to the swing on the front porch, and they sat together. "So...Cooper's not your boyfriend."

"Nope."

"Friend with benefits?"

She shrugged.

"You're interested in boys?"

"We try not to label ourselves, Taylor." Belle's voice was dripping with condescension.

Taylor could hardly blame Belle. She also thought her questions were invasive and out of place. "It can be hard to know who to trust with your...with your heart..."

Belle laughed. "Don't be gross. I know Hudson saw me last night."

"What did he see?" Taylor stared into the distance, afraid of how Belle might answer.

"He saw me come out of Maddie's room. I'm as embarrassed as you'd expect, but I was freaked out last night. Mom died here. She died, you know? And it's an old place. It creaks and makes noises in the night." Belle pushed the deck floor with her feet, and they swung back and forth. "I got scared. That's all."

"I'm sorry I made you stay here." Taylor also pushed against the floor. Knowing Belle went to Maddie for comfort didn't really answer the question. "So…what happened when you went to Maddie's room?"

"She was asleep. I didn't want to wake her up, so I just turned around and went back. I didn't mean to wake up Hudson either." She caught Taylor's eye and grinned mischievously. "Though, since I did, maybe he could have made me feel better."

"Belle…"

"If I'm going to engage in risky behaviors, I should aim a little higher than Cooper, or even Maddie, don't you think?"

"Come on, Belle. Hudson was worried. I guess he was right to be. How many times do we see this crap come up in the news? Teachers, youth leaders, scouts, and stuff seducing vulnerable kids."

"I may be grieving but I'm not vulnerable."

They rocked in silence for a few minutes.

"About this friends with benefits thing…" Taylor didn't want to keep digging at this hole, but she figured she'd better since they were already at odds with each other.

"Yeah, it's a wild world, isn't it?" Belle said. "I let him use my library card and he lets me use his Netflix password."

"And?" Taylor waited.

Belle hesitated. "Okay. We made out one time. Just once. I didn't like kissing him. It felt like kissing a relative, a cousin or something. It wasn't any fun." Her voice was unnaturally deep.

"Okay." The tension that had built up in Taylor's shoulders dissipated.

"And the only inappropriate thing Maddie asked me was if she should give Hudson your number. Since I'm only two years away from being legal, I said she absolutely should not. Hudson seems like a patient guy."

Taylor slugged her in the arm. "Not funny."

Belle laughed again. A little, cynical laugh, but still, better than nothing.

"Can I go finish my poppy seed muffin? I want to freak out the school if they have a random drug test."

Taylor groaned and followed her inside.

At the breakfast table Maddie was showing Grandpa Ernie pictures of herself and her husband on their recent trip to Butchart, Gardens. It was such a normal, healthy married person kind of thing to do that Taylor wanted to laugh. But also, she promised herself she'd never again put Belle in that kind of situation.

Hudson was wrong about Maddie, but he was right to worry that Taylor didn't have a sweet clue what she was doing as stand-in parent to a teen.

After breakfast had been cleared, Hudson and Grandpa Ernie went to the front room, which Hudson called the lounge, to watch golf and drink more coffee.

The girls went back to the dock.

"Tell me everything you learned from Hudson last night. Was he here the night Mom died?"

"He was just leaving when the ladies arrived, but Andrea, his aunt, called him when they found Mom the next morning, so he came back," Belle reported.

"Did he notice anything unusual about any of the ladies that afternoon?" Taylor watched the water flowing sedately in front of them. It made little, happy noises where it met rocks. It didn't know the damage it had done to their family.

"Not that he could recall. They all seemed happy, laughing and comfortable. Amara had her canoe on top of her Subaru, but didn't want help taking it down." Maddie leaned on the dock post near the shore.

"The girls mentioned some other folks staying there at the same time. Did you learn anything more about them?" Taylor sat on the dock and traced that gash in the wood that may have been made by her mom's kitten-heeled sandal.

"The two other ladies were a mother and daughter. He checked the register and confirmed they're Gina Croyden and Nancy Reese," Maddie said.

"Melinda and Amara said they knew them when they were younger." Belle turned to Taylor to confirm her statement. "The register said Gina lives in Troutdale and Nancy lives in Sisters."

"So, they met halfway? Seems like there are more interesting places to stay than here."

"Not if you're headed home for a visit, but don't have a house in the area anymore," Maddie said. "This is a really nice location. Good views, good dock."

"And that's all we learned from the night. Maybe Andrea will come back today, and we can ask her more questions." Belle sounded dejected. She was also staring at the water.

"You need to talk to Gina and Nancy." Maddie's tone was optimistic, though she might have been putting on a front for Belle. "Just knowing those names is worth it. I don't think Hudson would have confirmed with the book if he hadn't been here, getting to know us."

"He did seem to hang out with us a lot." Belle smirked at Taylor.

Taylor blushed, the levels of embarrassment were too thick to parse, but Belle hit all possibilities with her short sentence and impish smile.

"He kept asking when you were coming back. I think he might be interested." Maddie smiled as well.

"Yeah…" Taylor caught Belle's eye. Belle snorted.

Maddie frowned. "If you're not interested…"

"You're married," Taylor reminded her.

"I wasn't talking about me. I was just thinking there are more single girls around here than you'd suspect."

"Should we be getting Gramps home?" Belle asked.

"I guess so. I'll go take care of the bill." Taylor walked slowly back, loath to take her eye off the water, as though it might change its character when she wasn't looking and take someone else she loved.

Grandpa Ernie was asleep in a rose-covered wingback chair.

Hudson took her to the old-fashioned register at the check-in desk by the front door. "Everything okay?" he asked, real concern still etched into the fine lines that radiated from his eyes.

"Yeah. Belle said she went to Maddie's room because she was creeped out. You know, her mother did die here."

Hudson chewed his bottom lip.

"But Maddie was asleep, so Belle went back to bed."

He nodded, seeming to process her story.

"She said she noticed you wake up and considered popping in there for a little comfort." Taylor teased him a little. She couldn't help it. He seemed almost too concerned. She wanted their loss to be taken seriously, and yet, she could only handle so much kindly empathy.

He blushed again. It was cute.

"She also said she's legal in two years…"

He didn't take the bait—just calmly wrote a receipt for her. "I'm sorry we couldn't be more help to you, but I'm glad everything was okay last night."

His hand brushed hers, and then lingered there as he passed her the slip of paper.

"Thanks." Taylor shoved the receipt in her purse with the card she'd used to pay for the useless trip.

LATER THAT AFTERNOON, after they'd delivered Maddie to her office, helped Grandpa Ernie find Mayberry on the TV in his bedroom, and made Belle check her school issue iPad for assignments from her teachers, Taylor took the receipt out to file.

Hudson had written something on the bottom—his phone number followed by a note: For you, not Lolita.

Instead of saving the receipt carefully in a file of expenses related to Belle's counseling, she crumpled it up and threw it away. How dare he call her baby sister Lolita?

Taylor needed an outlet for the anxious energy Hudson had drummed up in her so she hunted Gina Croyden and Nancy Reese on Facebook. She found them quickly, both accounts were mutual friends with her mom's old Facebook account, so she sent friend requests. If she was lucky, she could chat with both Gina and Nancy tonight.

She put the books back and left her laptop on the bed. It was just about time for dinner and, if she recalled correctly, they were pretty much out of food. Tonight was as good as any to take the three of them to Reuben's.

Grandpa Ernie lit up at the idea and offered to pay. "It's my turn." He slipped his feet into well-polished loafers and hunted for his wallet while Taylor hunted for Belle.

Belle wasn't around and hadn't told her she was leaving. With a grimace of annoyance, Taylor sent her a text. Then she called her. Then she called Cooper's mom, Sissy.

"I don't know why you think it's best for her to be out of school." Rather than answering the simple question about Belle and dinner, Sissy tore apart the only decision Taylor was actually proud of making. "She needs routine and friends and support. What kind of life is she going to have holed up in that house with her grandfather?"

"I just want to know if she's eating with you. That's all."

"There's a lot more than that you should want to know."

"Of course there is, Sissy, but what I need to know right now is if she is eating dinner."

"She's not here, and I'm not surprised you've lost her again."

"Does she happen to be out with Cooper?"

"He said something about going out, but he didn't mention her. I'm sure he's with Dayton."

"Maybe they're all three together." Taylor drummed her fingers on the counter and wondered if Sissy and her mom had gotten along. She couldn't imagine it, herself. "Can I have Cooper's number? Belle isn't answering her texts."

As Taylor asked, a text came through. "Never mind. Have a nice evening."

But the text wasn't from Belle.

"Reminder: you have an appointment with Maddie Carpenter Tuesday at noon. Respond "yes" to confirm."

An auto text from Maddie's office.

Taylor responded *"yes"* and then sent Belle another message. *"Meet us at Reuben's in ten minutes or you'll pay."* It sounded threatening enough to her, but also like she could play it off as a joke. If she were a real mom, that's the kind she'd want to be. Firm but funny, but firm. But funny.

"Come on Grandpa, Belle is meeting us at Reuben's."

CHAPTER EIGHT

*B*elle neither responded to her messages nor showed up at Reubens. By eleven o' clock Taylor had run the full gamut of emotions from fear, to acknowledging the depth of her love for her sister and how devastated she'd be if anything happened, to laughing at memories of her own teen sneak-aways, to flat out anger after she remembered the kind of stuff she got down to when she'd snuck out as a teen.

How dare Belle pull that kind of nonsense?

She'd hit 'numb' by the time Belle snuck in at midnight.

"Hey." Taylor's voice was as excited as her feelings. That is to say, not even a little bit. This crap Belle had just pulled? The same all kids everywhere do, and not worth giving attention to. Especially since attention is what she was seeking.

Belle fell into the chair at the old kitchen table. "Oh my gosh, wait till you hear what I have to say." Belle raked her hand through her hair and whipped it into a quick ponytail.

Taylor yawned.

"Sorry it's so late. My phone was turned all the way off. I couldn't risk having it do anything at all."

"Pity you brought it at all." Taylor yawned. She knew the

anger would come back but seeing Belle safe and alive in front of her seemed to tell her brain it could go to sleep finally.

"Yeah, if I had been thinking I would have left it in the car."

"Whose car?"

"Dayton's."

"I thought Dayton hated you."

Belle laughed. "You talked to Sissy, then?"

Taylor shrugged.

"Dayton doesn't hate me. Dayton is not in love with Cooper. Sissy has some ideas about their future because Dayton's mom is Sissy's best friend. But that's all beside the point. Dayton and I were at the Kirby house tonight."

Taylor sat up. If Belle was seeking attention, now she had it. "Oh?"

"She fed us dinner, and we talked for a long time. Family pictures, family history, that kind of stuff."

"Must have been real fun for Dayton." Taylor wasn't proud of being snide, but it was better than screaming. Probably.

"Dayton's a sport." Belle's lips curled in a smile. "We drank a lot of juice and had to take turns going to the bathroom, over and over. And every time we slipped away, we snooped."

"What thoughtful guests you were."

"Taylor...what's the matter?" Belle's shoulders slumped.

"You didn't come home. You didn't answer your phone. You disappeared without telling me. What do you think is the matter?"

"You're kidding, right? I don't have to check in with you, and...I did this for us."

"Oh, spent a happy family evening with your...with Colleen as a favor for us?"

"Yes. As a favor, or did you not remember we are trying to find out if she killed our mom?" Belle's face went red. She drummed her fingers on the table, and her knee was shaking.

"You're my responsibility. Can you imagine what I was thinking while you were missing?"

"Excuse me, Taylor. I am sixteen years old. I've got almost two years of college out of the way. I hardly think I need you to babysit me."

"You're a junior in high school, what are you talking about?" Taylor pressed the ball of her hand to her eyes. Was her sister delusional?

"You've never heard of dual credit? I've been taking classes for college credit since eighth grade. Some schools don't know what to do with kids like me, but Comfort is okay. I stick the high school out for three years and leave early with an associate degree. Surely Mom told you I'm starting college next year as a junior. Or don't you pay attention when she's not talking about you?"

The vitriol in Belle's voice was deserved. Taylor hadn't known that Belle was gifted. Belle was their girl and brilliant at everything she did, but Taylor had sort of assumed they were seeing her through rose-colored glasses. That the giftedness was the same kind all families saw.

"So, if you think I'm going to report to you every time I pop out to see a friend, you're nuts."

"Fine." Taylor was tired of apologizing. She was tired of finding out she had no idea what was going on in Comfort, Oregon. She was tired of being a stranger in the house she had grown up in. "What did you learn at the Kirby's?"

"The house is huge, like four of ours stacked together. Her little boys each have a room, there's a guest room and an office and a room set aside for me. It was kind of child-like, but still sweet, I thought."

"She sounds like a fortunate woman."

Belle ignored the sarcasm. "Part of me thought it was sweet, but the other part thought it was highly suspicious. Don't you? Why have a room ready for me if you aren't sure, I mean really sure, I'm moving in? And how could she be so sure?"

"I suppose she just thought she'd revoke the guardianship

and come get you anytime she felt like it, even if Mom was alive."

Belle pressed her lips together and inhaled. "I wondered about that too. It looked like she really wanted me." She dropped her eyes to her lap. "But I wasn't fully adopted, why did she never come back for me?"

Taylor swallowed. When she was in middle school, her mom had read her a book about kids of adoption to help her understand what Belle might wonder about as she grew up. This was one of them. The main one really. The book had suggested they say that biological families who keep distant, do so because they want what's best for their babies. She opened her mouth to say it, but couldn't. Instead, she shrugged. "Who can ever know what someone else is thinking?"

"If...if she didn't kill Mom, I'd like to ask her."

"She didn't say anything about it while she poured out all the old family stories and stuff?"

Belle shook her head.

Maybe Colleen hadn't read the same book they had. But it seemed if she'd set a room aside in hopes that Belle would want to move in, she'd have some kind of answer. "So, did your spying pay off?"

"Maybe. We learned Colleen is on Abilify. I recognized it from commercials, but Dayton and I confirmed with Google that it's an anti-psychotic commonly used for bi-polar disorder." Belle seemed to find strength in reporting facts.

"Interesting. How did she seem?"

"Really, really hyped. I don't know if I'd call it manic or anything, but she seemed both excited and scared. Like how you feel on a first date or something."

"Which makes sense, since this was kind of a first date with you. Are you sure the Abilify was hers?"

"Yeah. Dayton didn't have a phone either, so we don't have pics, but we read it right. The prescription was for Colleen Kirby."

"And you really, really don't have any reasons not to trust Dayton?"

"Dayton and I danced together for a million years, and we were almost always in the same class in elementary. Dayton's trustworthy. Maybe not as smart as I am, but trustworthy."

There was no hint of ego in her statement. It was just fact. Most likely none of her peers had been as smart as she was, if she'd been taking classes for college credit since she was in middle school.

Taylor rubbed the back of her neck to ease the tension. Even she hadn't been as smart as her sister. "Okay. We trust Dayton. We know Colleen is being treated with a medicine commonly used for bipolar disorder, and she seemed both high energy and anxious tonight. What else?"

"Don't forget she already had a room for me."

"How did her husband seem?"

"Dave was really quiet. Nice, but he didn't say much. You might not be able to, living with Colleen and the boys. Those three made a lot of noise. The little guys never stopped talking. They had to show me their rooms, their train set, their bikes, their iPads. Even their baby books. It was intense."

"Family pictures?"

"Yeah."

"Anything funny about them?"

Belle nodded. "You're smart. In every family portrait Colleen was wearing the same necklace, a small gold bell on a thin chain. She wasn't wearing it tonight."

"Because the real Belle was finally with her." Taylor rubbed her neck again, but no matter how much she repeated that action, the tension was only getting worse.

"Yeah." Belle exhaled. "It was kind of intense. Out there, in the world, this woman has been constantly thinking of me, all the time. She had a photo album for me too, with the pictures Mom always sent to her friends. And…other stuff. Some early report cards, some ballet pictures. Some artwork from elementary school."

"Woah. How do you feel about that? Your life being shared without you knowing?"

"I'm torn. If, um...if Colleen didn't kill Mom, then I'm glad she had that stuff through the years. She seems like she really loves me." Belle's eyes were fixed on her hands.

That book their mom had read when Belle was a baby described the adopted child's feelings as a honeycomb—complex and strong, with flavors that range from sweet to bitter based on what fed the bees. At the time, Taylor didn't get it. Belle had been a baby, how complex could her feelings have been?

But she wasn't a baby anymore. She was sixteen and had just discovered that the woman who gave birth to her had indeed loved her just as much as the woman who raised her.

Again, Taylor found herself thinking about the dock on the sleepy South Yamhill River. Her mom's shoe had gotten stuck in the board, she had seen the chip in the wood herself. Her mother had fallen and hit her head on a rock, a terrible accident that could happen to anyone.

It didn't need to be Colleen Kirby's fault, did it? Just because they were arguing didn't mean Colleen pushed her in the river. "Tell me again why you didn't have your phones on?"

Belle smiled that sly smile of hers that Taylor now assumed meant she knew how much smarter than everyone else she was. "You didn't know where we were, so I figured you'd blow the thing up with texts. I didn't want Colleen to think I had to sneak away to visit her."

Taylor had several thoughts about that, including that being a sneaky and smart teenager was the worst combination ever, but she didn't say anything. It was too late, and she didn't have the energy for an argument. "I bet you're exhausted. Why don't you hit the hay and we'll go out for breakfast tomorrow and compare notes again?" Taylor stood up and pushed her chair in. "The best thing we could find out from all of this, is that it was all just a terrible accident, right?"

The look of appreciation that Belle gave her was worth avoiding a fight.

Taylor tried to give Belle a hug on her way to bed, but Belle didn't accept.

And that was okay too.

It wasn't, not really, but it would have to be.

WHEN TAYLOR GOT up the next morning at eight, Belle was fast asleep.

She managed to get some oatmeal fixed for Grandpa Ernie and get him his medicine.

"Your mom was wrong," Grandpa Ernie said sipping his coffee from the comfort of the recliner in the front room. "That girl isn't Belle, she's sleeping beauty."

Taylor chuckled. That wasn't a bad joke for someone who isn't always sure who he's talking to.

"I'll get her over to the store for you by the time you open. Give you time to learn how to make one of those videos."

Taylor exhaled sharply. There was enough work to do at the store without that.

"Trust me, you don't want to leave your fans without new content much longer."

"Okay." New content? Who was this social media guru sitting in her Grandpa Ernie's chair?

"What? You're agreeing just like that?" Grandpa Ernie laughed.

"You're not wrong. I'll get into the shop asap and figure this thing out."

"You're a good girl."

Taylor kissed his head and then went to get ready for a long day's work. She and her sister would have to have their more serious conversation later.

FORTIFIED with a cup of coffee and snuggled into Grandpa Ernie's recliner at the shop, Taylor decided to spend some time with her mom. It wasn't easy, but it was good. The videos were her, alive in a way that all the photos in the albums were not.

Her mom had a funny way of tucking her hair behind her ear using only her pinky finger. Taylor wondered if her mom had picked it up so she wouldn't get food in her hair while she was cooking. Taylor had forgotten about that little quirk, but her mom did it three times in the ten minute video. How could she have forgotten that? And her mom's habit of saying "anyways" instead of anyway. She had forgotten that as well. But she had these videos. A whole lot of them and what she really wished was that she had more. Many, many more. And that they weren't just about sewing.

The Quinns hadn't been a camcorder family when Taylor was little. And maybe her mom's phone had lots of videos of Belle on it now. Taylor knew it had a few, but her mom was behind the camera, not in front of it. She wanted a video of her mom playing dominos with them during a power outage, and of her weeding the garden with her funny old foam covered head-phones on, and of her buying groceries, and driving the old station wagon, and giving her love advice the time she and Clay broke up, and of both her mom and dad....

Nope.

That was one too many.

Taylor shut the computer. She desperately wanted video of her dad, and had wanted it for many years, but she didn't have it and wasn't going to get it.

Guiltily, she opened her computer again so she could play around with iMovie. That little app would be the key to keeping the online income flowing their way.

She had messed around with it just enough to feel like it wasn't the worst thing in the world, when she was interrupted by a call.

Maddie Carpenter's number was flashing so Taylor answered it.

"What's up?"

"You and I need to have an appointment without Belle so we can talk about this course of treatment." Maddie cut straight to the chase.

"What do you mean 'course of treatment'?"

"Our investigation into your mom's death is highly unorthodox. We need to come up with a firm plan, together, about how it is going to work, boundaries and all of that." She sounded very professional—even defensive.

"One question first. Did Hudson call you?" Taylor's hand clenched the phone. Was Maddie angry with her for something that man had said?

"Yes."

"Did he have concerns about the overnighter?"

"Yes." Maddie's single word answers were clipped.

"Did he...threaten you?" Taylor leaned forward in the chair, breath caught. What had she gotten them all into?

"You could say that. First, he questioned me about what I was doing, then he said if he had even a hint of suspicion about my actions toward Belle, he was going to call services to children and families."

"Is it even called that anymore?" Taylor switched hands on the phone, shaking her right hand to relieve the tension.

"No, but it's what he said. Listen, I think this is really going to help Belle, but it's not worth losing my license over."

"That's your concern?" Taylor's lip curled in disgust.

"As a matter of fact, yes." Maddie's voice lacked what little warmth it had had last time they talked. It was icy cold. "I did nothing wrong and will do nothing wrong, but a complaint like that and an investigation would ruin me, even though they would find I was innocent. He's such a jerk."

"He was concerned for my sister." Taylor stood and began to pace. If she had been back home, she could have gone to the chiropractor to work the knots out of her shoulders. She could have gone to the gym and used the sauna or the hot tub to help ease the tension. She could have hit the mall and walked off her anger, and shopped until her anxiety was gone.

She longed for nothing more than a long day downtown replenishing her work wardrobe at Nordstrom's. Filling her bookshelves at Powells. She glanced around the dated quilt shop. Everything in it was her mother's taste, and from at least fifteen years ago. To run from store to store in a town that *had* stores just to fix Flour Sax up would have been powerfully healing.

Instead, she replied to her angry friend's demands. "When do you want to meet?"

"I'm free right now. Why don't I come to the shop?"

"Fine." Taylor hung up.

Taylor was surprised Maddie didn't just fire them as clients. She wondered if she was sticking this out because she actually did care about them as friends. Then again, psychology was a field that highly regarded innovation and getting articles published. If this crazy idea of Maddie's worked, she could get famous.

Or not.

What did Taylor know about the world of child psychology?

Maddie knocked at the back door of the store not ten minutes later. She was dressed for a jog and turned down Taylor's offer of a cup of coffee.

"First things first." She and Taylor sat across from each other at one of the worktables in the sewing class area. "The only place I will be alone with Belle is my office, with you in the waiting room. I am not going to stand in as a chaperone, and there will be no more overnighters."

"Suits me." Taylor sipped her coffee.

Maddie was flushed, partly from her run and partly from her chagrin at getting caught being unprofessional. "If I weren't seeing her as a client, it would be different."

"Totally."

"Second, after any research together, we will meet at my office to make formal notes on it, both for the file and so we can talk with Belle to process it. This experience will be useless if she isn't able to process it with me."

"Fine." Taylor's heart was sinking as Maddie spoke. Even though she had anticipated this terse conversation, she had hoped it would be different. That face to face the old friends would be...friendly.

"And finally, any evidence of criminal activity discovered will be reported to the police immediately."

"That's only reasonable. Hey, do you know how to make a good YouTube video?" Taylor spun her phone in Maddie's direction. Yes, she was being passive aggressive. She didn't like this black mark on her sisterly-parenting skills any more than Maddie liked it on her professionalism. They had both screwed up, and it was frankly embarrassing.

"What? No. Are you paying attention?"

"Yes, I am. You need to have an appointment with Belle soon. She went rogue and investigated her primary suspect last night. Can we get in later today?"

Maddie gritted her teeth. "I suppose you can't leave the shop while it's open."

"Roxy has the day off since she covered for me while I was gone. It will have to be after we close."

Maddie checked her phone. "Can't. I'm sorry, my husband has a business dinner tonight and I have to go." There was an emphasis on husband that felt like an insult to Taylor.

"How about tomorrow around this time?"

"Okay." Maddie added it to her calendar then stood. "I still think this will work."

Taylor turned her phone over and made eye contact. "Why? It's not normal. Why do you think this will do any good at all? No one has investigated themselves out of grief before."

"No, you misunderstand." She scooted her chair closer. "We're not trying to bypass the grieving process. I'm wanting to help her start it healthy. She's a wreck right now—not a healthy wreck. I can help her the traditional way, but I think this is better. I really, honestly, do. We can't be careless. That's all." She had slipped up, sounding soft and caring in the middle of her speech, but she fixed it fast.

Taylor sighed. "I don't know how I could possibly care more. I know you're saying let's not be sloppy, but nothing felt sloppy. I'm just...I'm not her mom."

"No, you're not, and you're only going to be the person responsible for her well-being for a very short time. Let's not screw it up, okay?"

"I am honest to God doing my best."

The front door to the shop jangled as someone tried to get in. The shop was hours away from opening. Taylor didn't turn around to see who it was.

"You'd better get that." Maddie was facing the door. "It's Grandma Quinny."

Her grandmother was bundled up against the crisp spring morning in what could only be called English tweed. That and a paisley pashmina. None of it looked springy. Taylor welcomed her to their little worktable and offered her coffee.

"Thank you, indeed. It's not warm out there."

Taylor agreed.

"Darling, I had so much to say when you were over, but I really didn't get to the heart of things. Not after our talk about..." She glanced around and tucked her pashmina a little tighter. "But there was more, and here it is: If Belle is giving you too much trouble, you know what you need to do." She jutted her chin out and lifted her eyebrows.

Taylor frowned. "You wanted me to move back to Portland, right?"

"In an ideal world, you would be back home shortly after your sister graduates. But in the meantime, if you find her a challenge too big for you to handle, you are to move in with me."

Taylor caught Maddie's eye. To say she was shocked was selling her feelings short. "That's really kind of you..."

"If I were in charge, you'd already be there. I have plenty of room."

"To be honest, Grandma...I didn't know we were invited."

Her eyes went wide. "Well!"

"I mean, you hadn't said anything."

"I would think a grandmother wouldn't have to ask. You should know my door is always open to you and your sister."

"Thanks." Taylor tried to wrap her mind around what her grandma was offering and the implications. Belle claimed Grandma Quinny wouldn't even say hi to her on the street, but Grandma was saying she had expected them to move in with her. Then again, she said the door was open to her and "her sister". Was that a weighted term? Was Belle's value to Grandma Quinny only that she was Taylor's sister? She didn't know. She couldn't tell. "It's only been a few weeks, and I think I've already made every wrong decision that could be made."

"Taylor..." Grandma Quinny's tone wasn't any softer, but that was just the way she spoke. She couldn't help it. "I'm here for you, always."

"I guess I just worry about Grandpa." Taylor waved her hand toward his empty recliner.

"Why, love? He'd be thrilled to have you. We haven't seen nearly enough of you in years."

"I mean Grandpa Ernie."

"Ahh." She pressed her lips together and nodded. "I don't know what his finances are like, and I don't dare to pry, but it is likely time to consider a home. He values his independence too much for any other option right now. but he's a good ten years older than we are. Bible Creek Care Home is lovely. The Methodists run it and do a good job."

"He's not a Methodist." Even Taylor knew that was the wrong complaint, but she wasn't ready to kick Grandpa Ernie out of his home so she could run off to her other grandparents. It felt an awful lot like cheating on him. Too much like how Clay had so quickly found another woman to live with after telling her he wasn't willing to move here. For heaven's sake, he was in someone else's place after only a week.

One week.

Lila must have been waiting in the wings all along.

And no matter how many times he said they were just friends and he was only crashing at her place, she had seen the way he looked at Lila when she left. If they had been 'just friends' before he moved in, they certainly weren't still 'just friends'. "I'll look into it." Taylor spoke up before Grandma Quinny could respond to her other, more nonsensical comment. "But I can tell you I don't think I'm ready yet. It's just so many changes at once. I know Grandpa Ernie and Belle are a lot of responsibility for me, but I'm used to being independent." She laughed, embarrassed. "I'm almost thirty, Grandma. I haven't needed someone to look after me for quite a long time."

Grandma Quinny nodded in approval. "I thought as much. We Quinns don't raise weak women. But the second it gets to be too much, and not one second later, you call me, do you understand?"

"Yes, Grandma." Taylor wanted to invite her to dinner with them. She had hosted those friends of her mom's. She could make another pot roast. But Grandpa and Grandpa Quinny didn't go to other people's homes. It would be silly when theirs was so large and comfortable. Grandma Quinny wasn't much of a cook, but that was okay, since they could afford catering.

"Now, Taylor, I was just headed to the market and I don't have a lot of time today. Remember, Grandma is only a phone call away." She stood and gripped her purse in a carefully manicured hand. She might live on a hobby farm, but you'd never know it from her fingernails.

Taylor gave her a kiss goodbye and let her back out the front door. Grandma Quinny wasn't one to use the back entrance.

"Whew!" Maddie made a dramatic sigh of relief as Taylor locked the door behind her grandma. "She's always terrified me."

"Rightly so. No one messes with a Quinn woman."

"That's a lot to live up to." Maddie gave her a practiced look of compassion. "I suspect you'll be changing your name when you get married."

Taylor thought back to all the ways she had come up with to write her new signature once Clay married her and made her a Seldon. "Maybe. It'll depend on the name, I guess."

Maddie also stood. "Sadly, I was heading to the market too, but I think I'll put it off a bit. See you tomorrow, same time, but at my office, okay?"

Taylor let Maddie out the back door but didn't say okay. She was tired of agreeing with everyone.

CHAPTER NINE

$\mathcal{B}$elle was hanging out in the living room that evening. An unusual thing, her being in the house at all, much less being out in the living room with the rest of them.

Taylor put a kettle on and joined her.

Belle stretched on the old hardwood floor of their front room. She could still do a front split and lay her chest on the floor.

"Do you ever miss dancing?" Taylor sat on the sofa with her legs tucked under her. The muffled sounds of the news floated in from the TV in Grandpa Ernie's room.

"Sometimes." Belle sat up and stretched her arms over head.

"Why did you quit?"

"There's only so much dance you can do here in Comfort. Mom was willing to drive me wherever a stronger studio was, but I didn't love it that much. There's plenty to do without dance."

The kettle began to softly whistle. "Can I get you a cup of something?"

"I'm good."

Taylor went to the kitchen and made herself a cup of tea, then went straight back to where she had been. She wouldn't have left, if it hadn't been for the insistent whistling.

"What did you replace dancing with?"

"Lots of hiking, mostly. Some kids think it's boring, but I like to follow the creek and stuff. Be outdoors. This is a great place to be outdoors."

"Man, you are so right." Taylor sipped the tea. "Do you hike much still?"

"Too much school."

Considering Belle had been skipping classes she didn't think were worth her time for most of this year, Taylor wondered how much she could trust her. "So...I took you out of school for a little while, not realizing you were in some kind of crazy college thing. Are you going to be okay?"

"Yup. I've got it under control."

"Even the classes you were skipping?"

"I wasn't getting dual credit for gym, don't worry."

"Can't help it, sorry. I suspect I've entirely ruined your life, and I hate that feeling." Taylor picked at the seam of the slip-cover. It would need to be mended. She didn't love big projects like this, but overall it was still in good shape. Worth saving. Plus, her mom had made it.

"You haven't. Mom was really pushing for me to graduate with my class next year instead of graduating early, since we've all been together forever, but I don't see the point. I got early acceptance to OSU this December and can start in the fall. Why would I stick around one more year? For sentiment?"

"Yeah, Mom's sentimental. She would have wanted all the cap and gown pics and stuff. Are you going to walk this spring?"

"I was going to, but now, I don't know. I don't care. Grandpa doesn't really care. Do you care?"

Taylor closed her eyes for a moment and pictured Belle, black lined eyes, inky died hair, but in the silver cap and gown girls wore at graduation from Comfort High School. She wanted to see that. To take pictures of her sister and frame them so her friends would ask about her, and she could brag about how smart Belle was. "I care about what you care about."

Belle laughed. "No, you don't."

"I want to, does that count?"

Belle shrugged. "September's not long from now. Does it really matter if you and I care about the same stuff?"

"I guess I just want you to know you're still loved and watched over and thought of." Taylor sipped her tea.

This was hard.

She found herself saying that way too often. What had she expected? The sudden loss of her mother to be easy? "So what? Who cares that you're moving out in the fall? You're here now and you deserve someone in your life who thinks of you and tries to help."

Belle narrowed her eyes and considered this. "Will you be here still, when I go away?"

Taylor's original plan had been to stay in Comfort for the year and a half Belle had left of high school. She had pictured a long stretch of sisterly togetherness, grieving, laughing, loving. In her mind, it was going to be intense and beautiful, and when they loaded up the car and drove to college, Taylor would go her own way too. Whatever way that was. Maybe she would sell the shop. Maybe by then she'd be attached and want to stay. Hudson's handsome face passed fleetingly through her mind, then the bank teller whose name she had forgotten. It wasn't like this was a singles wasteland.

That's what Clay had called it—a wasteland. He hadn't wanted to leave his job to help her run the family shop and raise her sister. It was a dead end…the shop, the town. Somehow, he had even dismissed Belle.

Taylor hadn't brought Clay around here much, even though they had dated for over four years. He hadn't gotten a chance to get to know them, or this place.

Not that she hadn't invited him.

The point was, it wasn't a wasteland. Comfort was one of many small places spread out over a glorious fertile valley, and sometimes you had to drive a ways to get to all of it, but that didn't matter because it was lovely.

"That's what I thought." Belle responded to her silence. "Neither of us are planning on sticking around."

"I don't know the future, but I'm not planning on running out on Grandpa Ernie."

"Good." Belle nodded in approval. "I'll be done with college in about two years. Maybe three if I get a masters, and then I'm going to follow work, you know?"

"I do know." Taylor had followed work, sort of. She had taken her education and experience and gotten in on Joann's management track with the hope of moving to corporate sooner rather than later. It had been getting later and later and seemed less likely than ever. Impossible now that she had quit, but that didn't matter. Flour Sax was a fabulous store and Comfort was a lovely town. With her master's she could even teach at the college, maybe. There was plenty to do in this area. "So, thinking of you and what you might want, where do you think we should take this investigation next?" Taylor needed this change of subject. She wasn't ready to think beyond the now.

"We need to talk to the owner of the Riverside Getaway, Andrea Millson. I think she knows more than she says she knows. Also..." Belle whipped out her phone and Googled something. "Are you or are you not going to get that YouTube channel back running? Our ad revenue has really slipped."

"Why did no one tell me about this?"

"Mom told you. I sat in the kitchen and listened to her while I did some statistics homework. I don't think you listen well."

"I suck." Taylor traced the subtle plaid pattern of the creamy linen slipcover with her thumb. Her mom had matched the pattern perfectly. When Taylor repaired it, it wouldn't be as good.

"Yup. Even though I have scholarships and stuff, the YouTube money was going to be very useful for paying school fees, and also for Gramps as his dementia gets worse."

"Can you help me?" Taylor joined Belle on the floor and looked at her phone. She had the Flour Sax website open.

"Sure. I can walk you through what they did. Mom's old school—was old school—and has a bunch of spiral notebooks with her notes in them up in the apartment." Belle referred to the apartment above the store. "We'll need to get those and figure out what's next. She was very organized, methodical and so on."

They spent the rest of the evening messing around with iMovie. Taylor pretended she hadn't figured it all out already. She needed this time with her sister.

THE NEXT MORNING Belle talked with Maddie alone while Taylor read through her mom's notes in the waiting area. It was easier on her emotionally than watching the videos, but she had to do both. She didn't want to duplicate content, or even worse, contradict. She was feeling pretty good at the end of the hour. Ready to test her hand at it, in fact.

Belle invited her into the counseling room, but both she and Maddie were standing.

"We discussed Belle's visit to the Kirby house. In the future it makes sense for Belle to make sure you know where she is, so you won't worry."

Taylor refrained from saying "duh."

"It was a lovely gesture on Belle's part." Maddie continued.

"Excuse me?"

"I apologize if I in any way contributed to the idea that Colleen is responsible for your mother's death. While I still believe finding out exactly what happened that night is the right thing to do, I decidedly will not be pinning blame on anybody. And, as Belle and I discussed, if any of us finds any evidence of wrong doing, we will immediately contact the police."

"Indeed." Taylor sneered at Maddie like she was her enemy. "You're embarrassed about what Hudson said to you, but you don't have to take it out on us." She slipped her arm into Belle's. "We've got enough problems without your cold attitude."

Belle laughed. "Maddie's embarrassed about it. I'm embarrassed about it, you're embarrassed. What's a little embarrassment between friends?"

Taylor turned to look at Belle but didn't let go of her arm.

"We can do the investigation without Maddie, if you insist on making her an enemy." Belle patted Taylor's hand. "But I don't think we can do the grief processing stuff without her. Sorry, Taylor. It's just...they didn't really cover that stuff in your MBA program, did they?"

Taylor shook her head.

"That's what I thought. I need Maddie more than she needs me right now so let's play nice."

"When did you turn thirty-seven and become a better grown up than me?" Taylor asked.

Belle smiled. "I have moments."

Maddie cleared her throat. "It's not uncommon for a younger sibling to step up significantly in maturity during a time of crisis. Let's make our next appointment, shall we?"

Maddie and Belle compared phone calendars while Taylor stared at a painting of water bubbles. It didn't soothe her troubled spirit.

"Maddie agrees. Talking to Andrea Millson next is the right thing to do." Belle and Taylor walked the six blocks home from Maddie's office on Third and Mill.

"I'll call to see if we can meet her soon." The day was chilly, and Taylor folded her arms. Spring seemed determined to stay in hiding, despite the tulips being in bloom.

"Sure." Belle nodded. "I've got some schoolwork to do, but I can bring Gramps over to the store around eleven when you open."

Maddie's help with Belle was supposed to make everything better, but Hudson's stupid misinterpretation of an innocent overnighter had ruined it. Taylor wished she hadn't thrown out his number. She would have liked to give him a piece of her mind.

Taylor called Andrea before she left the house for work. Andrea didn't sound excited to talk with them, but was willing. All they had to do was meet her at the bed and breakfast for dinner the following night.

WHEN THEY RETURNED to the bed and breakfast, Taylor wasn't surprised to find Hudson outside flipping their burgers. But Belle gave her an obnoxiously knowing look when she spotted him.

Andrea looked about their mom's age. Her wispy hair was styled with blonde highlights and beachy waves. She leaned in hard to country chic, pairing a high-end western snap front shirt and Wranglers, with wedge sandals and fake eyelashes. She had a huge aquamarine colored stone on her right hand, but nothing on her wedding finger.

On greeting, Andrea embraced Taylor in a surprisingly comforting hug, and then Belle as well.

"Girls, I owe you an apology. I chickened out when you stayed here. I just...I couldn't. I've known your mom a long time."

"We can't blame you. None of this is easy." Taylor reached for Andrea's hand and gave it a warm squeeze. "I didn't realize you had known Mom."

"I went to high school with her and the girls. I drove into school from our place out on Moon Creek."

Andrea led them to their seats at the old farmhouse style table.

"I guess Mom didn't do these getaways very often now that Grandpa Ernie's kind of heading downhill." Taylor had a view of the patio from her seat, and of the grill master who was focused on his work.

Andrea said. "Aging parents is probably the hardest thing a person goes through."

Taylor caught Belle's eye. She would have given everything she owned to have to deal with the problem of aging parents. She swallowed the ache and continued. "Had Mom and the girls stayed here before?"

"Sure, lots of times. They used to do this as a regular getaway. They came here every couple of years. Sometimes it's nice to get away, but still be near home."

"I agree."

Belle pinched her mouth in a way that indicated she didn't.

"Soup's on." Hudson carried a tray full of burgers that smelled like the perfect summer dinner into the dining room. He set the tray down on a quilted table runner—an elegant dogwood flower pattern.

Taylor trained her eyes on it, trying to decide if it was hand appliqué or machine. Also, it kept her from looking up at Hudson.

Once the formalities of building their burgers was over, Taylor dug back into the investigation. She had hoped Belle would have questions, so she could have an emotional connection to this process, or whatever, but Belle could not take her eyes off Hudson. He seemed to have left her speechless.

He was handsome, but Taylor didn't think he was leaves-a-girl-speechless handsome.

"I hear Mom and Colleen were fighting the night she died." After the question, Taylor took her first bite of the burger. It was perfect.

"I was upstairs bringing fresh towels and heard them in the hall."

"Any idea what they were angry about?"

Andrea had just taken a bit of her burger and couldn't answer.

"How are you doing, Belle?" Hudson smiled kindle at the girl.

"I'm doing quite well." Belle sat up, her chin out. "For a vulnerable teen likely to be taken advantage of by adults in positions of power."

"Belle!" Taylor almost dropped her burger.

"Would you rather folks not care?" Hudson wasn't bothered by Belle's mouthy answer. He smiled, even with his eyes.

Belle didn't have an answer, despite being the brightest one in the room.

"Sometimes caring what happens to people is embarrassing," Hudson said casually. "But it's always worth it."

"I think Laura was mad at Colleen about the food." Andrea jumped in, her own cheeks red.

"What?" That wasn't what Taylor had expected to hear.

"Not my food, but the picnic stuff she had in the cooler. I know for a fact I heard her say cooler, and also hot, and nacho."

"They brought nachos in the cooler and she was willing to fight over it?" Taylor muttered.

"Nachos should be served hot." Hudson offered her a cheeky grin.

"It doesn't sound like Mom. Like, I can't see her getting mad about the food." Belle turned to Andrea and seemed to consider her for the first time.

"All I can say is what I heard through the door, and it wasn't much." Andrea's large eyes were apologetic.

"But we know she was angry and went out to the dock, probably to cool off, right?" Taylor asked. "And Colleen followed her out?"

"Colleen came downstairs but I don't think she went out. I think she was just pacing, cooling down." Andrea clarified.

"Amara and Melinda said she went out."

"Did they see her?" Andrea asked.

"No," Belle said. "They just heard her go out."

"You can't hear the doors from upstairs. You can check before you go, if you don't believe me. My hinges are smooth as butter."

After they finished their burgers, they tested the doors. Even with the windows in the bedrooms open, Taylor couldn't hear the back or front doors opening or shutting.

"I've got ice-cream," Andrea said as they hovered in the front room, unsure of their next step. "Let's have sundaes and really talk. I feel like there's more that needs to be said or asked or just remembered."

It was getting on nine and they had a bit of a drive home, but it was worth it. Cooper was at the house with Grandpa Ernie. He'd agreed to say he was looking for Belle and was happy to wait around at the house for her. They didn't want Grandpa to feel like he had a babysitter, though they were paying Cooper ten dollars an hour and all the snacks he could eat to do it.

They were scattered around the room at a comfortable distance. It didn't quite make for an intimate share-your-secrets setting, but they all had a little room to breathe in the otherwise tight quarters.

Hudson passed around classic sundaes—vanilla ice cream, hot fudge, whip cream and a cherry on top, then sat next to Taylor on the Victorian style loveseat.

She scooted a little to make room for him.

"What I'd really like to know," Belle paused to lick a dab of whip cream from her finger, "is how all of the guests interacted with each other."

Taylor nodded her approval. It was a great question.

"Like, were the other ladies annoyed about the fight or anything?"

"They seemed...normal." Andrea swirled her spoon in her dish, making a soup of her dessert.

"But how would you define normal?" Belle pressed.

"There was a little chit chat, maybe some light laughter. The two groups of women didn't linger together, but they didn't seem to want to avoid each other."

"What kind of chit chat?" Taylor asked.

"Let me think...Nancy and Amara compared sweaters. They

had similar cardigans, knock-off Pendleton wool, I think. Maybe Gina just said hi to the other three?"

"Did they say hi back?"

"I suppose, I don't remember it all, just that they were smiling."

Taylor leaned back, but the little loveseats' cushions weren't very firm and so in leaning, she shifted into the arm Hudson had draped over the back of the couch. He gave her shoulder a pat and then politely removed his arm.

"What were Mom and her friends doing before the fight?" Belle asked.

"Maybe just looking at the river?" Taylor suggested.

"Shh," Belle said. "Let her think."

"Sorry."

"Drinks." Andrea nodded, proud of herself. "One of them, I think it was Amara, had a small cooler and they all had margarita glasses in their hands."

Belle seemed satisfied. "They had already started drinking, but were happy, and not fighting."

"Yes. Very much."

"And the two groups were the only ones staying that night?"

"Yes, though, I was here as well." Andrea leaned forward. Her face was scrunched in concentration. It was clear she was trying as hard as she could to remember everything.

"But not Hudson?" Belle asked.

"I was here when they checked in but went home. I do odd jobs here, but it's not my main gig." He directed his answer to Belle, who blushed when he looked at her.

"How long after this did the fight start?" Taylor asked.

"A few hours."

"But what was everyone doing all that time?" Taylor thought sitting around a Bed and Breakfast must have been a dull evening.

"I was in the kitchen doing prep work for the next day's

breakfast. Gina and Nancy had tea by the fire in this room for most of the evening."

"And the other party?"

"Amara and Melinda went for a walk. Not long after, Colleen and Laura—your mom—came down together. They were quiet and asked for tea. I offered them an electric kettle for their room, their choice of teas, and a fresh muffin each. They accepted. It took a minute to put it all together, but then they went back upstairs."

"How did they seem?" Taylor asked.

"Fine...or...a little bored, actually. I remember hoping they thought the bedroom tea party was fun."

"Did all of the ladies see each other again before the argument you heard?"

Andrea held her hands up and shrugged. "I wish I knew. When I was done with my baking, I grabbed the fresh towels for the hall bath and headed upstairs. That's when I heard the fight."

Taylor's sundae cup was empty, as were the others.

Hudson gathered them and took them to the kitchen.

"I guess that's all we can learn." Belle was hiding behind her shaggy black hair still, but the lines of her mouth suggested she was unhappy with the conversation.

Andrea stood, frowning. "I wish I could have helped more."

"You said you could hear footsteps when people use the stairs. We know Mom and Colleen both went downstairs. Did anyone else?"

Andrea raised her eyebrows. "Yes! Don't know who, though. My suite is here off the kitchen." She waved behind her to where a square addition that jutted from the side of the Queen Anne home. "When Nancy and Gina went upstairs for bed, I had gone to clean up their tea, but they had taken the cups with them. I just assumed Gina was bringing their teacups back downstairs."

"Why Gina?" Belle asked.

"I suppose because she was treating her mom to a special

trip. She had booked the rooms, paid for them, asked for the tea. Nancy didn't seem to do much but chit chat quietly with her daughter."

"And you couldn't hear the front or back door open if someone else went outside, even though you were downstairs."

"No. Those are quiet doors, plus I had the TV on. You know how stairs are, hollow and echoey if folks aren't trying hard to be quiet, so I do hear that, but otherwise I don't really know what's going on in the inn when I go to bed."

"Who was it that found Mom in the morning?" Belle appeared to have no interest in getting up.

Andrea squeezed her eyes shut. "It was me." Her voice wavered. "I had opened up the house for the morning. There are little outside jobs I need to do, like sweep the patio, and fill the bird feeders. I was out there, on the patio, when I saw her. Her shirt was bright pink, and it stood out against the murky water and the stones." She stopped and pressed her hand to her mouth.

Belle inhaled.

Taylor wanted to take over for her sister, save her from having to ask questions like this, but she found her own voice was missing.

"What did you do next?" Belle's voice was a little breathy, but she was hanging on.

"I moved her head out of the water. Checked her pulse and called 911. I had my phone in my pocket. She was gone though. No pulse at all."

"Did you try CPR?" Taylor's voice rang out in anger, surprising even her.

"She was so cold. Her lips…were blue and swollen…if you had seen her."

Taylor took a deep breath.

"But I did try. Chest compressions. I tried so hard I broke her rib. I swear to you I tried. She was my friend."

Taylor collapsed back in the sofa, not sure where that spurt of adrenaline had come from.

Hudson moved slowly across the room till he was next to her. His hand was on the back of the sofa as though he wanted to offer her comfort but wasn't sure he should.

"What else do you remember?" Taylor asked quietly.

"All of it. Every detail. After 911, I called Hudson. I heard the sirens. The guests heard the sirens and came running. Amara fell to her knees, sobbing. Melinda sat, slowly—I can see it like in a movie—she was hyperventilating."

"I got her a lunch sack to breathe into." Hudson's voice was low and sad.

"Colleen came to me and held my hand. She stroked your mom's cheek. There were tears. I remember so many tears."

Tears burned Taylor's eyes. She wiped them away with the back of her hand. She hadn't realized how much she had not wanted to hear all of this.

"Did the police interview everyone?" Belle's voice was small but determined.

"Yes. They took over my suite so they could talk privately. Then they let everyone go. It was an accident, sweetheart. Her heel caught on the board. It was sitting there, on the dock next to a splinter of old wood. This white, pretty sandal, all alone. She'd been drinking. She hit her head. It was a tragic accident."

Andrea's eyes were sparkling with unshed tears.

Belle's eyes were about to spill over.

Taylor was afraid to look at Hudson, if he was crying, she was done for. She'd never be able to drive home.

She took a deep breath and held it.

She counted, slowly, but only made it to seven.

Then she let it out.

Her head cleared a little.

She needed to be the adult now, so she stood and offered Andrea her hand. "Thanks so much. I'm sure this was the very last thing you wanted to do tonight."

"It was the least I could do after what you all have gone through." Andrea squeezed her hand again.

Their ride home was mostly quiet. Their emotions were too raw, too exposed to leave room for any kind of conversation. But as they turned into town, Belle had one more thought. "All of the women there went to high school together, except Nancy. I don't think that was a coincidence."

Taylor nodded, glad for something practical to rest her mind on. It reminded her of another practical question. "Belle, there's no denying you were closer to Mom. Understood her better. Why on earth was she fighting about nachos?"

Belle pursed her lips. Then replied. "She wasn't. That much is obvious. But what were they really saying that sounded like nachos when heard from a distance?"

The answer was obvious: not yours.

But Taylor wasn't going to be the one to say it.

CHAPTER TEN

*B*elle and Maddie met privately in the little counseling room attached to Maddie's house. It was a shabby addition, the paint starting to peel on the outside. The space was split in two, a waiting area and a counseling room. The waiting area had large armchairs that looked suspiciously like they had come from a Starbucks. The floor was cheap laminate that made a hollow tapping sound when Taylor walked across it in her penny loafers. The dim lighting was meant to either calm them or distract from the lack of trim around the windows and lack of baseboards. Maddie probably told herself the little mister puffing out essential oils would have a therapeutic effect, but Taylor suspected it was masking something. Maybe the dusty odor that comes from older heating systems.

When they were finished, Belle and Maddie both joined her in the waiting area.

"Did she tell you how our visit with Andrea and Hudson went?" Taylor asked.

"She said you learned details of the fights the ladies were having." Maddie wore a suit jacket buttoned up. Her arms were crossed.

"What did you make of it?" Taylor leaned back in the chair.

Her arms also crossed. She could do the closed-off body language with the best of them.

"We decided it meant there were definite tensions that night, but not enough to draw any conclusions." Maddie managed to say all of that without moving a muscle of her body, and barely even moving her face.

"But I think we need to get the ladies alone and ask them more specific questions." Belle leaned on the wall. Her silky black button up was buttoned all the way up. "Maybe you and Maddie could take Amara out. What do you think?"

"Why Amara?" Taylor asked the first question that popped into her head.

"She's the lawyer," Maddie reminded her. "You could discuss the custody situation. Even without the complication of Colleen's invitation, you must have a million questions about things you need to do to handle legal guardian issues. But I don't have any reason to be there."

"Sure, but she knows you're helping us. Won't she think it's weird you haven't just sorted that out for us?"

"Then get together with Melinda first. It really doesn't matter. I'm sure you're capable of coming up with an invitation that makes sense."

"I like Amara better," Belle said. "Always have."

"Any particular reason?" Taylor asked.

Belle shrugged. "Melinda spanked me once, when I was little and ran into the street."

Taylor laughed.

Maddie frowned.

Belle rolled her eyes. "Hudson has a lot to answer for if you two are going to keep arguing like this."

Taylor heaved a dramatic sigh and pushed herself up out of the chair like it was difficult. "Maddie and I made a stupid decision because we've known each other so long, we forgot we're not family. That's hardly Hudson's fault."

Belle pursed her lips. "Interesting take." She popped the door open and left.

Maddie sighed as well but not quite as dramatically as Taylor had done. "She's going to act out, it's okay." She didn't make eye contact with Taylor. "We're going to keep this professional, and that's okay too."

"Makes perfect sense. Two girls that used to 'borrow' your brother Brace's car when they were fourteen are going to totally professional amateur detective work to come to terms with my mom's untimely death. That's reasonable and logical."

"What's Brace's car got to do with it?" Maddie's façade cracked as her face pinked with the memory. The car had gotten them into more than a little trouble back in the day.

"I'm just saying, if you wanted to have a totally clean slate so we could have a completely professional experience together, you're going to have to erase a lot more than just one night at the bed and breakfast. And, yeah, I'm hinting your idea of grief counseling is bonkers."

"Fine. Do it on your own." Her lips thinned out as she pressed them together.

"Fine." Taylor clenched her fists and took a deep breath. "No, it's not fine, and you know it. You know I need you. So stop being a bitch and help us, please."

Maddie's lip curled as though she were suppressing a snarl. "We need to make Belle's next appointment. Two days from now, same time?"

"Fine." Taylor agreed to the appointment with a terrible feeling of defeat.

BACK AT FLOUR SAX, Belle and Grandpa Ernie sat together in his little corner of their world, but Belle was glued to her phone. Grandpa Ernie seemed to have great patience for her, despite her generational addiction to the internet.

"Hey, Roxy…"

Taylor's dedicated employee was cutting fat quarters from almost empty bolts. She wore a vest Taylor swore she recognized from her teen years—a spring flower patchwork. Her mom had made it, but she had never worn it.

Roxy sighed. "I'm doing my best."

"What? No…. I'm not going to criticize you! You're doing great."

"Oh…" She seemed down, and Taylor didn't like the way she assumed she was in trouble. Her mom hadn't managed by fear, had she? "It's just I saw you had the sales records with you when you came in. I'm really working on selling, but everyone just wants to browse. Or come in to gossip about Laura. They go over there," she indicated the corner where the YouTube show was streaming, "watch the videos and talk about her…"

"I hadn't thought…"

"You would hate to hear the things they're saying." Roxy's face was red, anger and sadness mixed.

"I haven't heard any of it." She had seen the way people whispered behind their hands, but she hadn't wanted to hear what they were saying as they looked furtively in her direction and scuttled out of the shop.

"They don't talk openly when you're in here, you're her daughter and all. I'm just an employee. But I was her friend too, and I don't like hearing them call her a drunk or whatever."

Taylor shuddered. "No, I don't like that either. Who is it? Locals?"

"Yeah, townies and others from around here." Roxy folded the quarter yard square of fabric over and over again.

"I could turn off the show." Taylor had considered doing this anyway. The sound of her mom's voice coming from the notions display brought sharp biting tears to her eyes at unexpected times.

"They'll still talk,"

"But they won't loiter gawking at her and gossiping. I'm sure of it."

Roxy nodded, accepting her word for it.

"Speaking of the videos, I think I need to start making more."

"Oh, good. I'm glad to hear it. I wasn't sure if you'd want to." A lilt returned to Roxy's movement and a shine to her eyes as though a million pound weight had lifted from her shoulders.

"The only thing is, I have no idea how she did it." Taylor chewed on her thumbnail, embarrassed. Here she was, the eldest kid, her mom's partner in crime for so many years, and she had to turn to an employee to find out what the heck her mom had been doing to make such good money online.

"We did it together." Roxy wrapped the fabric in the paper label.

"That's fantastic. I'm so glad to hear it. Did you film and edit and stuff?"

Roxy cut another square of fabric with one quick slash of the Ginghers. "I filmed it, then Jonah, my son, did the edits, and Belle managed the channel."

"This is the best news I've heard in a while. You're saying all Mom had to do was prep and practice and do the show?"

"Yes." Roxy paused, mouth slightly open like she wanted to say more but was afraid.

"I'll pay whatever she was paying. We'll get back on the same schedule. We'll do everything exactly the same."

Roxy smiled. "I'm so glad to hear it. This was the only job Jonah could find in town and he can't drive right now. Auto insurance for teenage boys is way too expensive, so I can't afford to put him on mine. This show has been such a blessing to us."

Taylor swallowed. "Of course. I've been doing my best going through all of the store records, but I'm still behind. Is there any way you could let me see your invoices or pay stubs or anything? I want to make sure you have everything you need."

Roxy's eyes went wide and soft. "I'll do anything you want, whenever. Just let me know and we'll take care of it."

"If you don't mind, I think I'd better go back to the office and get at it."

Roxy waved her away.

Her mom's office was merely a desk with a safe under it at the back of the shop, next to the stairs to the apartment. Taylor wanted to turn the whole apartment into a proper office, but before she jumped into big jobs like that, she needed to focus on the store. It was one thing to play detective to help Belle get closure. It was another to get so wrapped up in the search for the truth that she let the family business fail.

And she had a terrible feeling it was failing, like so many other parts of her life right now.

Last time she'd visited for more than a day, there had been three employees at the shop, Roxy who had been here forever, Willa who had retired from the business office at the college, and Roberta who could only work when she wasn't babysitting her grandson. Taylor couldn't remember the last time she had seen Willa or Roberta. They weren't on the books anymore. In fact, they hadn't been this year at all. She'd assumed they were still around, and possibly coming back for their busy season. But they weren't. The sales records were clear on that. Roxy was the only employee because she was the only one they could afford. She and her son who handled the video edits.

Taylor took a deep breath and squared her shoulders. Things weren't good at Flour Sax these days, but she could turn it around. She wouldn't let them down. Flour Sax had always been a good little shop, a good little employer. She just needed to remind people the store was out here. The internet had killed a lot of businesses, but quilters still needed fabric, and they liked to see it and touch it before they bought it. Quilt fabric was not something better sourced online.

In the meantime, she didn't like that Roxy couldn't afford auto insurance for her son on what they paid her. She had hoped to leave the world of overworked and underpaid employees behind her at the corporate chain store.

"I'm so glad you aren't mad at me." Roxy appeared around the corner. "We just need that cash cushion, that's all. Your mom was a big believer in that, but I'm sure you know. With a cash cushion it's easy to weather a slow spot." She patted the little half wall that hid the desk. "But really, anything you need, I am here for you."

"Thanks, I'm making a list. It's gonna be long."

Roxy chuckled and went back to the front of the store.

She was right though. A cash cushion had been Laura Quinn's motto. And she definitely had one. But Taylor's motto was advertising, and she was going to have to dip into that cash cushion if she wanted to see good things for this store this fiscal year.

Roxy worked till closing—eleven to six just wasn't a long working day. When they parted ways, Taylor had a much better idea of how this filming business would go and some ideas for what she could make videos about.

DESPITE A POSITIVE END to the workday, Taylor's feelings of insecurity got the better of her that evening. She was not just overwhelmed and cranky, she was angry at the world for doing this to her. Not even to the family. Just her. Her shields were up, and she didn't have room for anyone else in her little fortress of frustration.

Grandpa Ernie had been asleep when she got home, ready to go to the bank. And a quick check at the local small town credit union website had reminded her that they weren't open anyway. She couldn't solve any larger problems for their family, and she could hardly keep her head above water with the regular household work. The laundry had piled up, the dishes had piled up, and Belle was ignoring her phone.

She was doing her best, but it wasn't good enough. In the middle of her private tantrum, her phone rang.

Her hands were slippery with soap suds—she was attempting to take control of at least one part of life—so she couldn't get the phone before it went to voicemail. She dried them as fast as she could and drug her phone out of her purse. The number didn't show up on the screen, but she checked the message anyway. Between vendors she was trying to establish new relationships with and legal issues for the family situation, there were any number of strangers calling. She chalked up her inability to keep track of the necessary details for business and life to the fact that her mom had passed less than a month ago and the seams of her mental health were definitely fraying.

Taylor put the phone on speaker and went back to the dishes.

The voice came on strong, and she dropped a plate. "I don't know what game you think you're playing, but it stops now. I'm not letting that little—" the message was interrupted by a crashing noise and the sound of the caller swearing, but not into the phone. It stopped there, some emergency on the other end aborting his threats.

Taylor wasn't in the mood to be threatened or trifled with so she returned the call, but it rang indefinitely and then said the voicemail was full.

She slammed a freshly cleaned stainless mixing bowl into the dish rack. Then, feeling like this guy deserved to be harassed, she called the number again. And again. And again. She had called it fifteen times in total, not getting an answer, when another call came through, distracting her from her mission to annoy the hell out of what had probably been a wrong number.

She didn't recognize this number either, but at least it was listed. "Yes." Her voice was not friendly. She hoped it wasn't a vendor.

"Taylor?"

"This is she." Taylor paced the kitchen hoping to walk off the aggravation she had built up against her anonymous threat-caller.

"This is Amara. You called recently to talk about your mom's will."

"Ah, yes. Sorry. I did. But actually, I wanted to talk about the custody situation for Belle more than anything. When can we meet?"

"I have a free appointment in the afternoon two days from now, would that work?"

"I can make it work."

"My office is in Newberg, still okay?"

"Not a problem."

She gave her the address and Taylor jotted it down.

"Even though you're only asking about custody stuff, we need to talk about the will. I think you'll be glad we did."

"Wonderful." Taylor didn't sound like she meant it, but that was because she was still spitting nails.

"But regarding custody, don't let your heart be troubled." Amara's voice was friendly and soothing in a way Taylor had wished Maddie would be.

"Why not?" She stopped in the middle of the kitchen.

"Changing legal guardianship can take well over six months at which point Belle will already be a student at the university. There is no way any judge is going to force her to change that situation. In fact, it's most likely he will grant her an emancipation. It only makes sense, don't you think?"

Taylor scrunched her mouth, hard. "She's only sixteen. I'm not sure emancipation is a good idea."

"I can see why you'd feel that way, but don't forget that Belle isn't your average sixteen year old. Let's not worry over that right now. We can discuss the details at your appointment, in addition to the will."

"Thanks Amara." Taylor softened her tone a little. "I appreciate it."

"See you then."

They ended the call and Taylor stared at the phone. Emancipation? Emancipated minor? She thought that was just for abuse victims or spoiled rich kids with absent parents. Belle didn't have absent parents. She didn't need to finish her teen years legally alone. The anger Taylor had almost controlled beat against her rib cage.

Her phone rang again, this time unlisted. She snatched it. "What?" She snapped the one word like a dried twig.

"I'm returning your call to the bank." The voice on the other end seemed to find humor in the way Taylor answered the phone. "Am I speaking to Taylor Quinn?"

"Ah." Taylor cleared her throat. "I'm not sure I want to admit to that right now."

"I'm returning a call about the Flour Sax account. If you'd like to have Taylor Quinn call me back, I'm John Hancock, this is my number." He gave her his phone number plus extension.

"John Hancock?" Taylor stifled a much needed chuckle. "Sorry about that. I had a bizarre threatening phone call moments ago from an unlisted number."

"Did this one show up unlisted? Jeeze. I'm sorry. It's not supposed to do that, but I did use a back line since it's after hours."

Taylor hoped this John Hancock was the same good-looking guy named John she had met not long ago at the bank, and in that hope, she settled comfortably into a chair.

"Can I help you with something now?" John Hancock asked.

"I've taken over the family business—Flour Sax Quilts up in Comfort. I'm going to need to be put on the business account. What do I need to get to do that? Something from a lawyer?"

"That's easy. Ernie's on the account as an administrator, he can just add you. Bring him down soon and take care of that. No lawyer needed. Sorry we didn't do that when you were down the other day." Some papers rumpled on his desk. It was a nice old-fashioned sound.

"I don't know if you remember from when I was in before, but my mother Laura Quinn passed away, so I'll need to remove her…"

"That's a little more complicated, but still not hard. Unfortunately, we do need a copy of the death certificate."

"Got it." In fact, it was still waiting at the funeral home for her to pick it up.

"If that's everything, I'll let you go. Who knows when your phone enemy will call again."

"Yeah, I should probably get all riled up again just in case, huh?"

He laughed. "Hope to see you soon."

The call ended and Taylor smiled.

Funny thing to smile after a call about getting her dead mother off her business account, but she welcomed it. This grief business was killing her.

Her phone enemy didn't call back, but Belle texted. *"eating with Cooper."*

Taylor wanted to think of something terribly clever and a little curt to reply, but she couldn't, so she just said *"cool"* knowing full well that her text wasn't cool, and that she wasn't cool with Belle's dinner plans.

CHAPTER ELEVEN

aylor had a hard time falling asleep that night. She chalked it up to getting so mad about what had probably just been a wrong number. She ought to have taken a long walk to get over herself, but Belle hadn't come home, and she wasn't sure she could leave Grandpa Ernie by himself for the length of a walk. He seemed fine, but then, before he went to bed, he asked her if she thought Todd and the boys had the fires under control yet.

Todd was her dad.

Taylor dozed on and off a little, but she was awake when Belle slipped into her room. Belle had on some baggy winter themed jammies and padded her way in quietly. She sat on the floor, leaning her head back on her bed. "Are you awake?" Her voice was a whisper.

"Mm hmm." Taylor fluffed the quilt aside, an invitation for Belle to join her like she had done when she was little.

"Ever since this morning with Maddie, I keep thinking about Amara."

"How so?" Taylor propped herself up on her elbow and stroked Belle's soft hair.

"Now that Mom is gone, why hasn't Amara brought up Colleen with me?"

"It's not really her place, is it?"

"But she was their friend so she must have known. What does she gain by not telling me about it?"

"You're just a kid."

Belle shifted her head away.

"Let me finish before you get mad. You're underage. Maybe there's some kind of legal reason she can't say anything to you."

"There's not."

"Maybe Colleen asked her not to."

"What does Amara get out of Mom being dead?"

"I'd think nothing. She lost a good friend." Taylor yawned. Tomorrow would kill her if she didn't get any sleep."

"But she's the family lawyer, right? Doesn't she get a lot of work out of this? Doesn't that mean we have to pay her a lot of money?"

"I hope not."

"What if she gets something else out of it? Something we can't see yet?"

"I'm going to see her in a couple of days. Want to come?"

Belle pulled on the Barn Dance quilt that was folded at the end of the bed for decoration and wrapped herself up in it. "No. I don't. If she's keeping secrets from me, the only way we'll learn them is if you go alone."

After a few moments of silence, Belle climbed onto the bed and lay on top of the other quilts. She rested her head on the spare pillow. "I miss Mom."

"Me too."

TAYLOR MANAGED to get through the next day's work, though it was so quiet in the store, she almost fell asleep more than once.

But the day after that Taylor was well-rested and drove expertly to Amara's office on the first try, thanks to her phone.

Amara worked out of a newer brick office building with a rock garden and fountain area out front. Once inside, a receptionist shoved her glasses up the bridge of her nose with a bandaged finger and asked Taylor to wait.

Taylor was about ten minutes early, so she sat in a chrome and black pleather arm chair and pretended to read something on her phone. After a moment, it rang, the number unlisted. She answered it softly. "Hello?"

"Taylor?" The voice might have been the crank from two days ago, but it was hard to say. He didn't sound angry when he said her name.

"Yes, to whom do I have the pleasure of speaking?"

"This is Dave Kirby, Colleen's husband." His voice was so kind it was hard to believe he had been the angry caller. But he could have been.

Suddenly the message came roaring back to her, the way it had said "I'm not letting that little" ...little what, girl? Sister? Had the caller been talking about Belle? Had Colleen's husband called to yell at her about Belle? "What can I do for you?" Her words were correct, but her tone was guarded. She stood and moved to the doorway, not sure if she wanted to go into the hall to have a private conversation with this guy or not.

"Colleen and I are taking the boys to Neskowin to spend some time at the beach—we have a place there. We wanted to invite you both. For the weekend, if you'd like, but even just dinner," he continued in the same tone, soft, kind. Welcoming.

Amara came into the waiting area and nodded at Taylor.

"I'm so sorry, Dave, I'm about to go in and talk to my lawyer. So much to do since Mom passed. Like, the lawyer literally just came out for me. Will you text me the info so I can call you back after I check our schedule?"

"Will do." He sounded relieved.

"Thanks so much. I appreciate it." Taylor ended the call and followed Amara to her office.

Though small and with an indifferent view, Amara's office felt substantial. The wall of legal books and the solid wood furniture helped, as did the deep green velvet drapes. Large potted ferns with the gleam of real live plants stood in the far corners of the room on either side of the window.

"Thanks so much for coming down." Amara sat in an old-fashioned, wooden desk chair.

Taylor took a seat across from her. The chair matched the one out in the waiting room and felt solid.

"What I said on the phone about guardianship and probate being slow is really all there is to say. By the time any of you come before a judge, she will be living on her own, handling her own finances, and half way through university. No judge will demand she suddenly be under the care of a woman who has no relationship with her."

Taylor let out a breath. "But there's no reason for her to get emancipated?"

"No." The corners of Amara's mouth turned down. "But if she requests it, there will be no reason to deny it."

Taylor laced her fingers together. "I guess it's up to me to make sure she doesn't feel like she needs it."

Amara nodded, her eyes round with sadness. "I don't want you to worry about it. At least not right now."

"You look like you have something else for me to worry about instead."

Amara let out a long breath. "This is the will. I know I gave you a brief rundown after the funeral, but it's time we discuss it in detail, and privately."

Taylor found her eyebrows drawing together in the start of a pinching headache. She made an effort to relax.

"The first thing, as an old friend of your mom, I need to say that she dearly loved Belle."

Taylor smiled, but it felt tight. "That goes without saying."

"Money has a way of tearing apart good relationships and so I want you to look this over with me to see if we can figure out ways to prevent that."

Taylor closed her eyes for a moment. There was no avoiding the headache.

"First of all, as you now know, Belle was never adopted. Laura was just her legal guardian. As such, Laura was not in a position to name a legal guardian on her demise, and so didn't. She did recommend you, but that doesn't mean much."

"Yes. I get the picture."

"And that recommendation is the last place your sister is mentioned in the will."

Taylor stared at Amara, waiting for her to explain what she meant, but she didn't. She just looked across the desk, her carefully coiffed head tilted ever so slightly, the corners of her mouth still turned down.

"I briefly showed you your part in the will, but it's time to talk about Belle. Laura made the will a couple of years ago." Amara spun a page of paper her direction. "I explained to her at the time how disastrous it would be if something happened, but she just laughed."

"That doesn't sound like Mom." Taylor's eyes refused to focus on the text in front of her.

"She was laughing at the idea that anything could happen to her."

"It still doesn't sound like Mom. Explain to me what you mean by Belle not being mentioned in the will." Taylor set the papers back down and shoved her shaking hands under her legs.

"You'll need to read that eventually, but I can summarize. Laura left everything to you. The businesses, the house, all of her belongings and investments, the insurance policies. She made the note that you were who she recommended to look after Belle. The implication is that you would use the family resources to do so. But legal guardianship doesn't come with any legal inheritance. Belle would have to have been mentioned by name to get anything."

"All of this is to take care of her." Taylor pulled a hand out and waved it at the paper. "That's all I'd ever use any of it for."

Amara smiled, but her eyes were still sad. "You sound just like her, you know?"

"How do I fix this?" Taylor looked at the paper again, but the words were a blur of legalese three times worse than any business jargon she had learned in school.

"I'm glad to hear you say that. When Laura made the will, she didn't know that Belle would start college early."

"I'll take care of her college fees. That's a given. Half of all of this," Taylor poked at the disastrous paper, "belongs to my sister."

"We can do that. We can make her a partner in the business and split the assets. That would be fair minded and generous of you."

"And yet your voice tells me it's not wise." Taylor's mind went to the several hundred thousands of dollars of YouTube money sitting in the bank. It was for college, and part of it would be a massive advertising campaign as soon as Taylor had time to plan it.

"Belle is a genius, but that isn't the same thing as being mature, or wise. I would not split any cash with her right now."

"So, a trust?" This wasn't bad. It all made sense. Trusts were things people had. Belle could have one. Taylor repeated it over and over to herself. This was a problem, but she was a problem solver.

"That is what I would recommend."

"I can do that."

"And you should put the money for her college in a trust as well…in good faith."

"Obviously. That money is for her and her alone." Her dream advertising campaign seemed to dissolve in the air, but maybe not. It wouldn't take three-hundred-thousand dollars to put a genius through a couple of years of college.

"I can make a plan and present it to you. If you'd like to split the assets directly in half, we'll need to have everything appraised. Then you can split the current value of the items rather than each having half a share in the house and having to worry about buying the other out."

The house.

"What about Grandpa Ernie?"

"He wasn't in the will either. You'll have to sit with him and discuss his finances. I'm not his lawyer."

Taylor crossed her arms, not out of defiance, but to keep herself still, and to feel like she was a solid person and not in the middle of some bad dream.

"This can all be complicated to understand. Give yourself time." Amara passed her a slick navy blue folder. "All of the information is summarized in that report. I'm making it sound more difficult than it needs to be. When businesses are involved, the total value of an estate can seem daunting."

"You seem like you have more to suggest." Taylor didn't open the folder yet.

"I suggest you look carefully over the approximate value of all of the assets, and then look at the expenses to run those assets, such as the business and the house. You'd need to do that, I think, to get a fair split of assets."

"Flour Sax could be a white elephant?"

"Yes, it could."

They both looked at the blue folder.

"Alternatively, your mother had one generous life insurance policy. Five-hundred thousand dollars. You might consider putting that policy in the trust for your sister."

The slick blue folder crinkled in Taylor's grip.

Amara was right.

That would be the best way to correct her mom's terrible mistake. "I could tell her that Mom expected me to run the business and finish raising her, but that the life insurance was special for Belle's inheritance."

"She may not believe you." Amara scrunched her mouth up, in a look of frustration. "But it still seems like the kindest thing to say."

"It's worth the risk." Taylor sat up, correcting her posture and feeling the strength that came from it.

Amara and Taylor locked eyes. They understood each other.

Her mother had left such a terrible will because she hadn't expected to die. Ever, apparently. At least Taylor hoped that was the reason.

TAYLOR WORKED till closing time that evening. Seeing the lawyer was an item off the to do list, but like so many of those kinds of items, it only led to more work.

Roxy had handed her a flyer before she left that informed her of the meeting of the Quilt Shop Guild that evening.

Taylor didn't want to go. First, their use of the word guild was both pretentious and wrong, so she didn't want to be a part of it. Second, shoppers kept coming into Flour Sax carrying bags from the other shops and leaving without buying anything. Why would Taylor want to team up with her competition?

Quilt Shop Row, or the south side of downtown Main Street, boasted four unique stops for quilters. Bible Creek Quilt and Gift was the first. Though Bible Creek itself was named for a pioneer salesman, A. S. Bible, Bible Creek the store leaned heavy into Bible related merchandise. If it was fun for church ladies, they had it.

The next quilt shop was Dutch Hex, which tried so hard to be the cool, goth-Amish version of Flour Sax.

Flour Sax stood right on the corner of Main Street and Love.

In one direction, Love Street led to the Quinn house and

Comfort College of Art and Craft. In the other, it led to the k-8 school and the high school.

Flour Sax had been the first quilt shop in this town, but their position as the third on Main Street was bad for sales. Always had been.

The last quilt shop on the road had popped up about five years ago and seemed to have a strong presence. Quilters made a point to make it all the way down to Comfort Cozies because they gave free wine samples and sold souvenir glasses for fifty cents.

Her mom's aesthetic both as a quilter and shop owner was strong. The vintage print thing had been really hot for a long time, but seemed less popular now. Taylor longed to use what she had learned ordering fabric for Joann's to update their stock. She didn't want to alienate their loyal base, but their loyal base couldn't keep the shop afloat. It wasn't like she'd quit stocking the thirties reprints they were named after, but they needed to branch out.

As much as she didn't want to hobnob with the Guild, she knew she had to. She locked up, sent a quick text to Belle, and called Grandpa Ernie to let him know where she'd be.

"Aren't you picking me up?" he grumbled.

"I can. Do you like Guild meetings?"

"A bunch of young ladies making terrible decisions for their businesses and my town? What's not to love?" He sounded like he loved it, despite the gruff words.

"I'll be right there." She stopped off at the house where Grandpa was waiting for her in his suit jacket and best shoes.

"Let's go prevent foolishness in the business world." This time, there was no doubt. The smile on his face indicated the Guild meetings were a favorite of his.

THE QUILT SHOP owners met in the town hall, a small board building with a western façade that was original to the pioneer days. It was only a couple of blocks from her little house, so Taylor and Grandpa Ernie walked.

Taylor had, like any kid, wanted to live in one of the faux craftsmen houses in the new development by the old mill museum rather than the little, real craftsman house so close to Main Street, but now that she was an adult, she saw great value in being able to walk just about anywhere she needed to be. Especially since Belle was out somewhere with the car.

Taylor walked arm in arm with Grandpa Ernie, his slow steady gait was about how fast she wanted to show up there anyway.

"Grandpa, we need to talk about finances. Mom didn't leave a lot of notes."

He huffed into his mustache. "What do you need to know?"

"I feel like a nosey parker," Taylor used one of his favorite terms for a gossipy old lady, "but I think I need to know how your finances work. I'd hate to leave important bills unpaid."

"My money is my business."

"Indeed, and there's no one I'd rather have in charge. But I bet Mom knew all about it, and now…"

"You're not your mother." His mood was souring, and they were almost to their destination.

"No, I'm not, but I do have to do her job. Can't you help me a little?"

He huffed or grunted. Whatever you'd call it, it was the old man version of Belle rolling her eyes.

Taylor helped him up the wooden steps to the Town Hall.

"Listen young lady, you mind your business and I'll mind mine."

"Yessir." Taylor opened the door. She wasn't giving in just yet, but she didn't want to bring their fight to the meeting.

She hadn't been in the Town Hall since Belle's bridging ceremony from Brownies to Girl Scouts. Belle quit Scouts that winter, in time to not have to sell cookies again.

The room was exactly the same but decorated differently. Taylor stood near the door and looked around. Three large quilts hung from rolling displays creating a cozy nook for a round table. To one side was a table that appeared to hold potluck cookies and two plastic water pitchers. It also held a Kleenex box with a sticky label on it that said "DUES."

"Pay up, young lady. Have to keep in good standing with the Guild." Grandpa Ernie shuffled into the center of the group. Three ladies came to him, arms out, cooing. No wonder he loved this group. Her mom's rival, Shara from Dutch Hex, remained seated. She wore a Wednesday Addams-like black dress with white Peter Pan collar. Her hair was rolled into a low bun at the back of her neck, and like all costumed women, she had big dark glasses on. Taylor couldn't see her shoes, since she was seated at a table covered with a long piece of batik quilting fabric, but she would bet money Shara was wearing Doc Martens.

A motherly woman with a large bosom and sparkly flowered top took Taylor's arm and led her to the table. She placed a brochure in front of her. "That's just a little something to explain how all this works. I'm sure it's terribly different from the corporate store you used to work for." There was just that something in her tone that made Taylor's old corporate job sound like something she should apologize for. "Tonight, June will be presenting new business." She indicated the woman helping Grandpa Ernie to his seat. "She has a midsummer idea for us. We want to keep the meeting short and sweet to honor your mother."

June was her mom's age. Her pale skin was soft and glowing, just the slightest bit of wrinkling around her mouth that made her seem older. She wore a button-down cambric shirt with an embroidered Comfort Cozies logo on the shoulder.

A lady wearing a Bible Creek Quilt and Gift shop polo shirt with "Carly" embroidered in a curling font, brought Grandpa

Ernie a plate with a lemon bar, a chocolate chip cookie, and handful of pretzels. "Must keep your energy up, Handsome," she simpered.

The motherly woman who had taken up her cause sat between Taylor and Grandpa Ernie. The rest of the group filled up the eight seats—the owner of each shop and a plus one, Taylor supposed.

Carly called the meeting to order. They made quick work of "old news" with embarrassed faces when mentioning the loss of Laura Quinn to their group. Carly stopped after the old news was approved and looked to Taylor. "We want to have a memorial for her, if you'd let us, but it's so soon. We didn't want to pressure you and yet her passing had to be addressed today, you understand."

Taylor nodded and waved a hand feeling vaguely like Princess Diana.

Carly's eyes glowed, possibly with unshed tears, and she sat.

June stood. "Christmas in July."

The folks around the table who were not Grandpa and Taylor murmured happily.

"We didn't do it last year and I think we all know how that went."

A slender man possibly in his mid-thirties had the seat next to their rival, Shara. He chuckled. His plaid shirt was too vivid to be a Dutch Hex employee, so Taylor guessed he belonged to Carly, who sat on his other side. Maybe her son.

"It's a great old stock event." June continued.

"Oh, definitely. One of the best we do all year. And we all know what a bother old stock can be, don't we? I say we should do something like it on New Year's too....something with our unsold fall stock maybe? What do you think, Ernie?" Carly smiled at Ernie.

"No such thing as old stock. Fabric can't go stale. What's wrong with you people?"

The little crowd laughed indulgently, but also honestly.

The man in the bright plaid shirt shouted, "Preach!"

Shara scowled darkly at her, then raised her hand.

"Yes?" June pointed to Shara.

"You have the floor."

"I yield it to you." June's smile was tense.

"No, I mean you have the floor, hang onto it better or we'll never get done."

"Got somewhere better to go?" the young guy in the bright shirt asked.

"Yes. Home. So let June talk."

He shrugged.

"We all have stock set aside for the event, as we agreed in January. And we are going to use funds from our dues to pay for co-op ads in the Corvallis and Eugene papers." She paused, but no one interrupted.

"In addition, we agreed to split the cost of radio ads to be determined, and we are all agreed to use Christmas outdoor decorations for the week of the sale." June stared at Shara.

"Whose hare-brained idea is this?" Grandpa Ernie scowled.

June turned a much more natural smile to him. "Laura loved the Christmas in July sales."

"Laura doesn't know a sale from a hole in her head. Wait till Delma hears you want her to dig out all her Christmas decorations in July. She'll have a fit. I'll never hear the end of it."

Taylor swallowed. It was evening. He seemed to get a little more lost in the evenings. And first thing in the morning. Taylor mouthed an apology to June, but her attention was all on Grandpa Ernie.

"Delma likes this, I promise."

The young man in plaid choked back a laugh.

"You're all crazy. Who's going to come to a store just to buy blanket fabric? No one. That's who." Grandpa pushed his chair back with a terribly grating scrape. "Come Laura, we're leaving."

Taylor knew she should stand, but she couldn't. She felt glued to her seat.

He had been so with it. Seemed to follow what was going on. Seemed to want to be here. When had he slipped away from them? Were there signs she should have seen?

Carly patted her back. "Darling, it will be okay. We all love Ernie."

Grandpa Ernie didn't seem to hear Carly, and was stumbling his way to the door.

"But you should call me as soon as you can. I had some ideas for your mother that I think you should hear. For Ernie." She watched Grandpa make his way to the door, then mouthed the words, "For his care."

Taylor swallowed and nodded at her. "Sorry." She also stumbled out of her seat.

Shara sighed. "In the future, maybe Ernie can stay at home."

"Shara! You're heartless," the plaid guy said.

"Before you go," June interrupted them, "are you in for the sale?"

"Yes, yes. Definitely, and whoever is planning the ads, I'm happy to help."

"Wonderful!" A woman whose name Taylor hadn't caught, but who wore a macramé vest, clapped her hands together. "I'll call you."

"Great," Taylor tossed the word over her shoulder as she hustled after Grandpa Ernie. Outside she took his arm and they started the now, much longer seeming, walk back home.

CHAPTER TWELVE

*R*oxy texted Taylor the next morning at 7:30. *"How about filming today. You ready?"*

"Yes. Good. Fine. Okay."

Roxy responded with a laughing smiley.

Taylor had the rough outline for a class on color theory. Her mom had done one about six months earlier, but she'd do a different take on it and show a fun fabric color wheel she had invented in college. She was sure someone else somewhere had also "invented it", but it felt like it was all hers. She met Roxy in the shop at 8:30.

Taylor had the simple wheel of cotton fabrics on the work-table and was digging through a basket of scraps to make the sample for the show.

"That looks like more than ten minutes of work." Roxy greeted the bright morning in a tank top and shorts, her small wiry self all muscles and excitement.

"I won't do the whole thing at once. Today I'll just show how to cut the diamond shape and then sew three together."

"Hmmm. That could work." Roxy held her chin as she considered her color wheel, then nodded.

"I hope so." Taylor set aside three good scraps. She was getting there.

"Here." Roxy placed a cardboard carton on the table. "Dig through this too."

Taylor hoped she'd find bright and cheerful solid colors, but instead she found hats and scarves. "Help me out here…what am I supposed to be finding?"

"Costumes!" Roxy grinned. "I always wanted your mom to wear them, but she wouldn't. She didn't have that kind of spunk."

Taylor lifted an eyebrow.

"I've always seen you as the real spunky one in the family. You could pull this off." Roxy reached in the carton and pulled out a pill box hat that looked like a pin cushion, right down to hat pins sticking out of the top.

"I'm not sure…" Taylor narrowed her eyes. That hat was cutesy. She wasn't cutesy. Was spunky another word for cutesy?

Roxy stuck it on her own head. "Cute, right? I've sold quite a few of these on Etsy."

"Ah." It looked adorable on her, but maybe only because Roxy with her big eyes and bigger grin in a petite package would be cute in anything. "I think…you know…this is the first video since I lost my mom. Maybe this time we need to be a little more sedate."

"Oh…" Roxy nodded in sympathy and placed the hat back in the carton. "What about this one?" She held up a black beret that hosted a small cluster of blue and brown feathers held in place with a pewter broach.

Taylor tried it on and turned toward the mirror behind the register. To her surprise, it flattered her face shape and matched the colors in her blouse.

She looked like her mom.

She'd aged over the last couple of weeks, but there was something about it that she liked. Some kind of character or strength she hadn't had or needed before. "Sure. This is nice." She nudged it in place.

Roxy put the pin cushion hat back in the box. "I had another idea, since this is the first show since we lost Laura."

"Shoot."

"I binged on her show last night and noticed that she often had these little bits of life wisdom. They just came out as she worked, real natural. I thought we could clip those moments and do a Laura feature at the end of each sewing show." She blushed and looked at the ground.

"That's brilliant, Roxy. It really is." Taylor gripped the edge of the table.

Roxy was smart. She was worth so much more than they were paying her.

Roxy looked up again, her eyebrows lifted. "Jonah will do a great job. He'll do all the editing on today's show and then send it to you. Give him a couple of days since he has to find the clips."

"And Belle handles the rest?"

"Um hmm." Roxy shifted the box off the table. "We were due a team meeting when your mom passed. Would you like to have one?"

"It sounds like the sooner the better. And please, please get me those invoices. I don't want to short shrift you."

"Will do, Taylor. I promise."

With that, they began the shoot. Taylor stumbled over words and her hands were unsteady. She forgot lines and steps in even this simple project, but Roxy was patient with her and promised the half-hour's worth of material would be edited into a fantastic ten-minute show.

"We usually filmed about two hours so we could do several episodes at once. It's good to get ahead of the game for these."

"Does that mean you have some unaired shows?"

Roxy pressed her lips together, as though holding in a bit of emotion.

Taylor had been making that face herself quite a lot recently.

"Yes. We have five. I wasn't sure if it was tasteful to upload them during the crisis."

"Of course not, but…can you send them to me?"

Roxy nodded and put away the tripod and lights she had rigged for filming.

They had plenty of time before the shop opened, but Taylor wasn't sure she could fill it with chatter just yet. "Can you do me a favor?" She grabbed her purse and pulled out some cash. "I could use a pick me up after all of that. How about coffee and donuts from the place on the corner of Main and Temple?"

"You got it." Roxy took her box of hats and scarves with her as she left, though when Taylor glimpsed herself in the mirror, she spotted the attractive beret still on her head.

IT WAS A SLOW DAY, but a rush of women at noon made her more optimistic about their future. They came in small groups, three or four women, one after the other. The jingling of the bell over the door sparkled like the hope that bubbled up in Taylor. They laughed with each other and smiled at the fabrics.

Roxy sold all four of the Mother's Choice wall hanging kits they had put together over the weekend, and Taylor sold three of the Bubbling Creek kits. Their electric fabric sheers were practically smoking from all the yardage they had cut, and when the final little group of happy quilters left, they both sighed deeply. "That's what season ought to feel like," Taylor said.

"I so want the good times back." Roxy sat on a stool at the cutting table, her chin resting in her hand. "This store has always been the most popular on the block, and our little town can do so much."

"The co-op ads for Christmas in July will help."

"True. I guess we'd better start making up the Christmas kits."

Taylor had seen the fabric that her mom had set aside and the list of kit plans for pillow cases, advent calendars, wall hangings, and aprons. All solid promotions for a summer event. Nothing too big or overwhelming in the hot weather. The quilt shop equivalent of impulse purchases.

Taylor was about to head up to the apartment where the materials for the kits had been stored when the bell jingled again. She turned a smiling face to the customer.

Rather than a happy little group of crafters, she found herself smiling at a stout, red faced man whose deep frown seemed to start at his bald head and go all the way to his booted feet.

"Good afternoon." Taylor kept her smile on like a mask. Surely he was just grumpy because he didn't know what it was the woman in his life had sent him after.

"You are very difficult to get a hold of."

She raised an eyebrow and looked at Roxy.

Roxy frowned and her hand went to her apron pocket where she had a phone.

"You've got me now, what do you need?"

"I need you," he sneered like it pained him to speak to her, "to keep Belle away from Dayton."

Taylor recognized that voice. Her angry caller.

"Taylor, is everything okay?" Roxy was at the register and looked ready to jump over the counter and tackle the guy.

"Why don't we talk somewhere a little more private?" Taylor's smile was fixed. She couldn't have abandoned it if she had wanted to. "Come around back with me and I can get you a cold drink. Is generic okay? It's all I've got at the moment." Taylor didn't give him the chance to say no. She walked back to Grandpa Ernie's area and grabbed a cold can of cola. Grandpa was asleep so she continued on to the back stoop.

The angry man followed. "I am a patient father." He stood with his feet apart and his arms crossed, back to the door. "I put up with a lot, let me tell you."

Taylor handed him the can, dripping with condensation.

"Just one moment, are you Dayton's dad? I don't think we've met. I'm Taylor, Belle's sister."

"Yes." He took the drink and held it without opening it. "I'm Dale Reuben. Listen, Dayton has a bright future and I don't like to see Belle being a distraction."

Taylor sat down in an umbrella chair they kept outback for breaks. "Would you like to sit?" She indicated one opposite her.

Dale sat. Disarmed now with the cold drink in one hand and seated on a less than stable chair some of the steam seemed to go out of his approach. "Dayton told me all about how Belle is dropping out and that she hasn't been to school in weeks. You might think that's fine, but it's not. Not for my kid."

Taylor nodded, pushing her smile down into a sympathetic frown. "It's been very difficult for Belle since our *mother died*." She emphasized the dead mother.

He had the decency to blush.

"The ROTC will pay for Dayton's school and give my kid a real future, but not if Belle continues to be a bad influence."

"I'm glad you're a patient father," Taylor's voice was cloying, even to her, so she tried to stiffen it up a bit, "because whatever evil influence Belle is holding over your...over Dayton...will be done in September when Belle is in college."

"Excuse me?"

"Belle's very bright. She's skipping senior year and going straight to college in the fall. She already has two years of college credits out of the way, so why bother graduating high school with her class?"

He licked his lips and sat back a little.

"I don't usually endorse dropping out either, but I want to honor the plans Belle made with my mom." Taylor popped the tab of her own generic soda, the fizz felt like worthy punctuation. "Perhaps, if Dayton is struggling in school, the kids could meet in the afternoon and Belle could offer tutoring."

Dale grimaced. "I don't know what game you are playing, but I've been getting phone calls from the attendance office daily and when I ask Dayton the answer is always the same. Belle, Belle, Belle."

"Not Cooper? I'm surprised it's not a three amigos situation."

He set his unopened can on the ground and stood. "If you're not going to take this seriously, I guess I'll just have to forbid Dayton from seeing Belle."

"It sounds like you already have. Were you wanting me to do likewise?" Taylor stood also, sick of the conversation.

"Yes."

"Okay."

He stared at her, frowning.

"Is that all?" Taylor made her way back into the shop, and he followed her again. For a man with a huge chip on his shoulder he certainly seemed easy to lead. They walked all the way back to the cash register where Roxy was still holding down the fort.

"If you can keep Belle away from Dayton then yes, that's all."

Taylor laughed. "I can't. That must be obvious. I'm not her mom. She has no obligation to do anything I say." Her throat closed over the statement, but she rallied. "I can certainly forbid them seeing each other. Most likely they'll only get together more once I do, but I'm happy to say whatever you would like me to say."

He slammed his fist on the countertop. "You might not care about Belle's future, or Dayton's future, but Dayton is my only child and I will not see...." The front door jangled again, and he paused.

"Oh jeeze, Dad!" A plaintive voice called out.

A young person with short hair, a denim jacket, Levi's, and checkered slip on Vans looked at them.

"Dayton, you do not have permission to be here." Dale stared at his child.

Dayton waved a piece of paper. "Mom told me to come get some unbleached hand quilting thread."

"Get it from Dutch Hex." He strode across the shop and

pushed Dayton back out the door with the force of his personality.

Taylor exhaled and dropped her chin to her chest. Poor Belle. No wonder she wanted to leave town now, instead of graduating with her class.

Roxy lifted an eyebrow, a silent offer to talk, but Taylor wasn't up for it. She hid at her little desk by the stairs and began to brainstorm a list of ways to keep Belle and Dayton apart. Midway through, her phone rang. She answered it hoping it was Belle herself.

"Taylor?" The deep, manly voice was not her sister.

"Yeah?"

"This is Hudson East from the bed and breakfast."

"Ah."

"How are you doing?" His kind, deep voice was disarming.

Her hackles smoothed out from his one little question. "As good as could be expected."

"I've been thinking about you." He cleared his throat. "Just... well. That sounded weird, but it's true. You've kind of been through it recently and I was thinking of you."

"Thanks." In a world where a quick text usually conveyed this kind of message, his call was unusual. She wasn't angry with him about suspecting Maddie of wrong-doing, but she was still a little annoyed he had called Belle, 'Lolita.' It seemed mean spirited, and she didn't have room in her life for people who were mean.

"I'm headed out to Comfort to pick up a piece of furniture for Aunt Andrea and was wondering if maybe you'd be up for a coffee."

"When are you headed this way?"

"About an hour, but no hurry. I've got things to do once I get there."

"Ahh...I'm sorry. I'm working."

"Oh, sure. Sorry. Not everyone has my random schedule." He

sounded embarrassed, even gentle. Maybe the mean Lolita joke was out of character.

"I could take a break, though, if we aren't busy. Roxy will be here."

"I can stop by the store. If you're busy, it's all good. I'm going to be across the street anyway."

"Yeah, sure. If I can take a break, we'll get some coffee."

"Great. See you later." He sounded happy as he ended the call.

Her heart seemed lighter too. His offer was some sort of antidote to Dale's tantrum. She'd hoped she and Maddie would fall into step and take up where they had left off years ago, but that hadn't worked out. Taylor wasn't looking for a romance, but she could use a friend. Especially today.

As it turned out, the late afternoon was quiet, and Roxy was more than happy to cover her while she went for coffee with the good-looking guy who popped in.

On their way down the block to Cuppa Joe's they discussed the various merits of fancy coffee verses Folgers. Neither of them were snobs, but they both liked something that tasted good. It wasn't the kind of conversation that lit the world on fire, but it was a bit of a relief from discussing the Great Tragedy, The Trouble with Belle, or even How to Save the Business.

Over their big steamy mugs of brew, he ruined the mood. "Have you made any progress on your investigation?"

Taylor stiffened. "No."

"It'd be hard, I guess. I've always heard you can't prove a negative, and if no one's responsible, then that's the task you've got."

"An accident isn't really a negative, though. I don't mean that metaphorically. I mean that it's a thing that happened rather than the absence of a thing." Taylor was fighting for the side of the debate she wasn't really on, and she resented him for bringing it up and ruining her escape from her troubles.

"Have you talked to the other guests from that night yet? Gina and Nancy?"

"I've sent Facebook requests, but haven't heard back." Taylor wanted to say her coffee was bitter in her mouth, but it was just her attitude. The coffee still tasted great.

"I hope you hear from them. They might be the witnesses you need."

"Yeah."

"You haven't come across any good motives yet have you?"

"Nothing new." Taylor pursed her lips. How was he not getting the mood change here? Did she need to just up and leave so he'd get the point? She considered it, maybe even just excusing herself to the ladies would help him see she wasn't into this conversation.

"Hey, sorry about that um...the Lolita joke."

Taylor leaned forward like she hadn't heard him well. "Oh?"

"Belle's a good kid. That's what I thought made it funny. The irony, you know? But I'm assuming it was not funny to you."

"So you think the only reason I wouldn't call you is because you called my sister Lolita, huh?" He was too close to correct, but he didn't need to know that.

"You're not the first person who didn't call when I gave them my number." He shrugged lightly. Humble, but it was hard to believe. What girl wouldn't call this guy if he asked? "But after thinking about it, I did wish I had just said 'call if I can help in any way' because that's all I meant, and it wasn't really a good time to be funny."

"Yeah, that would have gone over better."

"Belle is sharp. And from what I saw, she's working hard to make sure folks don't see her as a pretty face instead of a brain."

"Forget about it. I can probably forgive you."

Relief swept across his face. "Awesome. I know you have to

get back to work, but before you disappear again, can I take you out to dinner sometime?"

Coffee with a friend was something she needed. Dinner with a guy? She wasn't so sure.

"The timing is just...."

He nodded. "How about this instead: call me anytime. Got a raccoon stuck in your garage? I'll get it out. Roof leaking? I can move some buckets under it for you."

Taylor sighed, but in a smiling way. "I know that's not as much fun as a date, but it's about as far as my mind can think right now." She paused and sipped her coffee innocently. "You wouldn't believe the raccoon problem we have in this town.

TAYLOR THOUGHT ABOUT THE COFFEE "DATE" quite a bit the rest of the afternoon, especially because Roxy had a million questions for her. Who was he? How had they met? When was he moving in? She seemed to be avoiding the troubled conversation with Dale. Her son Jonah was about the same age as Dayton, Cooper, and Belle. Whatever Roxy thought about the problem, the kids, or even the way Taylor was handling things, she kept to herself. Taylor again realized this lady was worth her weight in gold.

"Roxy!" Taylor swatted at her with the March copy of Quilt Shop Owners Monthly. "I'm not even on the rebound yet, much less ready to move some rando in."

"Leave the girl alone," Grandpa Ernie called from his station at the back of the shop. How that had woken him up and Dale hadn't, Taylor couldn't guess.

"Yeah, leave me alone," Taylor said.

Grandpa Ernie countered. "No, you leave Roxy alone. She's got her head on her shoulders. That's a nice boy what came in to take you out. Forget that city boy you used to see. You need a good feller like that Hudson East."

"You know him?" Taylor ambled over to Grandpa.

"Sure, I do. His granddad Boggy and I were in the Fraternal

Order of Odd Fellows together, and two odder fellows you never did see." Grandpa laughed. "Next time you see that boy, ask him if Boggy still has those rockets. He's not supposed to, that's a fact, but I have a feeling he's got them hid somewhere."

Grandpa Ernie was lost in memory. Taylor didn't know if she'd take Hudson up on his offer for help, but if she did, she would certainly ask about this Boggy and his rockets. It would be nice to talk about something other than her dead mother and her moody sister.

Not long after, the moody sister herself showed up.

"Hey Belle, come back with me and get a snack." Taylor wandered back to Grandpa Ernie's domain and dug around in his little fridge looking for something to offer her.

They hadn't talked since her accusation that Taylor had abandoned the quest for her mom's killer, and they needed to sort that out.

"Whatcha been up to?" Taylor's opener was not brilliant, and neither was the cold, stale Ding Dong she passed her.

"Nothing." Belle accepted the snack and ripped open the little white bag.

Her guess was that "nothing" meant keeping Dayton and Cooper out of school.

"So my friend requests to Gina and Nancy haven't been accepted yet. When they are, I'll get right on questioning them about that night."

"That will be nice for you." Belle's gaze was fixed on something in the room behind her, or maybe nothing, just so long as she didn't have to look at Taylor.

"But, um, maybe we should go talk to Andrea again."

Belle shot her a quick glance and then looked away. "Whatever."

"Or not." Taylor had thrown that out as a Hail Mary. There really wasn't any good reason to talk to the owner of the bed and breakfast again. "But maybe you and I should just like, go away. We could go away for the weekend even. When was the last time

154

you were in Portland? It would be pretty fantastic to get some real shopping in. When was the last time you've been to a Target, even? What about this?" She showed her phone calendar to Belle. "Grandpa Ernie could stay with Grandma and Grandpa Quinny, I bet."

Belle shrugged, then froze. "Hold on. There's actually a thing coming up..." She checked the calendar on her phone, blushing. "Um...prom is that weekend."

"Prom!"

Her blush deepened. "Yeah, I wasn't going to go, but Mom wanted me to."

"Do you need a dress? An appointment for hair? What can I do?" The excitement bubbled up in Taylor. She couldn't help it.

Belle looked at her with laughing, disdainful eyes.

Taylor wondered if Belle had looked at their mom that way... then her eyes softened, and the color receded from her face. "I'm wearing Mom's prom dress, and um, Cooper's mom is doing my hair."

"Sissy?" Taylor couldn't hide the disbelief in her voice.

"Yeah, she's a stylist. She's good."

"Did she give you that cut?" Taylor tried not to reveal how little she liked Belle's current look.

"No, I did this myself."

"Are you going with Cooper?"

"Nah, I made him take Dayton."

"And you?"

The color began to rise again. "His name is Levi. He's from Hillsboro. I met him at the OSU early admittance summer program last year." Her voice was quiet.

"Is he headed off with you in the fall?"

"He's already there."

And that, Taylor realized, was the real reason Belle wasn't graduating with her class.

No. That wasn't fair.

Belle wasn't graduating with her class because she had

outgrown this school. Maybe in a different town, with a larger pool of kids that could keep up with her, she would have done all four years, but then again, maybe not. She had options and she was wise to want to take them. This Levi character was a bonus.

At least Taylor hoped so. "Okay, so...not this weekend. How about next?"

Belle shook her head. "I dunno." Though she had reverted to caveman language, she looked relieved, probably because Taylor had changed the subject from prom.

"I'll see what I can come up with. Maybe..." Taylor remembered the invitation to go to the beach with the Kirby's and swallowed. Stupid. She should have brought that up. It's what they really needed to discuss. There was literally no reason on earth to go to Portland, no matter how badly she itched to hit every major mall and leave loaded with a bunch of stuff she didn't need.

"Whatever." Belle moved toward the back door.

"Real fast...before you go..."

Belle paused, hand on the knob.

"After you get your hair done, can you come back home? I'd really like to take some pictures of you and Levi. Please?"

"Do what your sister tells you," Grandpa Ernie said.

Belle patted his shoulder. "Yes, Gramps." She turned to Taylor. "Yeah, I'll come back here. I promised Mom." On that note she headed back out again.

CHAPTER THIRTEEN

$\mathcal{T}$he next morning Taylor's calendar said they had an appointment with Maddie. She had wanted to go together, but Belle was ready and out the door before she had a chance to get her shoes on.

Belle had taken care of Grandpa's breakfast and pills before she left so Taylor shoved her resentment aside for later. At least Belle wasn't neglecting what really mattered.

Once Taylor had Grandpa settled in his room with the paper and the TV news, she hustled over to Maddie's office to meet Belle so they could walk home together. This counseling deal included her, and she wasn't going to be cut out from it.

When the appointment ended, she stood in the doorway of the waiting room to block their exit. "Ladies." Taylor looked at each one in turn. "I had a run in the other day with Dayton's dad that I think we need to talk through."

Maddie looked at her watch a bit too dramatically. "I don't think we have time this morning."

Belle pointed her heavily lined doe eyes in Maddie's direction. "But this could be of value for me."

"Five minutes?" Taylor asked.

"Fine." Maddie shut the door to her counseling room and took a seat in the waiting area.

Belle and Taylor remained standing while Taylor recounted Dale's warnings.

"I cannot discuss any other clients with you."

Taylor lifted her eyebrow.

Maddie passed her hand over her eyes.

"Dayton is all right, but no big loss." Belle's eyes grew cold and she shrugged.

"Every friend is a loss," Taylor asserted. "Why are you encouraging Dayton to skip classes with you?"

"I'm not. I can't control anyone but myself."

"Good. That's true," Maddie said. "And Dale is in the wrong to blame you for Dayton's actions."

"So what do you suggest Belle do? Send Dayton away any time they're together? Not respond to messages?"

Maddie shook her head slightly.

"Are you ready to go back to classes?" Taylor asked while Maddie considered the situation.

"Sure." Belle's shoulders were stiff under her backpack.

"It's just I don't know how many days you can miss before I mess up your plans for next year." Taylor already regretted what had been intended as a threat.

"I said it was fine."

"I can go to the school and explain..." Taylor couldn't back peddle this one. She had given Belle a reason to get away from her every day, and Belle looked like she was going to take it.

"I can handle it." Belle made as though she was going to leave, but Taylor still stood firm in front of the door.

"Belle, the break was good for you, but I was wrong about the investigation. It hasn't achieved the goals I had for it. I think you should resume your regular life. Get back into your normal schedule." Maddie spoke calmly, her eyes warm, but not smiling. She was like a robot set to "care but don't invest".

Taylor wanted to knock the controlled look off her face.

Belle pressed her lips together and stared at the door.

"But not yet. She and I have one more thing to do together." Taylor opened the door.

Belle slipped out but waited for her at the bottom of the steps.

"Do you remember how to get to Colleen's house?"

Belle turned, her mouth a little circle. She took a second then said, "Yes."

"Great. I think it's time we have a long talk with your...with the Kirbys."

Belle nodded, her eyes hidden behind that shag of black hair. "Fine. After that I have to go back to school?"

"Yes, but if I start getting lots of calls from the attendance office, I will go to the school to talk to your teachers. Understand?"

Belle gave a half-hearted one shoulder shrug.

They went back to the house. Grandpa Ernie was pacing the living room, agitated.

"What's up, Gramps?" Belle asked.

"Your mother had a bank book and I need to see it."

Belle took him by the elbow and tried to lead him to his chair.

"Don't push me into that thing." His voice was firm, and his eyes were sparking. He didn't look confused like he did in the evenings and mornings. "She kept accounts in an old-fashioned bank book, and I need it. Where did you put it?"

"I didn't put it anywhere, Gramps." Belle let him go back to his pacing. "She used a computer for her banking."

"Not for her personal banking. She used that computer for the business."

"Do you mean her check book?" Taylor asked.

"If I had meant her check book, I would have said her check book." Grandpa Ernie's face was turning an alarming color—something between red and heart attack.

"Let me get you your...." Taylor didn't know what to get him

"The bank book? Because that's the only thing I want right now. What have you done with it? It was always right there till you moved in." He pointed a finger that only shook a little bit at the table by his chair.

"I'll go look."

"I looked." He raised his voice so that it rattled in his throat. "I've looked everywhere. She was stealing from me, Taylor. Your mother had been stealing from me for years and I want to see it with my own eyes."

"I think you need to sit down." Belle whispered.

"I do not need to sit down. I know when someone steals from me and I won't put up with it."

"I promise I will never steal from you." Taylor spoke firm, and in charge, though she felt anything but.

"You're living in my house, aren't you? And you aren't paying rent. What do you call that?"

"I'll pay you rent. I have plenty of money." Taylor tried to imitate Maddie's professional cool. She wanted to step away from the feelings of panic that were rattling in her brain.

He stared at her, his jaw working back and forth. "Spoiled. That's what your mother was. A terrible spoiled brat. Convinced my own wife to steal my business from me. Stole from me every day after my wife died. Stole the business right out from under me."

Taylor looked to Belle who seemed frozen in place. "What now?" she mouthed. She had never seen him so angry, never heard these kinds of words from him before.

Belle shook her head, then looked at her phone.

"Let me look anyway. I'll look in Mom's room. And I'll call the bank and have them send you all of the records."

Grandpa tilted his chin up and appraised Taylor.

"Do that. Yes, do that." He stood in place, the color fading from his cheeks, though little beads of sweat broke out on his forehead.

Taylor went upstairs. She shut herself in her room with her phone. Grandma Quinny had promised her if she ever needed anything, all she had to do was call. She made the request as succinct as she could.

Grandpa Quinny was on his way over.

She took a deep breath, then tore into the closet. If there was a personal bank book, where would it be?

Before she was halfway through the first box, the doorbell rang, the old door creaked open, and her Grandpa Quinny's charming, smooth, and loud voice echoed up the staircase.

Taylor ran down to greet him.

He pulled her into a side hug. "Taylor! Darling!" He kissed the top of her head. "My dear, I know you ladies need a man around, but could you spare Ernie for me?"

Grandpa Ernie stared at Grandpa Quinny, his junior by at least ten years.

Grandpa Quinny, the tall, distinguished gentleman farmer with a new, thin mustache. "Ernie, I have a problem with my seed-sorter and no one is better with small machines than you are. Could you spare me an hour or two at the farm? Ingrid will make dinner to repay you."

Grandpa Ernie frowned, but in a different, more satisfied way. "Sure, sure. I could look at it."

Grandpa Quinny passed Taylor some folded bills. "You girls go out and have some supper together, this might be a while."

"Thanks, Grandpa." Taylor slid the money into her pocket.

Ernie frowned a little deeper. "You keep looking for that bank book, you hear?"

"Yes, definitely Grandpa Ernie."

"You wouldn't believe the way that girl has been stealing from me all these years." He shook his head as he led Grandpa Quinny outside.

"Kids!" Grandpa Quinny was saying. "You never can satisfy them, can you?"

After Taylor shut the door, she pulled the little wad of cash from her pocket. Two hundred dollars.

"What made you think to call him?"

Taylor looked up at Belle. "Don't know exactly, but Grandma Quinny said I could call her any time I needed her. You know, she wants both of us to move in with her."

Belle snorted.

"Says we should put Grandpa Ernie in a home."

Belle sighed. "I don't know what set him off, but it scared me." She slunk across the room and flopped into a chair. "Maybe it is time. I mean, what will you do when I move out?"

"It's just so many changes at once…"

"Mom didn't steal from him, just so you know. His social security checks switched to automatic deposit, so he thought she was stealing his checks."

"Ah."

"I know where her bank book is."

"What?"

"I've heard them fight about this before. No matter what she said he couldn't get it straight in his head, but he'd never been that angry before. Anyway, maybe we need to look over family finances tonight while Gramps is gone."

"Good idea."

Belle led her upstairs to the room Taylor was staying in and took a brown leather-like three ring binder from the top shelf of the closet that still held so many of their mom's things. They sat on the bed with the bank book and the computer open to the online banking account.

There were a lot of numbers in a lot of places, but Taylor was good with numbers and it didn't take long for her to wrap her mind around their family situation.

"Her retirement account wasn't what I would have wanted to see. She kept way too much cash around."

"I agree. I stash almost everything I make from the video business in a Roth IRA."

"You're smart." Taylor shut the three-ring binder that held the monthly family budget. "It doesn't look like Grandpa Ernie gets enough each month to pay for a place in a nice senior home."

"Yeah, but it also looks like college won't take up very much of the video money."

"I was worried about that, but we do have far more than enough for college and to take care of Grandpa. Plus, there's something I need to tell you." Taylor swallowed nervously. "There's a trust fund for you. It will pay for college and still have plenty left over when you come of age."

Belle cringed and stared at her sister in disbelief. "What are you talking about?"

"The trust fund Mom had, I mean, it's um, a life insurance policy, but there are directions…"

Belle closed her eyes and tilted her head up, inhaling through her nose loudly like she'd had it up to here with her sister. A look her mom had given her plenty of times when she was a teen.

"Um…I don't have all the details yet."

"Oh, really? You don't have all the details to your bold-faced lie yet?" Belle stood, taking her time as she unfolded her crossed legs and stepped off the bed. "I thought we could trust each other."

"Wait, I'm confused…"

"You're lying to me. Mom didn't leave me a trust fund or a life insurance policy or anything like that. She's not crazy."

"What are you talking about?"

"Why would she set up some elaborate trust and stuff for me when she had no reason to think she was dying? Why would she leave me a life insurance policy when I was a minor and, there was a possibility some random genetic relation like Colleen would get control of it? Not Mom. Mom had cash and lots of it. She had no reason to think she would die, and anyway, she knew she could trust you to take care of me."

"That's what I'm trying to do," Taylor whispered.

"No. You're just lying to me, trying to pretend things were different than they are. You're the only legal daughter. I'm just…." She shook her head.

"Belle, wait. It's five-hundred-thousand dollars. It's more than all the other cash she had put together."

Belle stood, tall and brave. "And it's what you thought would buy me off while you got everything else? The house? The business? Everything?"

"You can have whatever you want. I don't need the house. I have the money from my condo sale. I don't need the business because I have an education and lots of work experience. You're just starting out your life. Whatever you want or need, Belle, it's yours."

Belle was shaking as she stared at her sister. "I want to get out of this town and go to college and never look back." She ran down the stairs.

Taylor was on her heels. "Fine. Do that. But first let's have dinner." With Belle's elbow firm in her grip she led her to the car and drove till she wasn't angry anymore, and they were in the middle of the college town that was about to be Belle's home. They had driven in silence, and even now, Belle's head was leaned against the window.

Taylor thought maybe Belle would have tearstained cheeks when they got out at the first restaurant she could find, but she didn't.

Once they had ordered food and were waiting for it, Taylor leaned forward.

"This is how it's going to be. You are going to school. Period. You only have a couple of months left. Then you're living in town and working in the shop till you start college."

Belle just stared in silence.

"I inherited everything. All of it went to me. I wrote a five-hundred-thousand-dollar insurance policy over to you. It's in a trust. You can send education related invoices to me to be paid. The money won't be yours till you're my age. Got it?"

Belle drew her eyebrows together.

"Yeah, that's what I said. Turns out in our family twenty-nine is the age of majority. That magical time in life when massive amounts of responsibility are thrust on us whether we want them or not."

Belle pursed her lips, but still didn't respond.

"I'm going to sell the house to pay for Grandpa's care. I'll live in the apartment above the shop and run it till you're.... eighteen. And then I'll decide if I'm selling the business or not. You'll be done with your bachelors by then, right?"

She shook her head. "Not quite."

"Fine, Then I'll wait till you graduate. When you're done, you can decide if you want to buy the business or not."

"With what money?"

"With what money? How about the interest half a million dollars can earn in two years?"

"I thought I could only use it for education." Belle's voice was flat, as though half a million dollars was hardly worth effort.

Taylor groaned. "Don't be pedantic. Once you have a bachelors then, I guess you're educated. If you want the business, buy it. I'll stick around till then. After that, I'll do whatever I want."

"Fine. Whatever."

Their food arrived and they dropped the subject of their futures. From where Taylor sat, that trust fund idea was going to be the only reason she'd ever hear from Belle again.

She almost wished she hadn't done it. She really wished she hadn't brought it up.

GRANDPA QUINNY KEPT Grandpa Ernie overnight, but called her the next morning. "Can we meet for breakfast kiddo? Do you have time before you open the shop?"

"Yes, I do."

They met at Reuben's and each ordered the Bible Creek Special, a plate with all the breakfast favorites, plus crawdads.

"Taylor, I don't know how to tell you this exactly." Grandpa Quinny, retired investment banker and hobby farmer, was an elegant man by any standards. Even the face he made when sad for you looked like a picture.

"Grandpa Ernie's not well, is he?"

"No, sweetie. He's not. I know you're going to want to do your best for him, but he's going to need to live in a memory care facility before too long."

"He's just not that old."

"I know. I hate seeing it. He's always been one of my favorite men."

"Does the Bible Creek Care Home have memory care?"

"Fortunately, yes. He won't have to move far. Your grandmother and I would like to offer to help pay for it."

Taylor nodded but knew she wouldn't take money from them. She didn't need to. "I'll talk to the facility and see what the situation is. We might be able to swing it. Mom was a pretty good saver." Not with her retirement, but everything else was ship-shape. And Taylor's own retirement was right where all the experts suggested it be for a thirty-five year old. Which meant, she was six years ahead of schedule.

Grandpa Quinny let her eat without pushing for details, and they parted ways, her to do some filming with Roxy and him to pull weeds in his acres and acres of strawberries, a task he credited his youthful figure to.

IT HAD ALREADY BEEN a long morning. After last night, Taylor hardly wanted to make an effort to bring Belle and Colleen together, but she decided she needed to try anyway. She called Colleen but got voicemail and left a message. Colleen seemed thirsty for Belle's attention, so Taylor trusted she'd hear back from her soon enough. The nervous energy from Grandpa's bad news and the unanswered phone call wasn't best for filming, but Taylor forged ahead anyway.

Her mouth seemed to stumble over every word.

Roxy was patient, but she looked as nervous as Taylor felt. "Take a deep breath, Taylor. And let's try that again." Her smile spread from ear-to-ear.

Taylor took a deep breath and exhaled slowly. She shook her shoulders, rolled her head from side to side, and held up the flip-book color wheel they had worked on in the last video. "My projects always have gaps. Even when I buy a kit." She flipped the pages of her color wheel mindlessly. "I always want my work to feel like it belongs...to feel like home. It only feels right when it's got fabric in it that I have like, um, a relationship with." Taylor paused. That wasn't smooth, but at least her smile felt natural now. "The fabrics that make you remember stories when you see them." She flipped to a pink and gray polka dot on the color wheel. "I bought that to make a doll quilt for my sister and later I used some in a pillowcase for my grandma." She paused a little too long. "It just makes everything feel like family." She was starting to repeat herself. "So, um, I like to make these now and again out of my stash. Then I can just slip it into my bag and take it shopping with me."

Taylor had created a miniature version of their store behind her using fat quarters as pretend bolts stacked in a miniature version of their shelves that she had hobbled together from Rubbermaid shoe totes. It took her three tries to get through the section of the video where she shopped in her miniature store with her color wheel.

First her back was turned to the audience too often.

Then she blocked the fabric by standing in front of the miniature store.

Then she got her words backwards or she didn't smile.

But after two hours of filming they had enough footage for at least one 10-minute video. Or fifteen minutes, if they were feeling brave. She'd heard fifteen minutes made more money.

"I like that about filling in the gaps." Roxy piled handfuls of fat quarters into powder blue wicker baskets. "It reminded me of Laura. There was something special to it that meant more than just sewing, don't you think?"

Taylor shrugged. "Maybe. Mom was so natural at that and her little wisdom moments were so much wiser."

"She had lived longer and had done more than you, so it only makes sense that she had more wisdom to share. You'll get better at this. You'll get faster, and, unfortunately, the byproduct of life is that you'll get wiser."

"Unfortunately?"

"Sure," Roxy said. "Do you really want to live through the kinds of things that make you wise?"

Roxy had a point. Taylor barely wanted to live through what she was living through right now, much less anything harder

"Sorry. You just lost your mom. Nothing's harder than that."

Taylor shook her head. "It's okay, Roxy. I know what you meant."

She'd never asked Roxy what happened to Jonah's dad. She remembered he was a short guy, but really good looking. She hadn't seen him in at least ten years. She didn't think he'd died, but something had occurred that made him disappear from her life leaving her with a son to raise on her own.

It was funny how the little stories of life in Comfort, Oregon were coming back to her. Each day another place in town reminded her of something or someone. Sometimes her own family who were gone, sometimes people like Roxy's husband. She tried to remember his name but couldn't. She could remember the dimple in his chin, though, and the way he had big, round blue eyes like a cartoon. Cute, more than handsome. But to her teenage eyes, that had been sort of the same thing.

"Jonah will have this edited and ready for your approval by tomorrow."

"That's fantastic. I'm starting to feel like we can make this work." Taylor had reviewed the viewer stats. They weren't very impressive. Going over the ad revenue accounts was something that she hadn't been able to get Belle to do with her yet. But since she had a video almost ready to go, surely she would be up for it this evening. And hopefully by then she would have heard back from Colleen.

CHAPTER FOURTEEN

*T*aylor was fixing dinner when Colleen returned her
call.

"It's so good to hear from you." Colleen's voice was breath-
less with excitement. "Yes, yes, a thousand times yes, we need to
talk. Can we please? Just you and me? I've been thinking quite a
bit, and you were right. You and I should have been communi-
cating before we brought Belle into the conversation."

Colleen's request shocked Taylor. It was such a turn-around
from before. "I'm happy to speak with you," Taylor said. "But
I'm concerned how Belle will take it if we get together without
her."

"I can imagine. Let's keep it a secret, just between you and
me. Will that work for you?"

"Probably so. Maybe we can meet somewhere halfway for
lunch."

"Anything you want. How's Salem?" Colleen suggested a
restaurant.

"That's fine. Tomorrow?" Taylor chewed on her lip. Was she
rushing this?

Colleen took a moment to respond. "Of course. Anything. We

can meet for lunch in Salem and we'll keep it a secret from Belle."

THE RESTAURANT WAS A BIT OLD-FASHIONED. A quiet family dining place that had private booths with tall backs. Taylor could see why Colleen had wanted to meet here. She joined her sister's biological mother at the table, sliding across the gold vinyl seat.

"Thank you so much for meeting me," Colleen began.

Taylor was glad she broke the ice. Sitting across from her alone again made her more nervous than she'd expected to be.

"Dave told me he called and invited you both to our family trip to the beach."

"Oh yes, I'm sorry I haven't responded." Taylor fiddled with the cuffs of her corduroy jacket. They were too tight, all of a sudden. She longed to unbutton them and roll them up, but the fabric was stiff and the buttons were stuck.

"I wasn't sure how to feel when he told me. I wasn't angry, but it seemed precipitous you know?" Colleen had a glass of water already. She pulled it closer to herself, but didn't lift it.

Taylor chuckled softly. "Yes, I agree. It did seem a little precipitous but, it was kind."

Colleen's shoulders dropped slightly and her worried look turned into a small smile. "Dave is very kind." This time she took a drink of her water, then straightened up again, but not nervously. "Before I spend more time with Belle, there's just one thing I hope you understand."

Taylor fought with the brass button of her cuff again. It just wouldn't budge, try as she might.

"No matter what happens, you are Belle's sister. And I know it doesn't seem like this from your perspective and I don't know if I can explain this right." Her cheeks reddened as she struggled for the words. "I know I'm not her mama... not like I am to my boys. She had a mama. But at the same time, she's still..."

"She's still your daughter," Taylor supplied.

Colleen exhaled sharply while nodding. "She has always been in my heart and always had my love. For me, this is a reunion. But for her, I appeared out of the blue at the end of her childhood. For her, this relationship is very different than it is for me." She took another sip of water, then continued. "Belle had a mother. But she's also always been my baby." Colleen's eyes were stopped on Taylor's hands as she wrestled with her coat.

Finally, Taylor just took it off, giving up.

Colleen looked up at her face again. "One day Belle lost her mother... and found me."

Taylor frowned.

"I've read books. I've watched videos. Dave and I even took a class about reunifications. I have a good idea of what's realistic, but can I be honest?" Her voice quavered nervously. "My heart dreams of a day when Belle runs into my arms and calls me Mama and loves me the way my boys do." She looked up at Taylor with big, wide blue eyes.

Taylor's jaw flexed till it hurt. For a moment, she saw Belle's face in Colleen's.

Colleen's gaze dropped to her water glass. "But I know it won't happen. That spot in her heart, the mother-spot, is filled."

Though Colleen paused, Taylor had nothing to say. The words felt like an attack.

Colleen rallied. "All I can hope for, realistically, is that someday she loves me like...like an aunt. Like an older woman who loves her and is there for her, no matter what." Colleen's hands lay still on the table in front of her.

Taylor didn't like the idea that Colleen wanted to replace her mom, but she understood. Colleen had given birth to Belle and watched her grow and loved her. What else would she have ever wanted besides the return of that affection?

Taylor's heart drummed in her chest like it wanted to escape. She didn't know if Colleen was asking permission or just talking.

She couldn't give permission to chase after Belle. It wasn't hers to give.

They sat in silence for a moment.

When Colleen finally moved her hand, it was to tuck her hair behind her ear. She used just the tip of her pinky finger.

"Did they use to offer cooking classes or home economics at Comfort High?" The question wasn't the most important Taylor would ever ask, and yet, it felt immense.

Colleen looked surprised but nodded. "Yes, I took it as a senior with your mom and Amara. Melinda didn't take it with us. She was in show choir. None of the rest of us could sing, but we made cookies and brought them to her concerts. We were her little cheering section." She did the thing with her finger and her hair again, her movements nervous and jerky, like her words.

Taylor didn't know who had taught the class, but she wondered if they had all learned to do that thing with their pinky finger as a way to keep food out of their hair, the way her mom had always done. The way Taylor caught herself doing now and again.

Colleen had a lot in common with her mother, as you do when you grow up in a small town that has its own ways and culture.

"What I wanted to say, but failed," Colleen took a deep breath, "is that you are Belle's sister and Belle is my family and so you are my family too. Your mother is gone, but if you need an aunt, I'm here." She looked at Taylor, waiting.

Taylor bit her bottom lip.

"See, if Belle decides that she wants a relationship with me, and wants to spend, I don't know, Easter or Thanksgiving with me someday, I hope with all my heart that you would also come. Because you're family." Colleen rushed through her words.

A young server with her hair in two braids interrupted them. They ordered coffee and sandwiches as though their meal together didn't hold their fate above them as the waters rose from below.

The server left and they waited again in silence, this offer of replacement family hovering over Taylor like a cloud, or maybe like an umbrella.

It was up to her to break the silence and she couldn't. She didn't know how. She couldn't say thank you because she didn't mean it, because she didn't want to replace her mother. She couldn't tell Colleen to go away or get out of her life, because she didn't mean that either, because the idea that there was this umbrella in the rainstorm waiting for her was something she'd be a fool to reject.

The idea that Colleen wanted them both, even though she was fully grown and full of whatever mistakes and problems adults have, was overwhelming.

It was good that the sandwiches came because it gave them something to talk about. Colleen said hers was delicious and she liked it.

Taylor ate for a while in silence, then blurted out, "Who's her father?"

Colleen set her sandwich down. She seemed to hold her breath, and it was many moments before she answered. "His name was Brick O' Doyle. He wasn't a good man. I don't have good memories of him. And yet in his life he did do one good thing. He created Belle."

Taylor nodded, absorbing the statement. It was true, he had created Belle. Without this guy, whoever he was and whatever he had done, there would be no sister for her. Her mom would still be gone, but she'd be so much more alone. "Is he someone I need to worry about?"

Colleen shook her head slowly. "No, I didn't put him on the birth certificate. He was out of my life by then, in prison actually. Drugs."

"And now?"

"He died in a fight shortly after he was released, about seven years ago. He never knew about Belle. After he was arrested, he and I never spoke again."

That was a relief. One less person to worry about taking Belle away.

"When would you like the three of us to get together?" Taylor asked.

"Will you ask Belle that question?" Colleen asked. "I'd like to do this on her schedule, in her time, as much as possible. I feel awful for rushing her. That was wrong. It was a mistake."

Taylor let out a slow breath, then gave her an apologetic smile. "I'll ask, but if we wait for her timing, we may be waiting forever."

She frowned. "But she came to see me…"

Taylor nodded. "I know, and who knows what exactly motivated her. At least part of it had to be rebelling against me. If it sounds like I want all of us to get together she may not want to."

Colleen sipped her coffee. "Okay. I've been a rebellious teenager, I get it. I'll call her. I'll make sure she knows that you are still very hesitant."

They looked at each other, that moment of honesty standing between them.

It was true.

Taylor might not think Colleen had murdered her mom, but she was still very hesitant about all of this.

SALEM WASN'T PORTLAND, but it was a big enough city to have shopping, and Taylor needed to shake the angst that meal had caused in her. She told herself she was just going to walk off the nervous energy, but she didn't. She went straight to Hobby Lobby and cleared out their shelf of chicken wire storage items. Flour Sax was looking dated, had been for a long time. She needed to replace all the wicker with something more stylish anyway, and this was a write off. Swiping her card through the little reader sent a shiver of relief up and down her spine. She inhaled, maybe for the first time since she sat in the booth at the restaurant.

Retail therapy indeed.

On her way back to Comfort, she passed the restaurant again.

It was very politic of Colleen to offer to be her "aunty" too. But she had aunties coming out of her ears, something Colleen knew very well as she had grown up in Comfort.

Sure Taylor understood how buying things could ease a little internal combustion, but she would not let Colleen buy her affection that way. Colleen would have to prove she was worthy of Belle.

BACK AT FLOUR SAX, Taylor acted like this mini-redecoration had always been part of the plan.

"These are cute." Roxy leaned her hip against the workshop table, her arms loaded with chicken wire baskets. "Where do you want them?"

"Ummm…" Taylor scanned the main shopping area. There weren't as many wicker baskets to replace as she'd imagined. Her first arm load had done the job. "Maybe save those for a minute? We could toss them in the small bedroom upstairs." The smaller bedroom in the two-bedroom apartment was the one her mom had grown up in.

Roxy stifled a giggle.

"What?" Taylor tried to get a stack of caramels to stay in a round chicken wire style bowl. The holes were just too big. With a small grimace of irritation, she dumped two handfuls of the soft, paper wrapped candies back into the wicker basket and stuck the whole thing in the chicken wire container.

"Sorry. That's where your mom stuffed stuff she didn't need after a trip to town too."

"Ahh." Taylor eyeballed the baskets Roxy was holding. It was a small number compared to what was still in the Audi.

"I thought when Amazon started its three day delivery to Comfort your mom would sort of ease up on the panic-shopping, You know, the thing where when you're in town you feel

177

like you need to buy all of something since you won't get there again any time soon."

"Yeah, I know the thing." Not only had Taylor picked up all the wire containers Hobby Lobby had in store, she'd also grabbed an excessive number of mirrors framed in decorative weathered arched windows because they were on sale and would make the store brighter.

All of the walls in Flour Sax were already either windows or floor to ceiling fabric shelves.

"I can put these upstairs," Roxy said, "but I'm going to town on my next day off."

"And you're offering to return them?"

"I mean, just if you accidentally got too many." Roxy's bright smile appeared judgement free.

Taylor felt judged anyway. She sniffed loudly to avoid answering for a moment. "I needed some stuff for home too. I'll just take it all."

"Sure, that's fine." Roxy set the baskets on the counter and shifted from foot to foot.

Taylor had never asked about her limp before, but remembered, again, that Roxy was not only a hard worker, but someone who never complained about the trials she faced.

"Don't worry about it, I'll just haul the extras back out to the car. They are cute though, right?"

"Adorable…" Roxy chewed her bottom lip. "But…"

"Don't say it." Taylor didn't have room in her small house for all of the stuff she'd just bought, or room in the shed out back, either, since it was filled with all of the great finds she had dragged with her from Portland.

"I say nothing. I just hope you know that if you um, need to talk or anything, um…" She offered a sympathetic grin. "I'm here."

Taylor attempted to appreciate the offer. Roxy meant well. But as she carried the haul back to her car, she felt her friend's overly concerned gaze on her the whole way. Shopping wasn't a real problem. Not like drinking too much. And anyway. It wasn't like she was going to town again any time soon.

THAT NIGHT TAYLOR stacked as many chicken wire baskets as she could on the only counter in the kitchen that had any room, then hid more in the backs of closets and under sinks. She had to accept defeat regarding the mirrors and left four of the four feet by two feet impulse purchases leaned against the wall by the TV. After realizing Roxy was right and she needed to take a trip back to Salem to return one or two items, she sent Belle a text imploring her to help her with the YouTube show.

THEY MET at the scratched up oak coffee table in the living room without argument, or enthusiasm.

Grandpa Ernie was with them, but he was reclined in his chair, snoring softly.

Belle opened her laptop, logged into the business account at YouTube, and showed Taylor how the website worked. The views and income had fallen precipitously since their mom's death.

Taylor actually staggered from her seated position, when she saw the numbers.

The most popular video from the previous month had over two-hundred thousand views.

The most recent video posted, the last that had been scheduled before their mom had died, only had twelve thousand views.

"Views have dropped because there isn't new content."

Taylor leaned in and read the comments on the videos.

Someone had posted their mom's obituary in the comments under the third to last video in the channel.

The last two videos had dozens of comments about their

mom's passing. Slightly over half were sympathetic little memorial posts from quilters around the world, but the rest were calling them ghouls and other terrible names for continuing to run shows without acknowledging her death.

Those comments told them they were heartless, money-grubbing monsters. They didn't consider that these videos had been scheduled before her mom passed and that logging into YouTube and canceling them wasn't their main priority during their time of crisis.

And yet, the drop from $1400 of income on one video to less than $100 made Taylor rethink her priorities.

What if they couldn't recover from this?

"Jonah's next video will fix this. He's making a memorial." The reality that some teen she'd never met was creating a memorial video for the fans stung. If she'd been a good daughter and followed her mom on her crazy internet quilting career, she would have her own favorite clips to use. But self-flagellation doesn't get the job done, so she dismissed the shame and tried to move on. Only productive thoughts and actions tonight.

Grandpa Ernie's soft, snuffling, snores were the only sound at the moment, so Taylor hit play on the last video.

Her mom was smiling at both of them as she stood over a rainbow of colored fabrics spread across her table. "It's a double rainbow isn't it?" She grinned in cheeky reference to the old viral video. "It feels like a miracle even though it's just fabric."

Taylor tried to catch Belle's eye to see if she got the reference, but she wasn't revealing anything from behind her shaggy black bangs.

"What did Mom do with the projects she made?" Taylor hadn't seen any stacks of stuff in the storage, certainly not a couple of years' worth of extra random projects.

"Roxy would know." Belle's attention had moved to her phone. She expertly typed and avoided eye contact while talking. A real multi-tasker.

As her mom was organizing fabric on screen, Taylor considered the years' worth of projects and the impact they could have on their little shop. If even half of them were still around, and they packaged them right, they might be able to draw some of these YouTube fans to Flour Sax to buy them.

She didn't say any of that to Belle, though. She didn't seem in the mood.

"I'll do my best to keep up Mom's filming schedule and hopefully we won't have lost too many viewers." Taylor paused the video.

"Wonderful." Belle didn't look up. "You'll be able to focus on the one thing you really love."

"I don't know that I feel that strongly about YouTube videos." Taylor tapped her pointer finger on the mouse pad. It would be nice to finish the project her mom had started in her last video. It would give them continuity. The plan she'd come up with was based on what she perceived as gaps in her mom's videos and her own strengths. She hadn't considered what the fans might actually have been looking for.

Belle sent her bangs flying with a strong puff of breath. They fell back over her eyes and then she spoke. "Not videos Taylor, money."

Belle's words made no sense. Taylor wasn't money obsessed. She was just good at business. And when you're good at business, you make money. And Belle had been the one saying they needed to get the show going again in the first place. Wasn't that so they could make money?

Belle gave her a headache.

"It's just so important for you to keep the business running, isn't it? You got me out of school for my mental health, but then put me back in as fast as you could so you could focus on work again instead of pretending you care about who killed Mom." Belle's mouth was set in what could only be called a grim line. She stood from her crossed leg position with the grace you only get after years of dance lessons but stomped up the stairs like she was mad at them.

Taylor stared at the screen. Her mom was frozen, paused with one hand on the fabric, her gaze directed just off camera.

Grandpa Ernie snored contentedly in his chair.

Taylor did care about how her mom had died.

She just didn't know what to do about it.

CHAPTER FIFTEEN

he Kirby house was everything Taylor had pictured it being. Huge, new, and on a tiny piece of property. There was no yard to speak of, just a slim patio and a deck above it. She felt a little sorry for Colleen's two sons till she saw the full basement "play" room dedicated to their need to run around.

Colleen gave them a tour full of nervous laughter and too many words. As Taylor watched her stumble up her own staircase on their way to the eat-in kitchen where she had prepared a cozy dinner, she realized Colleen was terrified.

Not of Belle, who was wearing gray instead of black and had a smidgeon less eyeliner on today, but of Taylor.

Taylor wanted to calm Colleen before they started digging into her story, but she couldn't suggest a drink, and couldn't think of anything else that calmed a person.

Belle slid into one of the cushioned French country chairs at the round breakfast table as though it was her second home. "Hmmm. It smells delicious. Is that fresh bread?"

Colleen nodded, her face bright with excitement. "Just Rhodes rolls. I'm not a great cook."

Belle helped herself to a roll and pulled it apart.

Taylor was embarrassed by her bad manners, but every little action Belle took seemed to do Colleen's heart good.

A timer chimed and Colleen removed a pan of lasagna from the oven. "This, I did make. It's Dave's mom's recipe. She's Italian." She carried the ceramic casserole dish to the table and set it on an ironwork trivet. "And let me bring the salad over, then we'll have a nice meal and just talk."

"Mmm." Belle made a satisfied sound, her mouth full of dinner roll.

"Can I get you something to drink?" Colleen asked,

They had glasses of ice water with lemon wedges at the table already.

"Soda? Something else?"

"No, thanks. This is perfect."

"It's no bother, really." Colleen stood nervously next to the fridge.

Belle kicked Taylor under the table.

"Do you have any cola? Coke, Pepsi?"

"Yes!" Colleen smiled broadly and took a glass from the cupboard. She added ice from inside the fridge door, then opened a can of Hanson's All-Natural Soda and filled the cup.

She joined them and passed the food around.

For someone who claimed to be not much of a cook, the lasagna was tremendous. Taylor said so, and Colleen again looked like she had been reprieved.

"I don't dare ask the secret, since it's probably an old family trick." Taylor wasn't sure how to bridge the gap between small talk and what they had come for.

"It's the sausage," Colleen said simply. "I buy Italian sausage from a deli downtown. It's amazing the difference having a professional season things makes."

"Colleen," Belle asked after making almost half her lasagna disappear, "that last night I've heard that you and mom weren't getting along."

She tilted her head. "No. I regret that fight so much now."

"Can you remember what it was about?"

Colleen flushed. "I'll never forget. It was just so embarrassing now that I realize it was our last night together."

Taylor felt awful for Colleen. To end a lifelong friendship with a fight would have been devastating.

"Was it about...nachos?" Taylor asked.

Colleen looked at her in surprise. "Nachos? No. Whatever gave you that idea?"

"We asked some of the other girls what they remembered about the night and they mentioned you fighting. One of them thought Mom had said nachos..." Belle helped herself to another roll.

"Nachos...." Colleen pondered the word. "I wish I could say I remember every word your mother said to me the last time we spoke, but considering it was a stupid fight, I'm glad I don't. But nachos...she must have been saying 'Not yours' don't you think?"

"It would make sense." Belle tore her dinner roll into tiny bits.

"Oh!" A look of alarm crossed Colleen's big brown eyes. "Belle, we weren't fighting about you, I swear."

Belle nodded.

"I'll tell you all about it, but I think you'll understand why I'm ashamed."

"We won't think less of you," Taylor promised, but she didn't mean it.

Colleen grimaced. "Okay, here it is. I've always felt insecure with the ladies, because of my troubles. They've lived good successful lives. Amara is a lawyer, Melinda is an accountant, your mom...well, she was a good mother, and a business owner. What was I? I was an addict and failure for a whole lot of my life. All of this security is only in the last ten years. Hardly any time at all from my point of view."

Ten years ago. Taylor glanced at Belle. She would have been six when Colleen got her life together. Taylor had been in college.

"I'm sure someone has mentioned Gina and Nancy to you."
Taylor sat up. They sure as heck had mentioned them.

"When they showed up, I got mad."

"You knew Gina?" Belle asked.

"Yes, Gina was at school with us. A little younger. Your mom had wanted to invite her, but it was hard enough for me to feel okay with the girls as it was."

"What about Gina made you feel insecure?" Taylor asked.

Colleen took a deep breath and held it. Then launched into her story. "Gina was very, very good. Just a good sweet girl. I was trouble. You guys get that. I'm sure. Gina's mother hated me."

"Because of your…trouble?" Belle's voice was so childlike. Taylor side-eyed her to see if it was an act. She couldn't tell.

"I knew your mom had wanted to invite Gina, and I had asked her not to. So when Gina and Nancy both showed up, I was angry. I felt like your mom had lied to me. But she hadn't promised me anything."

"You have your life together now though, surely Nancy can't still hate you." The rich, savory lasagna had dulled Taylor's senses. She wanted everything to be as pure and wholesome as their dinner.

"That's what your mom said too. She wanted me to keep my cool and just enjoy the weekend. She said she'd always liked Gina and that we ought to include her in our lives more. She said life in a small town was better if everyone was included."

"But Gina didn't live here anymore."

"I know. I said that too. She came back with something about Gina being insecure, needing friends."

"How did you feel?"

"Like your mom didn't care about all of those insecure feelings I was having. She only cared about Gina feeling included. Gina's probably the nicest lady in the world, but her mom…" Colleen shivered. "I sound like a fool, but she really hated me."

"But why would a random lady hate you so much?"

Colleen caught Taylor's eye. "Gina was sweet, and innocent. But not all of Nancy's kids were. And she blamed me for it."

"Ah." Taylor and Belle made the same understanding sound at the same time.

"She didn't want you to ruin all her kids."

"Exactly." Colleen scrunched her mouth up. "But I just don't think I'm to blame for everyone who did drugs in Comfort."

"When did you guys go your separate ways that night?" Belle moved on to more concrete points.

"We didn't want to fight. After we realized the conversation was just going in circles, we parted. It wasn't dramatic. The opposite, even. The wind had gone out of the argument. She went downstairs and I did too. I figured she'd head to the water, so I went to the porch to sit on the swing. I can't tell you how much I wish I had gone to the water."

"Do you think Gina might have had something to do with Mom's accident?" Belle's question hit Taylor as out of the blue.

"Oh!" The nervy look returned to Colleen, with a slight shake to her hands as she laid her fork down. "No, definitely not. Why would she?"

"If Gina was lonely and wanted to be included in things, she might have been envious also. And Mom was internet famous," Taylor mused.

Colleen was pale. She shook her head. "I never thought about it. Why would she be? She had her own life and family and career. Surely she didn't envy your mom's success."

Taylor knew folks her age could get very envious of others' internet success, but she wasn't sure how the almost-fifties handled it. She liked to think they were mature and stable. "As far as you know, Mom was agitated, maybe a little tipsy, and slipped and fell."

"As far as I know." Colleen turned away.

Taylor admitted her use of the word agitated was purposeful. She couldn't seem to pin the act of murder on Colleen, but she couldn't help trying.

Dave and the boys came home while they were washing up for Colleen—Belle's idea.

The boys, she guessed to be about five and seven, ran in full of words and hugs for their mom, but skidded to a stop when they saw Taylor.

Dave was a handsome man, the Italian heritage showing in big dark eyes.

"Boys, this is Taylor. She's our friend Belle's big sister."

The taller of the two boys waved. The younger one ran to the table and got a dinner roll.

"Little piggy." Dave laughed. "Good to meet you, Taylor." He offered her his hand.

Taylor found a towel, dried her hands, and shook.

"I'll get the boys to bed and come right back."

"Don't hurry," Belle said. "I have school tomorrow, so we'll be heading out in just a couple of minutes."

The boys had scooted out and Dave sat next to his wife at the table. "It really is nice to see you both here. I don't know if Colleen told you, but I have an older daughter as well. I think she's about your age, Taylor. She's twenty-seven."

"Yeah, that's about right." Taylor didn't confess to being almost thirty.

"She lives in Seattle and we don't get to see her enough, but I hope we can all get together one of these days. The boys are still a little shy with Ashleigh."

"They love her," Colleen soothed.

"Sure, it just takes them a while to warm up."

There was such sweet affection between Colleen and Dave. It was real and lovely, and if Belle had moved here when she was six to live with them, she would have grown up with a big sister named Ashleigh instead of Taylor.

Taylor wasn't prepared to like Colleen and Dave or their little boys whose names she refused to ask. She wasn't prepared to feel like Belle had missed out by not living in this giant house filled with people and love.

"Thanks so much for dinner," Belle was saying as Taylor wallowed in her thoughts. "Are you ready?"

Dave and Colleen took turns giving Belle a big hug. Colleen approached Taylor, but Tayor turned and gave her a half-hearted side hug. Dave took note and shook her hand again.

Taylor was quiet till they found themselves on the highway. "They're lovely," she finally said.

"Yeah," Belle said. "Like when you go visit a friend and their family is so different than yours, it feels weird, like a TV show and not at all like home." Belle looked up at Taylor with big, mopey eyes.

Taylor pretended not to notice, but it felt good, being looked at like she was home. "You pick the music."

Belle put on something new to Taylor, a heavy electric trap beat under a soft, sad female voice.

PROM NIGHT.

Taylor remembered hers like it was yesterday.

The long drive in Maddie's dad's Camaro, she and her date in the back seat. Stopping at the Arco at the far edge of town for coffee. Spiking the coffee with Kahlua from Maddie's date's mom's last trip to Hawaii.

The dancing, Our Song by Taylor Swift, all of the jokes you got in 2007 if your name was Taylor. The kissing under the lights.

The hotel that Maddie's mom had thought was the Quinn house and Taylor's mom had thought was Maddie's house. The way the boys' parents didn't care where they were.

The regret the next morning. The headaches.

The way her mom hadn't let her leave the house again till graduation.

Taylor sat at the kitchen table bathed in fear.

Who was this college kid coming to take Belle away?

Belle hadn't offered any kind of innocent plans that might be a cover for something dangerous. She hadn't said anything about it at all.

Taylor was tempted to call that overly polite Cooper to find out what was happening. Or Dayton's overly concerned dad, Dale. Surely a guy like him would have a handle on what Dayton's plans were for the night.

Belle had promised to come home after her hair was done by Sissy, but she hadn't said who was driving her to the dance, or where the dance was being held, or what they were doing after the dance. Nothing.

Taylor had asked.

She had texted.

She had gone to the school's website but, apart from the word "prom" on the school's calendar, there was no information.

And who was this "Levi" Belle had met at some college thing anyway? Belle *said* he had some genius kid early admittance thing, like she was getting. That didn't mean it was true. She could be lying. *He* could be lying. He could be some twenty-two year old college senior who had a thing for sixteen year old girls. Taylor shuddered.

She had herself worked up about as much as you could get when the creaky old front door opened. She jumped to her feet.

Belle stood in the doorway, hair in curlers, bangs off her face, with a garment bag slung over her arm. She had most of a full face of make up on as well. Taylor stared at her sister. For the first time since coming home, Taylor recognized her.

Belle stumbled into the room as though someone pushed her.

A blousy woman with frizzled blonde hair and ashy gray roots came in behind Belle. Sissy Dorney. It had been a few years, but Taylor recognized her. Sissy's face was round, dimpled, and remarkably young looking. She wasn't much taller than Taylor, she wasn't much bigger either, yet she seemed to fill the room, her big personality extending far beyond her physical person. Sissy rolled a large piece of luggage in and set it in the middle of the living room. She stared at the stack of mirrors in their window frames that Taylor had brought home from Hobby Lobby. "Sure hope you've got a mirror we can use." She laughed with a little snort.

"Hey there." Taylor stood awkwardly in the doorway of her own kitchen, trying not to let Sissy's tone annoy her. It was…a lot of mirrors. "Thanks for coming…"

"Belle said you'd like it better." Sissy opened her luggage and pulled up a rack. She began to hang hair dryers and curling irons from it. "Where's the best outlet if I want to work in here?"

"I'm not so sure there's a good one in here. The light's better in the kitchen anyway."

Sissy tilted the traveling styling station and rolled it to the kitchen. "Just like me, putting the cart before the horse. The kids seem pretty excited about tonight."

"Sure. Prom is exciting." Taylor hitched herself up on the kitchen counter so she could be out of the way, but still watch. "Where are they holding it, anyway?"

"Over at the ballroom of the craft college. They fix it up real nice."

The ballroom at Comfort College of Art and Craft was a fairly basic events space, but it could be made elegant. She remembered one or two events there. "So…no need to drive then?"

"Oh, some of the kids love to make an entrance, but I think the school is hoping the kids won't be drunk driving after."

Taylor suspected she was right. It was smart, actually, and she wondered why her class had gone to a place way out of town. Probably a parent got a deal.

"I'm real sorry your mom can't be here for this. She had so much fun helping the kids get ready for homecoming last year."

Taylor nodded but didn't say anything. No one had told her about homecoming.

Her phone buzzed a text.

She slipped it out.

Can I wear Grammy's necklace? It was from Belle.

"Excuse me." Taylor hopped off the counter. Grandma

Delma's jewelry box was somewhere in this house. And if Belle wanted to wear something from it, Taylor would turn the house upside down to find it.

A small box covered in faux crocodile sat on the top shelf of the closet she was sharing with her mother's old things.

She pulled it out and blew a layer of dust off. She couldn't remember what it held, and hoped her sister would be pleased.

Since tears had sprung to her eyes again, she took a few minutes to pull herself together. This was not the time to break down. Belle was making an honest effort and she did not want to ruin it.

By the time she'd calmed down and freshened up her face, Belle was alone in her bedroom.

She wore a strapless silver taffeta party dress with a charming poof of a short skirt. It was the one their mom had worn to her prom in 1988. Sissy had style her black hair in a chic updo, and though the makeup was heavy, it was lovely. A fancy evening look rather than a dark, intimidating look.

"You look…"

Belle went to smirk but caught a glimpse of herself in the mirror and looked away with an embarrassed smile.

"So, you really like Levi, huh?"

Belle nodded.

"You met him last summer?"

"Yeah."

Taylor tried to remember if Belle had been doing the heavy make-up thing last summer, but she couldn't. She remembered very short jean shorts, flip flops, and crop tops. Sporty-feminine-country had kind of been Belle's thing then.

She held out the jewelry box. "I found these."

Belle opened the box gingerly, took each item out and laid it with care on the bed.

She got to one of Grandma Delma's faux pearl collars from the 1940s. It was a Peter Pan shape that their grandma would have worn over a round necked satin dress to go to a wedding when she was a young lady. The faux pearls were tiny beads woven on strong silk. They had discolored through the years till they were almost the same silver as Belle's dress. Belle held it out in both hands, then held it against her pale, perfect skin.

It was funky, Taylor thought, but cute. Perfect for a sixteen year old saying a premature goodbye to childhood.

Taylor helped her latch it and then gave her a quick kiss on the back of her head.

Belle offered a more natural smile than any time in the weeks before.

Taylor left Belle with the jewelry and her dreams for the night. Downstairs she found Sissy having a cup of coffee and laughing with Grandpa Ernie.

Eventually Belle came back downstairs and before Taylor knew it, the doorbell rang.

Levi was a tall, slim kid with big black glasses. He wore a light blue suit that fit in a very modern way. The pants seemed too short and too tight and the sleeves of the jacket a bit too long. But Belle looked at him with a blushing glow that indicated she thought he looked just fine.

They only had a moment to greet each other before the door banged open again and Cooper and Dayton popped in wearing coordinating tuxedos, cut to fit precisely. Cooper's was black with an overall pattern of red roses. Dayton's was gray with a matching pattern in pink roses. Dayton's tux shirt was ruffled, Coopers was open at the neck with an untied bow tie.

"Ooh!" Sissy practically swooned when she saw them. "Aren't you two the prettiest?"

Cooper blushed.

Dayton kissed Sissy's cheek. "Where are the corsages?" Sissy stood with one hand on her hip, brandishing a curling iron like a pointer.

"Flowers are out." Dayton grinned.

Cooper pulled something from his pocket. "Flowers are timeless, darling." He tucked a small daisy, clearly picked from a yard, in the buttonhole of Dayton's jacket.

"Pictures!" Taylor called out, hoping she was saving Levi from the embarrassment of not having a flower.

"Just a sec." He also reached into his pocket—gentlemen, these teens—and pulled out a dainty enameled poppy pin, like you'd see on Memorial Day. "I thought this flower would last longer." He carefully pinned it to the side of her sweetheart neckline.

Her face was aloof, but Belle took his hand in his and gave it a subtle squeeze.

"How many of you are coming back to my house tonight?" Sissy asked, again brandishing the curling iron at the young folks.

"Not tonight," Dayton said. "My mom expects all four of us for games."

"Games?" Sissy snorted. "I was going to have pizza."

"No one's going out to a…" Taylor hesitated. She shouldn't put ideas in their heads. She was just surprised.

"Who has money for hotels?" Cooper interrupted her with a laugh.

"I've got to get back to school." Levi shrugged, a little embarrassed. "The program has a curfew for everyone under seventeen."

Even though she could tell he was young just by looking at his peach fuzz of a face, it was a huge relief to hear him say he was under seventeen.

"You all could come back here." Taylor was hopeful and crossed her fingers behind her back.

"No." Belle's one-word answer was firm. She took Levi by the hand and led him out. Cooper and Dayton followed.

When the door shut with a click, Sissy sighed. "Young love, isn't it wonderful?"

"So, Belle is in your good graces again?"

Sissy gave Taylor a stern look. "Belle was never out of my

good graces. But it is nice to see Cooper and Dayton together again..."

Taylor was kicking herself for not insisting on pictures. Perhaps if she was up when they came home, she could steal some. "So how long does this thing go?"

"They kick them out at midnight exactly. But they'll be fine. You're probably glad they're going to Dayton's. The Reubens are very strict. They'll be chaperoned there."

"Dale's letting Belle come over?"

Sissy snorted. "Dale. What a bag of hot air. If his wife wants the kids to have a party at her house, they will. He doesn't get a say."

"So, he just bullies the rest of us?"

Sissy packed up her bag of tricks and then gave Taylor another piercing look. "You're a mess. The kids will be fine. Let's go get a drink to relax you."

Taylor was about to say no thanks, but Sissy held out a hand to stop her. "We'll be quick. I know you don't want to leave Ernie here alone long."

Grandpa Ernie was asleep in his room. He'd be fine for one drink.

"But seriously, Dale said my sister was going to destroy Dayton's life."

Sissy paused in thought. "Then he probably went somewhere else for the duration of the party. Let's follow his lead."

Taylor followed, locking the door behind her, ready for whatever a drink out with Sissy Dorney looked like, when her phone rang.

"Is this Laura Quinn?" A very formal voice asked.

"No, this is her daughter, Taylor."

A pause. "Okay. You're on the list. This is the alarm company. The alarm went off at Flour Sax Quilts. The police were dispatched but say there's no sign of a break in. This is your official call."

"But how did the alarm go off? What do you mean?"

"The police confirmed that all of the doors and windows were secure. There's no sign of a break in, so they think it was the wind. This happens sometimes. We'll send someone over to adjust the settings on Monday."

"Thanks." Taylor ended the call. "The alarm went off at the shop. Do you mind stopping by with me real fast? They say there was no break in but…"

Sissy checked her watch. "Sure, we can go past, but I gotta get this stuff home." She loaded her luggage into her car, and then opened the door.

Taylor got in and they drove the couple of blocks to her shop.

Sissy pulled up along the curb and Taylor hopped out. The door to Flour Sax was shut and locked. The windows, which didn't open anyway, were untouched. "I want to go around back, hold on." Taylor hollered.

Sissy looked at her watch-less wrist dramatically.

"I'll just be a sec." Taylor ran around the corner to the back. That door was also locked and the windows were not only shut, but the bars that blocked them hadn't been compromised. The upstairs windows were unreachable from the ground and seemed shut tight.

The thing was, it was a windless night. So how had the alarm gone off?

She jangled her keys. It wouldn't hurt to go through the shop on her way to Sissy's car, just to feel safe.

She unlocked the door, telling herself that it was silly to worry, but wise to double check.

She pulled the door shut with a click, typed her alarm code into the pad by the door, and then exhaled.

She snuck past Grandpa Ernie's chair turning fast to make sure no one was in it. She was almost to the register when there was a large crash upstairs in the apartment.

Her heart lodged itself firmly in her throat, and she choked on it.

She squeezed her eyes shut for a second, then headed to the

front door. Each step felt like she was walking on glass. She hoping above hope that whoever was upstairs could not hear her.

At the front window, she waved frantically to Sissy.

Sissy didn't notice.

She texted Sissy.

Sissy didn't notice.

She put her key to the lock but spotted the bells. She could usually hear those when she was upstairs.

She texted Sissy again, and waved again, but Sissy didn't spot her.

Taylor was hesitant to walk to the backdoor past the stairs to the apartment, but it was they only way out that didn't make a lot of noise.

She made it as far as the worktable when she heard the feet on the stairs.

Her breath was snatched from her mouth. She dropped to the floor, hoping she hadn't been spotted.

After the count of three, she opened her eyes and scanned the staircase, looking for feet.

Instead, she spied a fluffy ringed-tail going around the corner.

She screamed.

The sound ripped through the air. Clawed feet skittered back up the stairs.

She texted Sissy again. *"raccoon!!!!!!"*

Sissy responded with a laughing emoji.

"COME HELP"

"HELL NO"

She ran to the front door and just barely waited till she got it unlocked to run through it. She didn't bother to shut it.

She pulled open the door to the car and jumped in. "I need to call animal control." She stared at her phone trying to remember what Google was.

"You need the sheriff. No animal control here."

"Crap." Taylor's phone was shaking. No, her hand was shaking. No, they both were.

"Are we getting a drink?"

"I have a raccoon in my shop." Taylor used two hands to hold the phone steady. It was just a raccoon. It wasn't a killer.

"And?"

"And he'll tear the place up."

"Listen, I feel for you, but not bad enough to get rabies. I'm going for a drink. Call the sheriff and let him deal with it."

"I don't think that's how this works."

"Suit yourself." Sissy started her car.

Taylor hopped out.

The sheriff seemed extreme. Surely there was someone else she could call to help her deal with a raccoon.

She almost laughed when she remembered Hudson. He had promised he'd help with anything, even a raccoon.

She called him as Sissy drove away.

"Hey!" He sounded happy and surprised. "Is everything all right?"

"Raccoon." Taylor only got the one word out because she saw the beast again through the window, but he wasn't headed toward the door. He was using his creepy little fingers to peel open one of the caramels by the register.

"You're kidding! In the garage?" Hudson laughed.

"No, in the shop."

"I'll be right there. You don't mind if I shoot it, do you?"

The raccoon spotted her.

Taylor would have sworn it did.

It stared through the window and locked eyes, then it pulled the sticky candy between its two hands.

"Please hurry."

"Got it, boss."

Hudson hung up.

Taylor wished he hadn't, but he did. She stood there,

watching the raccoon discover caramel. He was mesmerized and so was Taylor.

Things had gotten really sticky for the beast when a truck pulled up. Hudson hopped out and joined her at the window.

He whistled softly. "Cute little guy, hey? He can't be very old."

Taylor turned to him, full of fear and disgust. "The devil is as old as the earth."

He laughed. "I probably won't shoot him. We just have to lure him out of there."

"How do you lure a raccoon?"

"With a cute lady raccoon." He said it with a straight face as he walked to the door of the store. "He doesn't strike me as sick or scared. We probably don't have to be afraid."

"I do not have a cute lady raccoon."

Hudson opened the door, but Taylor hung back. "It's easy to trap a raccoon with marshmallows, but I don't know, this one's covered in caramels. He might not care about a lowly marshmallow."

The raccoon was sort of lounging on the counter now, licking its fingers.

"If I take the caramels away, he'll probably follow."

"But you'll have to get so close to get them." Her hand gripped the cold metal door handle. She desperately did not want to go in.

"Is your trash can full outside?"

"It's not empty."

"Can you go around back and find something very aromatic from it? We can probably lure him out with some half-rotten fruit."

She stared at him.

"If you bring me the fruit, I will lure him out with it."

Taylor nodded, not sure if she trusted him. What if this animal chased her to get it?

"You really don't have to be afraid. He's not going to hurt you." Hudson's smile was confident and full of humor.

The raccoon dropped off the counter and waddled down the room with his sticky hands.

"But the sooner we get him away from your fabric the better. You go find some trash okay?"

He was right. They needed to protect her stock.

She ran back to the trash and found a few apple cores on top of the can. Not rotten really, but they were definitely ripe. She grabbed them and ran back.

She stopped at the front door to assess the situation.

Hudson had his back to her, and crochet low. He was inching backwards towards the door, but for a moment that was all she could see.

He stopped. Then inched a little further.

She moved a little so she could see around him.

He had an opened caramel held out in one hand, and the box in the other.

The raccoon was shyly following him, reaching for the candy as Hudson pulled it away.

She pushed the door open but tried to stand outside.

Hudson heard the bells jingle and turned his head to give her an encouraging smile.

The raccoon leapt at him, snatched the candy and ran back to the register counter.

Hudson stood up. "Almost had him." He kicked the door stop into place. "Got anything really stinky for me?"

Taylor held out the pathetic apples. "He'll hardly want those."

"Do you have any heavy wool?"

"No..."

"Not even an old blanket or a coat?"

"Maybe upstairs." Her eyes were glued on the greedy animal.

"Let's go check. I can sneak around behind him and nab him that way."

"What? No! You'll get hurt."

He grinned "I'm a lot bigger than he is."

"But rabies…"

"If he bites me, you'll just have to rush me to the hospital. It'll be fine."

"This is the worst idea I've ever heard."

"I have my .22 in the car. I could just shoot him." Hudson ambled back to his truck as though they had all evening.

Taylor went out with him, picturing the blood and gore she'd have to clean up if she shot the animal.

"Catching him in a wool blanket isn't such a bad idea now, is it?"

"You could literally die. I don't think fabric is worth that."

He gazed down at her, sad and sympathetic. "Okay. I won't. I've got a live trap in the back of the truck. You want to sit in there while I set it up?

Taylor glanced at the cab of the truck with its safe steel doors high up off the ground. "A real feminist would say no."

"Feminists can be scared of raccoons." He opened the door.

Taylor climbed in.

He shut the door with a click and disappeared around the back for the live trap.

And she cried.

It came up from some hidden fountain of pain, some unexpected spring of feeling.

A month ago, she'd had a mother.

And she'd had a job at a nice big store in the city, and she'd had a long-term serious boyfriend who lived with her and did the man of the house stuff.

And now she had a raccoon eating candy in her shop and a teenage sister at prom with a college kid and a grandpa with dementia.

She cried those deep embarrassing sobs, the balls of her

hands digging into her eyes like she thought she could send the tears back where they came from.

She sobbed till she couldn't anymore because it was too ridiculous. She had cried at the funeral, and in her bed alone, and on the drive here when she'd moved. She'd cried plenty. It was time to stop crying.

A great thunk in the back shook the truck, then Hudson got in. "He really is a little guy."

"Please tell me you didn't catch him in your arms."

"I didn't have to. After all that candy, he really wanted water. I put the apples and the caramels and a bowl of water from the sink in the back of the trap and it only took a few minutes for him to check it out."

"What are you going to do with him now?"

"I'll release him back at my place."

She nodded, but wondered if the animal was cold in the back of the truck.

Hudson graciously ignored her blotchy and wet face. "It's been some kind of night. Can I buy you a drink?"

"Yes, thank you." Taylor buckled up and leaned back in her seat. "It's prom night."

"Oh yeah?"

"Belle's there now, and I don't know if she's coming home."

"Did you on prom night?"

"No."

"I did." He offered her a cheeky grin.

"Aren't you a good guy."

"Regular knight in shining armor."

He drove to the west side of town, to the last bar before you find yourself on the road to the coast.

She looked longingly toward the coast range mountains.

"We don't have to stop here." Hudson offered.

"It is prom night, after all…." Taylor murmured softly, not looking at him.

He turned the radio to the classic country station.

She hummed along to an old song. She wasn't the biggest fan, but the classics were different.

A deep rumble came from Hudson as he started singing along.

She joined him. They laughed.

He didn't force her to talk.

But he wasn't silent either.

"Do you have a favorite beach?"

Taylor didn't want to admit she wasn't much for the beach. She liked it fine but wasn't obsessed. Once a year she liked to get to the edge of the country, stare out into the vastness of the sea and contemplate her finite nature, but mostly she just wasn't into sand and the Oregon coast is always so cold. She just said "No, not really."

"Then I'll take you to mine."

THE SUN WAS SETTING, and it was that dusky gray time of night where the sky and the sea melted together. He led her across the sandy expanse to a large log, driftwood really, but as big as a tree. He tapped the coals of a recently abandoned beach fire with the toe of his Timberlands. "Shall we?"

"Sure."

They got up again and collected chunks of wood from the general area. By the time they had a fire going the night had grown chilly. But the clouds were breaking, and a few stars shone above them. She leaned back on her arms letting the fire warm her legs while she watched the sky sparkle.

"Have you guys gotten any answers about your mom's death?" He'd given her plenty of personal space, which was the opposite of what she had in mind when she imagined them reliving prom night at the beach. But this was probably better.

She leaned forward and tapped at the fire with a thick stick. "No one really knows what happened. Everyone has a little piece of the picture, but when we put it all together, we still end up with Mom heading outside alone and not being seen again till the next morning."

"That's rough."

"I don't know if having a witness would have made it better. Knowing whose fault it was doesn't bring her back."

"It's natural to want to blame someone." Hudson stared into the distance, though the sun had set and there was nothing to see but darkness.

"Especially for Belle. She's so young."

"She probably thinks it's her fault."

"Hmmm...I wonder what made you think of that." Taylor used her branch to draw parallel lines in the sand, near each other, but never connecting.

"I've been a teenager before. Don't you remember?" He lifted his face to stare at the stars instead of the darkness straight ahead.

She did remember. She hadn't paid attention to most of the underclassmen, but he'd stood out as a freshman.

"There can be such a black and white fatality to everything when you're an adolescent." He paused, then turned her direction. "My dad was in a car wreck when I was a senior. He drove into the creek."

"Bible Creek?" Taylor shuddered at the thought of the steep cliffs.

"Yeah. He was headed to pick me up. I'd been drinking with some friends and we got caught by a neighbor. He took my buddy's car keys and made us all call our parents."

"Was your dad okay?"

"No."

She reached out for his hand, letting her fingers weave into his.

"He lived but had to go on disability." His hand was firm, and strong, and warm. It felt safe.

"This is kind of different." She murmured. Belle hadn't been the reason their mom had gone away for the weekend. Not the primary cause anyway, not like Hudson's dad having to pick him up when he got in trouble. She knew her tone wasn't sympathetic, and immediately regretted saying it.

He let go of her hand. "It was my fault my dad drove out there that night. It was not my fault that my dad had also been drinking. I've learned after a lot of counseling that this means the accident was not my fault."

"You're right. I'm sorry." Taylor felt a little sick. She should have waited to hear the whole story before she judged.

"I don't know what your sister is thinking right now, but I'd guess from having hung out with her a bit that she thinks it's her fault. And not just for the death, but for everything you gave up too."

Taylor kicked the sand in front of her.

"Don't try to tell me it wasn't much."

"I won't."

"Home?" He was close enough that their shoulders brushed, and Taylor was warm sitting near him, but he didn't offer to hold her hand again.

"Yup. Sold my place in Portland."

"Career?"

"Not that it was all that great, but yeah."

He didn't ask what else Taylor had left behind in Portland, so she volunteered.

"Grandma Quinny called after the accident. I walked into work and quit, that second. The next day, I called a real estate agent and put the condo on the market. My boyfriend, who happened to live there with me, didn't like my taking those kinds of steps without talking about it first."

Hudson didn't say anything.

"You don't blame him, I'm sure."

"It's not my place to have an opinion on that. I do have an opinion on him not coming here with you though."

"We'd been together four years."

"Shit."

"Yeah."

The fire was going down. Taylor wasn't in the mood to relive her prom night anymore.

"How does Ernie feel about all of this?"

Taylor considered her grandpa, his condition, and how he must feel right now. "Confused mostly. His dementia has gotten really bad."

"It must be nice to be able to take a night off, even if it is just to escape a raccoon."

Taylor stared at the coals, feeling sorry for herself and glad about the raccoon at the same time. "He'll laugh when I tell him about it." She smiled at the thought and then frowned. "Oh, Hudson, crap, crap, crap. I don't have the night off."

"What do you mean?"

"I mean Grandpa Ernie's home alone. I'm an idiot."

Hudson wrapped her hand in both of his and brought it to his lips. They too were warm and felt safe. "Hold on a minute, okay?" He left her at the dying fire, in the dark.

She didn't want to sit there alone, not while Grandpa Ernie could be in who knows what kind of trouble, but Hudson returned quickly with a bucket of water. "Had a bucket in the truck and filled it at the foot wash tap by the bathroom."

He poured the bucket over the coals. They sizzled softly and turned black. Taylor helped him spread them apart on the sand.

Then they both ran to the truck and drove as fast as was safe...or maybe a little faster once they were over the mountains.

At her house, Hudson walked her to the door. "Do you want me to come in, just in case?"

Taylor nodded.

To her relief, they found Grandpa Ernie safely in bed, snoring softly.

In the kitchen a crumb covered plate sat next to the sink, and the peanut butter jar was still open with a knife in it. He hadn't gone hungry while Taylor was gone, and he hadn't burned the house down or left the gas on or any of the other terrifying visions she'd had as they raced home.

Taylor walked Hudson toward the door so he could leave, even though every little part of her wanted him to stay. They stood together in the front room, only the little light by grandpa's chair was on. Hudson took both of her hands in his.

It was such a gentle gesture from such a strong man.

"Thank you so much for your help." Her words were a low murmur that she suspected had a romantic tinge to them.

"You really loved him, didn't you?"

Taylor knew he was talking about her ex-boyfriend, but she wanted to pretend he meant someone else. Grandpa maybe. She didn't answer but stared at his mouth—kissable lips, whatever that meant, slightly parted. Firm jaw, scruffy with a day's growth of beard.

"You've probably noticed I'm interested." His low growl of a voice was barely perceptible.

She was drawn to him like a magnet, a palpable pull to this man.

He grinned. "And sensitive, insightful, and handsome."

She laughed, thankful that he had broken the moment. Glad for a release from her overwrought emotional state.

"I'd love to say that I'm sensitive and insightful enough to recognize that being your rebound would be a mistake. But I'm not, so, can we do this again?" His eyes were round, and just vulnerable enough to make her want to do something crazy.

She tipped up on her toes and kissed him, just a little.

He wrapped her in his arms and kissed her more than a little.

The front door burst open and laughing teenagers poured into the room.

He held her tighter, laughing into her neck.

"I don't think they noticed us," she whispered.

"Ug, we do." That voice could only belong to Dayton.

Belle flopped onto the couch and Levi took the seat beside her.

"I thought you were all going to Dayton's," Taylor said.

"We thought you might need a chaperone," Cooper's smooth, laughing voice responded.

"We want to watch Sharknado." Belle finally spoke.

Taylor tossed her the remote. "Prom is just not what it used to be." She walked Hudson out the front door.

"I have to work tomorrow morning," he said. "But I'd like to come by in the afternoon to see if I can fix the damage that raccoon did to your place."

"I would appreciate that very much."

He kissed her again and left.

CHAPTER SIXTEEN

There were no signs of debauchery in the living room the next morning. The prom kids Sharknado fun had been loud, but Taylor had been so exhausted she fell asleep within minutes of hitting the pillow.

The next morning, she nudged Belle's door open and saw her piled under quilts with one bare foot sticking out. Their mom's dress was hanging neatly on the back of a chair, and the faux-pearl collar was laid on the desk.

Taylor shut the door and checked on Grandpa Ernie. He was sitting on the edge of his bed putting on his favorite slippers.

"Morning, Grandpa."

"Good morning, Prodigal."

"Whoops. You caught me."

"I know I'm not your father."

This was a relief to hear.

"But it would be nice to know if you are coming home or not in the night." He huffed into a mustache. "Grandpas worry."

"You wanna go out for breakfast today?" Taylor asked.

He scowled though he couldn't hide his smile from his eyes. "You have a production schedule to keep."

"Then let's go downstairs and I'll make us some eggs."

Grandpa Ernie stayed lucid and alert through the breakfast and took his medicine without the ritual of the raisin bread. It was the kind of morning that made Taylor think everyone had been overreacting. Maybe he wasn't as confused as they thought.

She'd like to get him to the doctor and find out what was really going on. As he made his way through his scrambled eggs, she pondered how hard that might be. She also pondered how she could get anything done in life…in real life, not work life, with only one employee and open seven days a week. It seemed impossible.

The shop really needed two people all the time. She had stacks of notes for her mom's previous shows and notes for ones she wanted to film, but she didn't have her business plan. No notes on how her mom had intended to keep things going with the money she was stocking up, and right now, that's what Taylor wanted.

Belle stumbled into the kitchen just as Taylor was finishing up. She yawned, then kissed Grandpa Ernie.

"When did everyone leave last night?" Taylor plated some eggs and sausage and carried it to the table for Belle.

"Around three." She yawned again, then rested her head on her hand, eyes closed.

"You should go back to bed." It was Sunday, a fact Taylor hadn't realized till that moment. She didn't have a filming schedule this morning. Perhaps Grandpa Ernie wasn't as with it today as she had thought. Though…. She hadn't remembered what day it was either. That little mistake couldn't mean much.

Instead of going to bed, Belle sat up and began to eat. "I have some plans for the day."

"Oh?"

Belle glanced at Grandpa.

He was getting up from his chair.

"Need a hand?" she asked.

"No, I do not." He took his plate to the sink and shuffled off to his bedroom.

"So, your plans..."

"It's about Mom." Belle took another bite.

Taylor waited.

"Cooper and I thought we'd drive out to Nancy Reese's place and see if we couldn't get her to chat."

"But that's hours away."

"We've got all day."

"True, so you don't have to rush. You could go back to bed and have more than three hours of sleep today."

"Hmmm..." Belle considered this option while she ate. "I'm sure Cooper wouldn't disagree. I'll text him."

"I'd really like to come."

"Why don't you see if you can track down Gina?" Belle's voice implied this would be a real challenge for Taylor.

"But that's hours away in the other direction."

Belle sighed.

"I suppose that's the point, but I would like to have the whole picture and not just some sides of it." Taylor was too tired to fight, but she wasn't going to give in, either.

Belle ate in silence for a little while. When the eggs were gone, she seemed to have come to a conclusion. "That makes sense. We can go together. I didn't think Cooper was all that excited, to be honest. Dayton was, but...ug. I can only take so much Dayton in one weekend."

"Understandable." Taylor probably shouldn't have agreed. She didn't know anything about the kid. "How about we leave at noon? You have the address and directions?"

Belle tapped the back of her iPhone. "Yup." After delivering her plate to the sink she went back to bed.

When Taylor remembered Hudson was coming over this afternoon to check the apartment above the shop for secret raccoon entrances, she also remembered she was supposed to be working while Roxy had a day off. So much for a day with her sister.

She pattered her way up to Belle's room, not excited to ditch her immediately after begging to be included, but Belle was already asleep.

She went to her own room and slouched in bed considering options. She could text Hudson to let him know she wasn't going to be around, but that she could make any day next week happen.

Roxy was harder. She both needed and deserved a day off.

Belle barely wanted Taylor around, and Roxy really needed the family time. Taylor had made spontaneous changes to her schedule half a dozen times since being home and Roxy had been a complete sport about all of it.

The last thing Taylor wanted in this world was to disappoint Belle, but in the end, it probably wasn't a disappointment.

When she heard Belle stirring in her room half an hour later, Taylor got up to give her the change of plans.

Belle stared at her blankly from the little stool in front of her mirror.

"I'm sorry," Taylor said again. "I just, I had forgotten. I still don't quite have my feet under me running this store."

"Whatever."

"You can tell me how you feel." Taylor sat on the edge of her bed.

"Oh, can I?" Belle's words dripped with sarcasm.

"I'd like it if you would." Taylor braced herself for whatever Belle was about to say.

Belle twisted her mascara wand back into the tube and turned on her little dresser stool. "I'm not surprised."

"I've been disorganized," Taylor tried to acknowledge Belle's feelings.

"Your priorities are very predictable." Belle crossed her legs. The hole in the knee of her ripped black jeans got bigger.

"Go on." Taylor gritted her teeth.

"I'm going to find out exactly what happened the night Mom died, no matter what it takes. You, on the other hand, are going to make money. That's your priority and always has been."

Taylor took her time responding. Defensive anger was filling her brain and making reasonable or kind answers hard to find. Eventually she came up with something. "I'm responsible for a lot of things in this world. One of them is making sure Roxy and I have a job to go to every day so our families can eat." She stood. The weeks of taking Belle's attitude had done her in. "I don't need to know exactly what happened the night Mom died because I am a grown adult with real work to do." Taylor was going to swish out on that note, but her mouth wasn't done saying angry things yet. "And nothing they find out about that night will bring her back. She's not like Colleen. She didn't just disappear one day to come back later, rich and happy and ready to play mom again. She's dead. Actually dead. Like my dad." Taylor took a deep breath, ready for the shame to roll over her in waves, but instead, there was just more anger. "I don't have the luxury of mincing my way through school half-hearted because I'm better than everyone else and have something bigger waiting around the corner for me. I have real work to do, whether I want to or not." On that note Taylor stormed out, slamming the door shut.

The waves of shame and regret hit her at the bottom of the staircase. But she had apologized enough for things that weren't her fault. She held on tight to the anger and hustled outside to walk it off. She wanted to walk all the way back to the beach, figuring her anger could probably take her that far. She only made it as far as the Old Mill Museum, which was just before that bar they hadn't gone to last night. It had only been two miles of full out anger-walking, but it had been enough. She sat on the bench in front of the board building that memorialized their early days as a flour mill town and leaned her head on the rough-hewn replication wall.

She didn't cry though. She had done enough of that yesterday.

In six months, Belle would be off to college, and that sounded like the best news she'd ever heard.

213

❧

Despite the lingering self-hatred that came from having a massive tantrum, Taylor opened the shop at eleven as usual. The day was bright and cheerful, a little chilly, but not bad. She expected today's quilters would come by later, figuring church, brunch or lunch, and the drive over from whatever towns they lived in would still take a couple of hours.

Hudson was there before any customers and looking fresh, handsome, and as Belle and her friends might say, "like a snack".

"Good morning." He smiled and came over to the counter Taylor stood behind. He hesitated like he wanted to lean in and give her a quick kiss but wasn't sure if he should.

She took a small step back. She didn't deserve a kiss today.

"I'm alone in the shop, do you mind much running upstairs to check it out and telling me what you find?"

He hid any disappointment he might have felt. "No problem. How's Ernie?"

"He's good. I left him at home for now. Belle is going to bring him by before she leaves." At least those were the directions Taylor had texted her when she was done blowing off steam.

"I'll report as soon as I know what's going on."

"Thanks." Taylor turned her back, pretending she needed to do something to the boxes of thread on the shelves behind her.

Last night had been a crazed fever dream. The result of over-wrought emotions. Taylor hadn't once let herself truly consider what the loss of Clay, who she'd planned to marry and have children with, really meant to her. She had focused all of her energy on Belle and her needs.

To be a hero.

To not have to feel what she was really feeling.

All of the bad stuff had piled on at once and she had barely been able to see her own face in the mirror much less the total decimation of the life she had lived and the future she had planned.

Hudson's feet echoed on the ceiling.

She was curious what he would find. She suspected somewhere along the row of downtown buildings there was a hole in the ceiling, and that a family of raccoons were making their way through all of their attics and second stories. Hopefully all she'd have to do was a little patch work in a wall or ceiling or something.

Thinking about wall repair was nicer than thinking about the scene she'd had with Belle this morning, or about Clay and the girl he had moved in with mere seconds after she'd left town.

She had checked Clay's Instagram once, but he wasn't much for social media. His last post was still the selfie of them at the new pier on the Columbia river, sailboats floating gently behind them.

Clay had been a lot of fun. Good looking, but in a cute, harmless kind of way.

Love had snuck up on her with him. They'd been friends for almost two years, after meeting in the parking lot of the mall their two stores shared—her Joann's and his Dick's Sporting Goods. He'd moved on to an accounting job downtown, but they'd stayed friends.

His smile, that lopsided grin, had hooked her. Taylor remembered the day that lopsided grin had turned from a friendly smile to one she wanted to wake up to each morning.

He had been kicked out of his rental. The house was being sold. He needed a place to crash, and she had a place. Her condo had two bedrooms and he could totally stay in one.

But that night, he hadn't stayed in the second bedroom. Their best buddy love had blossomed almost instantly and had lasted four years.

It had lasted until she had needed more from him than a buddy during the day and a lover at night.

"Knock, knock."

Taylor shook her head to get out of her own thoughts and looked up. Hudson had a very apologetic look on his face. "It's

215

kind of a mess up there, I'm really sorry. I don't know how often anyone goes to your attic, but that's where they all live."

"The crawl space above the apartment?"

"Yeah. That one. The raccoons got in through a vent and made a nice little house. Two bedrooms, a hot tub, a satellite dish. It would get a lot of rent in Portland."

Taylor smiled.

"They tore up the wall in a corner and got into the apartment that way. Looks like a fresh hole."

"That is….That's really disgusting, isn't it?" She shivered at the thought of those giant pests living right above her all of this time. She might be from a small town, but she had never been much of a country girl.

"I'd like to board up the hole for now to keep them from getting back in."

"But?"

"You need to hire an exterminator to get them out before it's worth fixing the wall correctly, and then the cleanup….oh man. The insulation is disgusting. It has to come out and be replaced. I don't like the idea of you doing that."

"Because disease?"

"Yup."

"You do odd jobs….is that the kind of thing you'd do?"

"I like to say I do side jobs." He leaned on the counter, comfortably. "I do have steady employment. But yes, I could do that."

"Well…." Taylor tried to remember the huge pile of cash in the bank and not freak out about this expense. "Better sooner than later, right?"

"Call the exterminator first, get them out, and then I'll take care of the rest. I don't want you to have to worry about it."

"Can I get an, um, estimate?" It was suddenly very important to her that he not think she wanted the job for free.

"Yeah, sure. Just materials, okay?"

She couldn't argue with that. She'd be an idiot to. "Materials and dinner?"

"It's a deal." He held out his hand and she accepted. "I've got to run. More odd jobs ahead of me."

"Side jobs, you mean."

"Thank you. That is exactly what I mean." He left, a happy lilt to his step.

Hudson was a good guy. A person Taylor had known, or at least known of, for years. A person who would be a good friend to have when making her life in this town. She really didn't want to screw that up by having a rebound romance with him.

By the time Belle dropped Grandpa Ernie off, Flour Sax finally had some customers.

Grandpa grumped his way into his chair and turned on his little TV. The quilters wandered over to him to give their hellos. They were old friends of Grandma Delma's from back in the day.

"Did Cooper decide to go with you?" Taylor asked her sister.

"Yes."

"You have some cash? And maybe some food?"

"Yes."

"When will you be back?"

"That depends on how long the conversation with Nancy goes, doesn't it?" Belle looked at her, unflinching.

Taylor squared her shoulders. She wasn't going to let Belle get to her this time.

"How long is the drive?"

"Google says it's two and a half hours."

Taylor glanced at her watch. It was just after one. They'd be there at three-thirty, give them an hour to talk.... "I want you home by eight." This seemed totally reasonable.

Belle smirked, but her eyes weren't in it. She seemed hurt. The things Taylor had said back at the house would do that. They would hurt. "We'll be back when we get back." She sauntered out like she had no care in the world, which everyone in the shop knew wasn't true.

CHAPTER SEVENTEEN

*T*hat evening Taylor convinced Grandpa Ernie to sit with her in the front room to watch a movie together. They had pizza and popcorn and chocolate chip cookies.

He picked an old western. Taylor didn't care. She just needed to not think about where her sister was or when she'd be home.

Just after nine, or around the time the girl who was trying to save her ranch realized she had lost her heart to the wrong man, the kitchen door creaked open.

It had been a long day, and Taylor was pretty sure she needed to apologize to her sister, but she couldn't bring herself to do it, so she pulled the Log Cabin quilt over herself and snuggled into the couch.

"Hey-dilly-ho, neighbor." Cooper wandered into the living room and sat next to her. He helped himself to a slice of pizza. "I understand there is some chill between you and Belle right now, and that things are, in fact, not chill at the moment."

"Yes."

"So, I want to let you know that Nancy Reese wasn't home. We left a note with Belle's number and the address to the shop. That was my idea. I didn't think this stranger needed to know where you ladies live."

"Very wise." Taylor refused to ask if Belle had sent him in with the information.

"Belle is a good kid." Cooper got comfortable, slinging one arm over the back of the sofa. "It's going to suck when she leaves. I don't think she'll keep in touch."

Taylor glanced at him, wondering what was behind the heart to heart. She also noticed for the first time that there were no signs of life in the kitchen. "Did she come here with you?"

"Nope. She's at my house. I refused to take her to Levi's dorm, firstly, because Levi is a weird kid and wouldn't know what to do with a girl if you dropped her in his bed half naked, and second, because those programs for teens at colleges have fairly strict curfews.

"I bet your mom was glad you took Dayton to prom."

"Indeed, she was pleased."

"And what are your intentions at this point?"

He dropped his head back on the sofa, looking surprisingly young. "I've got to stick around here for another school year. I don't get to escape. I guess Dayton and I will have whatever fun can be had. I don't know. I plan to go somewhere sunny for college. It might be my only chance in life to see what the sun is like."

Taylor laughed, knowing that despite a reputation as a land of clouds and rain, summers in Oregon rivaled anywhere in the world. "And?"

"Dayton only cares about fabric design. One of the best fabric design programs in the country is at the craft college, so, that's that."

"No white wedding at Bible Creek Church for you two?"

"Not if I can help it. I like Dayton, but it can all be kind of a lot, you know?"

"Yeah…" Taylor, in fact, did not know. Dayton remained, as ever, an impenetrable enigma. "So, I really screwed up this morning with Belle."

"That you did."

"Any advice?"

He was quiet for a moment. "If I knew how to make her love somebody, I'd use that magic for myself, don't you think?"

Taylor reached over and patted his knee. "There's cookies too," she said.

Cooper helped himself to one.

Grandpa Ernie slept through the conversation.

GRANDMA QUINNY FOUND Taylor at the shop the next day promptly at eleven. Roxy and Taylor had filmed enough material for three more videos. Taylor was getting better, or maybe Roxy had given up on making her good. Either way they had fumbled through several of the projects Laura had scheduled for herself.

Grandma Quinny made her way slowly to Taylor, stopping to look at a little table display of pincushions, then at some patterns. She had almost made it when she stopped and looked up and around like a little bird dog.

Taylor knew what had stopped her. The sound of her mom's voice. Taylor had the video running in the corner again, just a little louder this time. You couldn't see it from where she stood, but you could hear it. Four women in matching t-shirts were crowded around the screen watching it.

Grandma Quinny didn't follow the sound but joined Taylor at the work table where she was cutting yardage for another customer.

"The funny thing was," Grandma Quinn said, as though they had been in the middle of a conversation, "when I first heard Laura's voice, I wasn't surprised. This is her shop and the sound of her voice belongs here." She set her purse on the table. "I'm glad you're playing it."

"Thanks." Taylor folded the three yards of creamy yellow paisley and pinned the ticket to it. "Did you want to do more shopping?"

The lady who's shirt said, "Quilters never Quit," and matched the other ladies looked back at her friends. "Yes, I guess so."

"I can hold this at the register for you." Taylor held it out to her, letting her make the decision.

She took the fabric, smiled at Grandma Quinn, and went to see what her friends were engrossed in.

"It was hard at first," Taylor said, "but I've gotten used to it."

"And I see you've started making your own videos."

"It seemed like the right thing to do."

"Have you given any more thought to what we spoke about? That little policy would make a nice down payment." Grandma Quinny looked around the store, then her gaze fixed on Taylor again. Grandma Quinny didn't look particularly pleased, but she did look tolerant. "Especially if you're buying something here in Comfort. There's a very nice new development on the South side of town you might want to look at."

Taylor knew the development. It was nice.

Knowing her grandfather was a retired investment banker, she had done some figuring of her own. That little $30,000 insurance policy, if she guessed correctly, was worth five times that now. Combined with the proceeds of the sale of her condo she ought to be able to get one of those smaller houses in the new development for cash.

One of the other ladies who had come with the group peeled herself away from the video. She brought a bolt of white cotton with a subtle all-over floral pattern in off white. "Five yards please. It's for the back of a quilt for my granddaughter. She's having her first communion and I wanted to do something special." The woman pulled out her phone and tapped the screen a few times, then held it out. "Isn't she lovely?"

The picture was of a clean and healthy girl in a bright pink Easter dress. Taylor remembered something Mrs. Quimby had told Ramona in some book, that healthy kids were all beautiful. "Yes," Taylor agreed. "She's beautiful."

The customer beamed and scrolled through more pictures while Taylor measured and cut her fabric. "Is there anything else I can cut for you?"

"No, this will be all." She accepted the fabric and went on her way.

Roxy was at the register ringing up a customer who was not wearing a matching t-shirt. The proud grandmother waited in line behind her.

"I should go look at those houses. Are there many available still?"

Grandma Quinny brightened immediately. "Yes, yes. I think the model home is still free as well as one or two near enough the creak to hear it."

"That would be really nice." One couldn't say she'd actually moved into her mom's house, since all of her stuff was still in storage. Reinvesting what she made selling her own place while figuring out how to care for Grandpa Ernie didn't seem foolish. Even if he lived in a care home, he'd need someone in town to visit him and make sure he was well looked after. And that shouldn't have to be Belle.

"We can tour them together." Grandma Quinny almost sounded unsure, like Taylor wouldn't want to. "I've been wanting to spend more time with you, sweetheart."

Taylor came around the table and gave her a hug. "Thanks."

Grandma Quinny picked up her bag, a bright smile on her face. "I have a project for baby Hattie. I'm going to do a little shopping."

"Let me know if I can help."

Grandma moved on, letting the ladies in line have their turns.

Grandma Quinny didn't buy anything, but Taylor wasn't surprised. Grandma Quinny really did prefer the fabric selection over at Bible Creek Quilt and Gift.

Flour Sax was busy most of the day, so Taylor didn't notice Belle come in to hang out with Grandpa Ernie. When they closed up shop at six, Belle and Grandpa were sharing a bowl of popcorn and playing war with a couple of old decks of cards.

Taylor pulled a chair up to the folding table they had between them and opened a can of soda. "Who's winning?"

Grandpa Ernie gave her a fierce look. "She's cheating." Despite the grump in his voice, his eyes sparkled, and Taylor knew he was joking.

"I'm merely very talented at this particular game of chance." Belle took the next hand as she said it.

"What do you two want for dinner tonight? We can go anywhere, get anything, or cook whatever you want."

"Pot roast." Grandpa Ernie took the next trick.

"Does Reuben's make a good pot roast?"

"Delma did," Grandpa Ernie said. "Don't you have her recipe?"

"Probably, but I think it takes an hour or so...."

"Where do you have to be in such a hurry that you can't spend an hour cooking?"

Taylor glanced at her phone. It was already 6:30. Roxy had closed out the till, but Taylor had a bit more work to do before she could go home.

"You did say *anything*, Tay," Belle said, taking another hand.

"Okey dokes. Let me finish up here, then I'll meet you back at the house. I'll have to run down to the market."

"It closes at six."

"Ah. So, I just made another offer I couldn't live up to."

"Yup." Belle banged her large stack of playing cards on the metal folding table to straighten the stack.

"In fifteen minutes I can be ready to go down to Reuben's and I'm sure and certain we can get pot roast there."

"That's a long walk," Grandpa grumbled.

"I'll drive." It was only a few blocks, but that was getting to be a long walk for him.

Taylor left them to their cards so she could do the glamorous work of closing up shop. From emptying the waste to tucking in all the little corners of the fabric that had been touched, and examined, considered, and abandoned through the day, to running the sweeper. She knew that properly taking care of the little things separated a great shop from a bad one, but nobody really likes doing them.

When they all headed out, she was surprised to see her mom's Audi parked behind the store.

Belle opened the passenger side door for Grandpa Ernie and took the driver's for herself. "It's a couple of blocks from the house to the shop," she said simply.

Belle backed onto Love Street and pulled up to Main, pausing to check traffic before driving the block or so down the street to Reuben's. A small woman in a raincoat stood at the door of the shop, looking in through cupped hands.

"Hold on, Belle." Taylor tapped her shoulder to get her attention.

Belle stopped and Taylor hopped out.

"Hey, I'm so sorry, we're closed. Was there something you needed?" Taylor didn't know what prompted her to offer help, except maybe that she wanted to do one thing right. She wanted to not have been making her grandpa walk too far twice a day. She wanted to not have blown up at her sister. She wanted to just help someone.

"I saw that. I just drove in from quite a way. I didn't realize the shop closed so early."

"I'm sorry. I think Dutch Hex keeps longer hours, it's just a few doors down." Taylor pointed down the street toward the rival shop.

"No, I was supposed to come here." She held a crumpled note in her hand. "I'm looking for Taylor and Belle Quinn. Do you know them?"

CHAPTER EIGHTEEN

*T*heir guest for dinner that evening was Nancy Reese. Grandpa Ernie couldn't remember her, but Taylor wasn't surprised. Grandpa couldn't be expected to remember everybody who'd ever lived in Comfort.

Nancy was an older woman, polished and put together in a linen suit and less than sensible heels. Her soft, flowing blonde and silver hair fell just to her shoulders in a chic wavy lob. It looked to Taylor as though she'd had work done, since her face was much smoother than her hands. But her hands were still elegant with long fingers and large stones in several rings.

"I don't want to interrupt your family time, but when I found this note on my door, I had to come. What a tragedy for you girls, and you as well." She reached a hand across the table to take Grandpa Ernie's in hers. He smiled.

"Thank you. It was very generous to drive all the way here." Taylor tried to picture this non-threatening woman as someone who filled Colleen with fear and anxiety, but it was hard to imagine.

Sadie, one of the many Reubens who waited tables at the family owned diner popped over, a swinging ponytail and polka dot button down shirt giving her a fifties vibe, even though the diner was stuck firmly in the late seventies.

"What can I getcha?" She also gave the impression of bubble gum-chewing, but Taylor suspected that was just the rubber bands on her braces. She couldn't have told you what she had ordered when Sadie went off again, but Grandpa Ernie was getting his pot roast.

"You might not know this, but I knew your mom when she was little." Nancy peeled open a little plastic pot of flavored creamer and poured it into her decaf coffee.

"The other ladies said they knew your daughter." Taylor didn't mention the tangled negative associations they had with her.

"It was lovely to see them. We come to the river once a year. Andrea does such a nice job with her little bed and breakfast. The weather was lovely, but we were surprised not to have the place to ourselves. That time of year we usually do." Nancy's eyes were wide and sincere as though she hoped that every word she said would help in some way. Like she really wanted to do a good job.

Maybe they all felt like that.

What was a good job in this circumstance?

Surely, Nancy hadn't heard her mom and Colleen fighting.

But Andrea had, so it was possible. "It was such a pity that their weekend was spent arguing." Taylor sighed, trying to hide that this was an investigation.

Belle nodded. "When we learned she and her friend were at odds...." She sniffled. A well-timed, but likely sincere act.

"Oh, yes. I was sorry about that as well. They were loud and I was so tired. I admit, to my shame, that I complained about it to Gina rather than doing anything. I feel now like...like I should have gone in and spoken with them instead. Maybe I could have prevented your mother going out that evening, agitated as she was."

Taylor appreciated her not saying drunk. "I hate to ask this,

but it nags at me. I never knew Mom to have a drinking problem," here she choked up, also well-timed, but real grief has a
way of making it unnecessary to "act sad" on command.

"Oh darling, I don't think she was drunk. Not the way you
might be worried about. The ladies weren't getting along, and a
little alcohol does loosen the tongue. She had a terrible accident,
but that doesn't mean she was drunk."

Grandpa Ernie was growing agitated. "I always told her not
to drink. My father was a drunk. A terrible drunk. I'd never
allow alcohol in the house when she was a girl. Where she got
off thinking she could handle it, I'll never know."

"She should have listened to you, Gramps." Belle gave his
shaking hand a soothing pat.

"It's a different world than it was in our time." Nancy shared
a long sympathetic look with Grandpa Ernie. "Somehow
drinking has become a social hobby for the average woman. I
don't understand it, truly."

Grandpa Ernie huffed into his mustache but didn't seem
appeased. "If she hadn't been drinking, she'd still be here."

Part of Taylor wondered if he knew who he was talking
about at this hour. He might not, but he did know he was
missing somebody and that was bad enough.

Sadie brought their dinners balanced on two trays, like a pro.
Her passing them around and asking what else they wanted
gave Taylor an opportunity to organize her thoughts.

She wanted to know every single thing Nancy had seen and
heard and done that weekend. Her hunger for knowledge of her
mom's last day felt insatiable.

"I sent flowers to the funeral. It was so nice of Andrea to
make sure Gina and I knew about it," Nancy said over her chef
salad.

"Mom always loved flowers. We thought about donations
instead, but she would have loved a room full of flowers so
much." Taylor swirled her spoon around the bowl of cream of

mushroom soup Sadie had delivered. "Did you see much of Mom and Colleen before they fought?"

"Just a little. They seemed happy. Your mom, especially, was sweet to Gina. Gina had connected with her from that show. We Reese ladies have always been quilters."

"That's wonderful…" Taylor tried to think of ways to spin this back to the actual accident, but was stumped. "Was Gina working on anything right now?"

"Gina? No, she just sent a bed spread sized quilt out to be quilted. It's gorgeous. I think it was a pattern she got last year when they came back for a visit. We like to come to bring flowers to the family vault. Our family has been in this area since the 1845 wagon train."

"That's very sweet."

"The quilt she sent out is a log cabin. All of the fabrics were from a collection of reprints…no colors or designs that existed after 1860."

"Please send pictures when it's finished." Taylor didn't want pictures. She wanted facts. She wanted this eye witness to tell them for once and for all that her mom's death had been….She didn't know. Was murder better? Because it would feel so good to have someone to blame? Someone to punish?

Yes.

She wanted to punish someone for their loss. She wanted to pin the blame on someone and send them to prison. She wanted someone she could hate. Someone she could point to and say, "This is why".

An accident was just too unsatisfying. Too painfully unfinished.

If her mother had died because of an accident, then anyone could at any time.

"I'd be honored to. I told Gina not to have it long arm quilted, so she hired a group of ladies that will hand stitch."

"That's…amazing." Taylor was desperate to get them off the

topic of Gina's wonderful quilt and tapped Belle's foot gently. She needed rescue.

"None of Mom's other friends quilt. It must have been pretty great to reconnect with Gina." Belle sat in front of her BLT and fries, all of the food untouched.

"Oh, Gina was thrilled. You know, your mom was quite the popular girl when they were in high school."

Taylor couldn't help but smile. Popular in a town this size didn't mean much.

"It's a pretty remarkable coincidence that Mom's new friend just happened to be at the same B and B the weekend she was there." Belle spoke wistfully, but Taylor wondered if Nancy would pick up on the investigative nature of the comment.

Taylor frowned and chewed her lip a little. "I was surprised too, but I wondered a little if Gina had known."

"Doesn't seem normal to bring your mom to a party like that," Grandpa said.

Nancy smiled, "Gina and I are very dear friends."

Taylor sipped her water and didn't comment.

"Did you happen to hear what the fighting was about?" Belle asked.

"Ah." Nancy picked at her salad, and then stabbed a little round tomato. "I only heard a little bit, but something your mom said did stand out. Let me see if I can remember the words more exactly." She paused to eat the tomato that hung on the end of her fork. "This is close anyway. She said 'Don't be such a snob' which I couldn't help but think was funny. I don't know much about Colleen, but she had seemed very humble. Casually dressed, had helped the others carry their bags, walked at the back of the group, that kind of thing. I'm sure there was something else behind the words, some reason she said them, but it had come as a surprise."

This kind description of Colleen did not fit with what Colleen had said. Where was the hatred and anger over her past drug problem? Why had Colleen tried to make this guest into a bad

231

guy? Taylor didn't like what she was feeling, that Colleen couldn't be trusted after all. "Could you hear how Colleen responded?"

"Not very well. Her voice was quieter, you know."

It seemed like everyone was dancing around the fact that this wasn't a fight at all, but instead was Taylor's mom being mean to her oldest friend. Taylor sighed. It wasn't like her mom, and it had to mean something. "Was that all?"

"No...I heard her say something wasn't her decision, I mean to say wasn't Colleen's decision."

"Could she have said 'not yours?'" Belle asked.

"Yes, funny you should ask. That's how she said it. "That decision is not yours."

"Nachos," Taylor muttered. But what decision? Belle moving? Where Belle went to college? Maybe it was as simple as that. Maybe Colleen was being a snob about the state school, but the decision wasn't hers, and...the other ladies had said something about the word cool...maybe mom had said something about "cooling it" as in, Colleen needed to cool it with her opinions on Belle's future. Or maybe they had just misheard her saying 'school.'

Maybe.

It fit, but did it make sense? Could it have led to her mom's death? If so, then that meant Belle would always think her mom's death was her fault. Taylor most definitely did not want that.

"The other ladies said you were a real comfort after Mom was found. Thank you." Belle held a French fry between two fingers but hadn't taken a bite of anything yet.

"I'm a mother. Mothering is what I do."

"It's getting late," Taylor said. "Would you like to stay with us this evening? I hate thinking of you driving all the way home."

"Thank you for the offer, but I'm going to stay with Andrea at the B and B as her guest. We've talked a lot since your mom's death, and it will be nice to see her. We've sort of bonded."

Taylor waited for her to say it was a bright spot in the tragedy, but she had the grace not to.

"Thank you for coming all the way here," Belle supplied the necessary goodbye.

The waitress spotted their guest standing up and brought over the ticket.

Taylor took it quickly. "Let me, it's the least I can do for your kindness to them all."

Nancy took Taylor's hand and held it warmly. "Please don't be a stranger. Remember, mothering is what I do."

When they arrived back home, Grandpa Ernie huffed off to his room, a tired, sad, old grandpa. Taylor wanted to go in and have a snuggle to make him feel better, but he shut his door firmly.

Belle paced the living room while Taylor checked her messages.

"It's clear they were fighting about Gina. Mom had invited her, and Colleen didn't like it. Probably didn't like breaking up the foursome. Mom told her she wasn't being cool and that it wasn't her decision to make." Belle stopped at the doorway to the kitchen and paused, hands clasped behind her back. "Now that we have that sorted, I think we can dismiss the fight as her cause of death. It just wasn't an issue worth killing over."

"Likewise, I can't see her getting so agitated over it that she'd fall like she did."

"No. If she fell it was for some other reason. A surprise maybe."

Taylor scratched the back of her neck, completely at a loss. "A falling tree limb?"

"No evidence of one."

"A possum? Or raccoon?" Taylor shivered.

"That's not unlikely, but Mom wasn't usually scared of that kind of thing."

"If she was a little tipsy, and the boards were a little wet, and some kind of animal startled her, and her heel caught in the gap..."

"If we got all of those ifs to line up, then sure. It was an accident. But doesn't it make more sense that someone pushed her?"

"It seems more likely, but not when you try to picture any of those ladies as the one who pushed her. Making all the ifs line up seems more likely than murder."

"Unless it was still an accident. Couldn't someone have pushed her in anger, hoping to make her fall in and get a little wet?"

"Ah." Taylor nodded. "Manslaughter."

Belle resumed pacing.

Eventually, the words sort of spilled out. Taylor hated that she'd hurt this kid and needed to say so. "I'm so, so, so sorry."

Belle stopped and sniffled.

"What I said was inexcusable."

Belle gritted her teeth.

"So, I won't try to excuse it. I only want to say how sorry I am that I said such cruel things to you." Taylor could go on like this forever. Maybe now that her anger had been replaced by shame, she'd be back to her old plan of just apologizing for everything till Belle felt better.

"Let's forget it." Belle's shoulders were stiff and her hands, still clasped dramatically behind her back, were white knuckled. She wasn't offering forgiveness, just...a time out.

"Okay," Taylor agreed, though she knew that like her, Belle would never forget.

"Andrea, Nancy, Gina, Amara, Melinda, and Colleen. Her three oldest friends and a new friend. A seventy-year-old who barely knew her, and the owner of the bed and breakfast. Who would have wanted to push her into the river?"

Taylor didn't have any idea. Not one she could share with Belle anyway.

"Colleen," Belle said sadly. "Being angry about the guest list for a special weekend away isn't enough to kill for. But if I am anything like my birth mom, it is enough to make you push someone hoping they'd get all wet."

"All we can do is ask."

Belle took her pacing to the staircase and headed up.

Taylor wondered if Belle was ever sorry she was so smart.

THE NEXT MORNING the fight they'd had hung heavy in the air. Their conversation with Nancy had done nothing to reconcile them. Taylor's apology hadn't settled her heart. The sisters moved around each other, wary, wondering who was going to take the first punch.

Taylor didn't have to go to work till opening. They weren't filming today. The only thing she could think to do to calm down was watch more of her mom's videos, so she nestled in her bed under the Dove in the Window quilt that had always been her favorite.

On the screen of her laptop, her mom ran her hands through a large pile of fabric pieces, the rainbow of pastels fluttered around her. "Quilters hate waste. We see these scraps and know we can make something beautiful out of them." She and the camera moved six inches down the table. "Foundation piecing a quilt is a fantastic way to use up scraps." She held up a piece of paper with several scraps sewn to it and flipped the fabrics back and forth so the audience could see how they were connected. "The paper shows us what the final shape should be, but the fabric determines how we get there. So long as we fit the bits onto the paper, we've done it right. And in the end, we can rip the paper off and no one will ever know it had existed." She set down the mid-progress block and picked up a completed one. It was a beautiful swirl of strips in various widths and lengths making an accidental windmill shape. She ripped the paper off the back. The camera zoomed in. "Those little bits in the seams might scare you at first, but they're just paper. They'll wash away."

Taylor's heart thumped in disappointment. Her mom's little wisdom moments had become her touchstones over the last few weeks. In each video she managed to say something that uplifted her and gave her courage that this was all going to be okay. But it wasn't working this time. There was a paper that was holding everything together, but then you washed it and it was like the paper had never been?

All Taylor could think of was that the legal guardianship her mom had been granted for Belle was the only paper that held the family together.

She didn't want it to wash away as though it had never existed.

In the video her mom was still talking, saying something practical about sewing. Taylor considered turning her off, but it felt like a betrayal.

She had tuned her mom out enough through the years.

"Listen, these are just scraps of fabric. Waste, by any other name. Don't beat yourself up trying to make everything fit perfectly. Sometimes you have to cut it up and lose a bit, that's okay."

Part of her thought her mom was horribly cold-hearted, but then she didn't know Taylor was trying to apply this video to life without her.

Laura Quinn, in the video, held up a finished lap quilt made with those topsy-turvy accidental windmills. "The paper disappears," she was saying, "when all of your hard work is completed. Your stash of scraps that felt like waste has become a quilt as real and beautiful and beloved as any other."

Her mom wasn't talking about family, but Taylor was listening about family. Surely...surely after all these years Belle and Taylor were real family, as loved as any other even though the paper that held them together had washed away.

"I know where that quilt is." Belle stood in her doorway,

wrapped in a silky black bathrobe. "She gave it to Gramps, but since his memory is going, he won't even notice when you sell it."

Taylor made a fist, digging her fingernails into the palm of her hand.

This was the kid she was so desperate to get forgiveness from? To keep close by her side? This moody, mouthy teen?

"I'll ask him." Taylor mirrored Belle's innocent look.

Belle's mouth shifted ever so slightly into a snarl.

In her fevered rush to come here and envelope Belle in a safety net of sisterly love, Taylor never dreamed she'd feel so very glad Belle was leaving for college early.

The mood was ruined. Taylor flung the quilt off and stomped to the bathroom, but it was occupied, by Belle. The idea of living in a bright and shiny four bedroom, four bathroom home in that new development sounded very good at this exact second. She stomped downstairs and made herself a cup of coffee.

Then the routine began, Grandpa Ernie getting his own bowl of cereal, Belle reminding him of his medicine and making his toast. Taylor, trying not to lose it as she watched two people she dearly loved who had become like strangers over the last decade.

Why had she done that? Why had she stayed away so long?

Why had she never made time for them?

Her phone rang saving her from a bout of self-pity. It was Dave Kirby. "Yes?"

"Hey Taylor. I wanted to catch you before work, to check in about the Neskowin trip. Do you think you'd like to come along?"

Taylor watched Grandpa Ernie laughing at something Belle was saying to him as she counted pills into his hand. "I'm so sorry. Can you give me another day to work out the details? I have been a little overwhelmed."

"You got it. And really, Taylor, anything you need, Colleen and I are just a phone call away."

"Thanks, Dave." They ended the call.

Belle was watching her closely. The one eyebrow Taylor could see under her shag of black hair was slightly raised.

"Want to go to the beach?"

She shrugged.

"What about taking a trip to the beach with the whole Kirby family?"

She scrunched her mouth up in consideration.

"You can if you want. I'm invited too, but I think I'd better stay home."

"Maybe." Belle left before Taylor could respond.

Well, fine. Just fine. A maybe is a maybe. Nothing to call Dave about. Taylor didn't need to go on the big family trip with them, no matter what the Kirbys said. She had adult responsibilities, something Belle would know plenty about soon enough.

Belle came back down the stairs with a back breaking back pack on. "I'll call Dave," she said, and then left.

CHAPTER NINETEEN

*a*s soon as Grandpa Ernie had his jacket and shoes, Taylor drove them up the street to Flour Sax. Belle would probably call Colleen and have the big conversation they needed to have without her. She'd learn exactly what happened that night with their mom, and never tell.

Taylor slammed things around as she opened the shop. For a moment it felt good.

"Knock it off or I'll put you in time out." Grandpa Ernie had ventured out of his little back area of the shop. He stood at the worktable, both hands pressed on its laminate surface.

"Sorry." Taylor shut the register drawer with care.

"Teenagers are a pain in the butt, young lady. You were no better than her, and she's not so bad."

"No, she's not." Taylor moved over to the notions display where she liked to have her mom's show playing and set it up.

A knock on the backdoor redirected her energy. Taylor hustled back and found a grinning Hudson wearing a canvas tool belt over his rather tight jeans. His plaid flannel sleeves were rolled up revealing half of his muscly arms. "Is this a good morning to do some patchwork for you?"

"I haven't had pest control in yet…" How that had slipped her mind, she'd never be able to explain.

"That's okay. I can do something temporary for now."

His truck was stocked with ply boards and sawhorses, probably a saw too.

"I'll take all the help I can get. Come on in." She opened the door for him.

He strode in, his tall, muscular frame filling the room.

"Morning, Mr. Baker."

Grandpa Ernie turned to face Hudson. He looked him up and down appraising him. "Morning." The one word seemed to grant approval. Taylor wondered briefly if Grandpa would have approved of the less manly Clay Seldon.

"I'll just head up and take some measurements first." Hudson took the stairs two at a time, his footsteps remarkably light.

Grandpa Ernie harrumphed and made his way back to his chair. "He's got his eye on you, young lady."

"I thought you liked Boggy's grandson."

Grandpa frowned for a moment. "Maybe I do, maybe I don't."

The front door jangled this time. Roxy wasn't scheduled till afternoon, and they were still an hour from opening.

A lady in her mid-forties stood at the door waving, shaking the handle, and mouthing something Taylor couldn't make out. She had bobbed black hair, wore a denim jacket, jeans and cowboy boots.

It couldn't hurt to go to the door and tell her they weren't open yet, but Taylor resented it. The hours were posted as clear as anything, and cute too, on a large chalkboard hanging in the front window.

The second her hand turned the lock, the lady pushed her way in. "Oh my gosh, thank you so much. I'm so glad you let me in." She brushed past Taylor heading straight toward the center of the shop, behind a long shelf of fabric bolts.

"We're not open. I'm going to have to ask you to leave."

"Oh no, no. I'm not here to shop. I need to talk. I'm Gina Croyden."

"This isn't a good time." Taylor walked past Gina, hoping she could lead her back out the front door again. "Why don't you call later and we can make an appointment."

"It's just that you spoke with my mom last night."

"Yes…." Taylor wanted this woman out of the store, and not just because they weren't open.

Gina's eyes were intense, fixed on Taylor's face, and round in an unnatural way. Her shoulders leaned forward and her chin tilted out, like a hen that was about to lunge. "I couldn't make it, but wanted to, badly. Mom…she isn't well."

"I'm sorry to hear that." Taylor stood between Gina and Grandpa Ernie. She stepped toward the unwanted guest hopping to maneuver her toward the door, but it didn't work.

In fact, Gina made the gap between them smaller and Taylor found herself backing up. "See, you can't really trust what Mom has to say. I assume she told you about the quilt."

"It sounds lovely."

Gina stopped and tilted her head. "Thank you?" It came out like a question.

Taylor took a firmer step forward.

Gina did back up this time.

"I'm going to have to ask you to leave, but I can meet you at Reuben's Diner at 12:30. We can have lunch and talk. Will that do?"

Gina nodded, continuing to back up as Taylor marched forward. They were at the door now, so Taylor opened it wide for her.

"See you down the street in a few hours."

"Okay, lunch. Yes. We'll talk there." Gina spun, heading down the sidewalk with the same intense energy she had come in with.

Taylor exhaled and realized it had been very nice to know that Hudson was just upstairs during that scene.

"You shouldn't kick customers out," Grandpa Ernie offered from his chair.

"Yeah, sorry. I won't do that again."

Taylor had intended on making sample projects for future videos this morning, but instead she went to her mom's show and scrolled through the many YouTube comments trying to figure out who Gina Croyden was when she was online.

It took most of an hour, but Taylor finally sussed her out.

Gina also had a YouTube show, but no one seemed to watch it, despite the many links she had been peppering the comments of Laura Quinn's show with. Taylor wanted to watch a few of Gina's episodes, but a cluster of quilters were chatting at the door already. Taylor switched back over to her mom's video feed and left it to auto play while she opened for the day.

Hudson had made some noise upstairs, but he didn't take long, and the sight of the tall, scruffy faced, plaid shirt clad handyman popping up and down stairs throughout the morning made her customers smile. Taylor wasn't ashamed to admit it made her smile too.

Roxy clocked in a little early, so Taylor was able to explain what Hudson was up to.

"Now there's an episode of Flour Sax..." Roxy's eyes glittered. "Have Hudson on to tell them all how to...oh, anything really. You'd get plenty of hits."

Taylor laughed, which also felt good.

Hudson himself was just coming down the stairs, so she put her fingers to her lips.

Roxy winked.

"Hey, Tay, you up for lunch?"

"Oh man...." Taylor was absolutely more inclined to have lunch with him than with Gina Croyden. Though she'd been wanting to see the woman, she found her more than a little scary.

He hoisted his hammer over his shoulder, nonchalantly. "It's okay if you're busy."

He had to notice that at the moment, the shop was empty.

"It's not that, it's just this crazy lady wants me to meet her for lunch so she can tell me something about...." Taylor swallowed, "about the night Mom died. Actually, it's Gina. She was there that weekend."

"Gina does have a weird energy." He scratched his jaw. "If you're uncomfortable, I'd be happy to eat with you both."

Taylor could feel the glow spread across her cheeks. "Yeah, that would be great."

"What about me?" Grandpa Ernie asked.

"We'll bring you a meatloaf sandwich." Taylor made her way to his chair and gave him a kiss on the cheek.

"You gotta stay here, Ernie," Roxy said. "I don't like being in the shop alone."

He nodded, his own face flushing a nice pink. "Smart lady."

"Smart to meet Gina in public." Hudson held the door open.

"When you met her that morning," Taylor swallowed hard, but kept going, "what kind of weird energy did she have?"

"For someone who just happened to be there at the same time your mom was, I found her reaction to the death pretty dramatic. She didn't faint, but there was a lot of face fanning, 'woe is me' crap. Nancy was a saint, but Gina was a pain."

They walked slowly along the sidewalk, side by side. It was a visceral relief not to be headed there alone. "Nancy implied Gina knew they'd all be there."

He paused a step. "Really?"

"She said they had become friends."

"It puts Gina's attitude in a different light." He walked in silence. They were almost to the restaurant. "I'd still say she was attention seeking, though. Maybe because she needed it, but more likely because she thought she deserved it."

Gina was waiting at a booth near the front door. Her face fell when she saw Hudson. "I was really hoping we could speak alone."

The restaurant was bustling with lunchers, both locals and weekend visitors. It was hot inside, and heady with the addictive aroma of burgers on the grill and coffee freshly brewed.

Taylor patted Hudson's arm and let her hand linger, savoring the feel of soft flannel over his hard biceps. "Can you give us a few?"

"Sure," he agreed, but took a seat at the counter while Taylor joined Gina.

"He's been doing some work for me at the shop. I owe him a meal."

Gina licked her lips and wrapped shaking hands around the coffee mug. "I know you talked to Mom."

"I did."

"You say she told you about my quilt." Gina moved her hands nervously from cup to napkin rolled around silverware over and over again.

"The log cabin one?"

"Not that one."

"That's the only one we spoke of." Taylor couldn't stop watching Gina's hands, so much fidgeting.

Gina pushed her sleeves up and rubbed her fingers over a recent scar on her forearm. Some kind of puncture wound.

Taylor wanted to nudge her hand away so she wouldn't scratch it and make it bleed.

Gina pushed her sleeves back down and began unrolling her silverware and rolling it back up again. "I watch your mom's show. I love her show. She's amazing."

Taylor had to agree, though she didn't think her mom was amazing in the "famous on the internet" kind of way.

"She has that spark, you know? The *je ne sais quoi*. The undefinable it. She could have been a star, but she had a shop instead. Do you ever think about what that cost her?" Gina looked down at her silverware so tightly rolled, then up at Taylor.

"I guess because she's always been 'Mom' I never really worried about her lack of fame."

"I tried a YouTube show. Did you know that?"

Taylor nodded.

"You had time to look at it, I guess."

"Just a little. I was working."

"I was so mad she stole the pattern from me, I was really mad. I told her I wasn't going to come to her weekend away."

"Ah." Now Taylor's hand was shaking. She felt like she should turn her phone on and record whatever Gina was about to say. She wished Hudson was closer so he could witness it too. She just knew she was about to have that moment you get in mystery shows where the murderer breaks down and confesses.

"But then I felt awful about being mad, because she was so nice and always let me share my links in her comments. She could have deleted those, you know."

"Sure." Taylor didn't really know.

"And she sent me some notes, not for my show, but for something we could do together. She was so amazing. She was going to help me."

"What was it you wanted to tell me about your mom?"

Gina took a hearty drink of her coffee and straightened up as though fortifying herself. "She called me and left a panicked voicemail, asking what she was supposed to do, because Belle left that note at her house. She was scared, said you'd all find out what I had done. But Taylor, I didn't do anything. I was as horrified as anyone that morning."

Taylor shifted in her seat. She wasn't getting a good read on this woman. Gina had beads of cold sweat on her forehead and she was quivering like a scared mouse, but her eyes were direct when they looked up from her mug.

They were interrupted by a waitress who took their order. Taylor found herself saying, "I'll have that too," without actually having heard what Gina had ordered.

When she moved on, Taylor took a deep breath. "Let me clear the air for you."

Gina nodded rather like a child to a teacher.

"Your mom told me what a good friend Mom had been to you. She said you reconnected over the videos. And she told me about how lovely your Log Cabin quilt was."

"She didn't mention our fight? Not at all?"

"No. Nothing at all."

A natural color seeped back into Gina's cheeks. "You can't know what it is like to live with someone who has mental illness."

"I didn't know you lived together." Taylor frowned. "I thought you had lived quite far apart, actually."

"Yes, yes. I didn't mean literally live with, but she calls constantly, and makes spontaneous trips to see me when I don't expect her. She came to my work so often that I lost my job."

"I'm sorry to hear that." Taylor exhaled slowly. She was pretty sure mental illness could be genetic.

"I wasn't angry with her about it. She can't help it, so how could I blame her?"

"And your husband?"

"He says he just worries about her and the effect it has on me, but I wonder."

"Understandably. Listen, did you hear Mom and her friend Colleen fighting the night before she died?"

"Just a little." Gina began to fade again, her cheeks a sort of grayish white.

"Don't be scared. Do you think they were fighting about your mother?"

"Yes." Gina pushed her coffee mug away. "I was in the hall. At first the door was open a little, and I heard Colleen saying something about how Nancy had always been crazy. I think she asked how the girls were supposed to have a nice time with her there."

"Had mom invited you both to come?"

"Your mother was a hard worker."

This seemed out of the blue, but Taylor didn't interrupt.

"We bonded, not only over quilts, but over how hard it can be when you're caring for someone with mental health issues."

"Grandpa Ernie." Taylor spoke under her breath, not sure how he fit into Gina's story.

"Yes. I used to live very near Mom, but it got to be too hard, so we moved up to the Portland area. My younger brother lives right around the block from Mom and Dad though. I didn't just abandon her."

"Of course not."

"I told Laura all about how I go away with Mom once a year to give my Dad and my brother and sister-in-law a break. I invited Laura—I mean your mom—to come with my mother and me on our little get away. I told her to bring your grandpa with her." She waited for a response.

Taylor didn't know what to say, so she just nodded.

"Your mom had the idea of doing a girls' weekend instead. She invited me and told me that I could spend part of the visit just with the girls and leave Mom to read books or visit with Andrea or what have you. She booked the trip for my regular weekend."

Gina was almost relaxed as she recounted the story, so Taylor asked another question, in her most soothing tone. "Tell me about the fight you had with Mom."

"She did a video about foundation piecing."

Taylor's breath caught in her throat, but she nodded for Gina to continue.

"She used my pattern. I created it. I entered it in a contest, but it didn't place."

"Copyright infringement is awful."

"It hurts, seeing your work uncredited."

"What did she say when you asked her about it?" Taylor had her doubts. There could only be so much truly original work in the world, and the foundation piecing video was merely scrappy windmills. Millions of women had done it through the decades.

"She acted surprised, like she had forgotten, but I don't think she had. When I was there last time, I showed her pictures of it and she told me how much she loved it."

"Do you have those pictures still?"

"Yes!" Gina took out her phone and found the pictures on her Google drive.

The quilt was similar, but the pinwheels were more literal, less organic. They looked purposeful instead of accidental, and they were dull. No vibrant spinning colors that looked like they were moving. Just tan and mauve and maroon over and over again. And yet, there was something satisfying about it, soothing even, in the steady stable design and the comforting secure colors. Taylor could see how this quilt could have inspired the one her mom made. And yet, it was also forgettable. If you had seen one quilt like this, you had seen a hundred. They had their place, but that place wasn't in your memory.

"I got so mad because she pretended she didn't remember it."

"It's a lovely quilt."

"Thank you. I made it for Father's Day."

Taylor closed her eyes. A wave of disappointment rolled over her. Her mom had also given the pinwheel-like quilt to her father. It didn't seem like her, to use an idea without crediting it, but that's what the story pointed to. "It's lovely that you were able to forgive her, even though she wasn't capable of apologizing."

"I just liked her. Really liked her. And when you like someone, sometimes you have to let go of things, things that hurt, you know? Her videos were always going to be more popular than mine. They were better. They just were. If she had credited me with that design, it could have helped me. Maybe. But it might not have. When I finally figured that out, I knew this pattern wasn't worth losing my friend over." The words spilled out, and Gina tripped over them, but she seemed sincere.

"So you decided to have some girl time with some ladies from your high school and your mom."

"Yes."

"It must have stung when Colleen didn't want you there."

Gina leaned forward and whispered, "I feel like I can trust you. Can I tell you something?"

Taylor also leaned forward, more than ever wishing she had a secret recording device.

"Mom has never forgiven Colleen. She blames her for my older brother's struggle with drugs, and even with his death."

Taylor's breath caught and she choked. Words wouldn't come out, so she took a drink of her icy cold water. "Your older brother?" She wracked her brain trying to remember who Colleen had said was Belle's father.

"Yes, Richard. We called him Brick. He's just about ten years older than me. And Colleen too. That didn't matter to Mom, she still blamed Colleen."

Taylor exhaled slowly, then asked, "What kind of trouble did Colleen and Brick have?"

"Brick was my half-brother." Gina's jaw was trembling with emotion. "And his father was no good, that's why Mom left him, and I think that's why Colleen left Brick too. Brick was never any good."

"Did something dramatic happen?"

"Oh, no. Colleen got tired of him and left. He went to jail sometime after that."

"Nothing else, nothing else remarkable at all happened that would make your mom and Colleen angry with each other?"

"Only that Mom thought Brick was an angel when he wasn't. That's all. Colleen was wise to get away. I wanted to be friends with her, if I could. I don't know if your mom knew about them. If she did, she wouldn't have brought us all together, would she?"

"I don't know, to be honest. I hadn't stayed very close with Mom."

"Would you ask Belle? I know she's just a kid, but maybe she knows something, something about why your mom would want all of us in the same place."

Taylor had no appetite for the sandwich the waitress brought them while they were talking. Gina seemed to be in complete ignorance of Belle's parentage. But that didn't mean Nancy had been. And fighting over Gina and Nancy gave Colleen another reason to have killed her mother.

Though Taylor felt for Gina, she did not inquire about where she was spending the night. She ordered a meatloaf sandwich for her grandpa, paid her bill, and left.

Hudson caught up with her pretty quickly. "Was that helpful?"

"Could you hear any of it?"

"No, and trust me, I tried."

"I don't know if it was helpful or not. Nancy is still at the bed and breakfast, I think. I'd kind of like to go down there and talk to her again."

"I can drive you."

"I can't leave till closing."

"That's all right. I'd like to do a little more work up in your apartment, if you don't mind."

"Whatever keeps the invaders out."

TAYLOR FLOATED through the rest of the workday, hardly aware of her surroundings. She hadn't heard from Belle by closing, which she should have noticed long before six. She called, then texted, then called again, then called Sissy Dorney. "Is my sister there?"

"Yes, and her phone is dead, so if you've been trying to reach her, it's not her fault. You should have called Cooper."

"If she's old enough to go to college in the fall, she's old enough to remember to charge her phone." Taylor was ready to take her aggression out on this woman who seemed to revel in keeping Belle away from her.

"It's not my fault, is it? No reason to yell at me. Belle, come talk to your sister."

There were voices of protest in the background and then a voice came on. "What?"

"You're not Belle."

"Yes, I am." The snotty, recalcitrant voice did not belong to Belle.

"I'm not playing around. Put Belle on the phone."

"She doesn't want to talk to you."

"That doesn't really matter, does it? I'm in charge and she has to talk to me when I say she has to talk to me."

"Actually, she told me that's not true. You aren't legally the boss of her at all. No one is."

"You sound like a seven year old. Put my sister on. I want to talk to someone intelligent."

"You're a jerk."

"You're a moron."

"I hate you." The phone call ended.

Taylor stared at it.

Had she just gotten into a name calling fight with a high schooler?

"That doesn't sound like it went well," Hudson's deep, husky voice sounded from behind her.

"I can't remember a time when I was more embarrassed."

"Don't be. Most of us want to talk like that to teenagers."

"I guess I'm not going to see Nancy tonight. Sorry."

He scratched his jaw. "Because Belle won't come home?"

"She won't even come to the phone."

"Do you know where she is?"

"It sounds like she's at her friend Cooper's house."

"Let's go get her."

Taylor lifted an eyebrow. It was impossible not to compare

him with Clay. Clay hadn't even been willing to come home for a weekend to hang out with her family. Hudson was willing to storm the enemy to drag her sister back home. "Can we bring Grandpa Ernie?"

"Sounds good to me."

Taylor had to look up the Dorney address, but as soon as she had it, she loaded everyone in her car, and they drove the six blocks to the house Belle liked to be at better than her own.

CHAPTER TWENTY

*H*udson was ready to charge the door and rescue the kid, but Taylor put a restraining hand on his shoulder. "I have a better idea."

Taylor walked to the front door with Grandpa Ernie and rang the bell. "She can't possibly say no to you, can she?" It was evening, the sun just starting to set. He didn't look pleased at being a pawn in her game, but he didn't argue.

Sissy Dorney's roots had been touched up since Taylor saw her last, and her frizz was under control. Like the shoemaker's children, Taylor suspected the hairstylist didn't always get to do her own hair in a timely manner. "Not surprised to see you here."

"You've got some nerve. Where's Belle?" Grandpa Ernie's voice was strong, even though his body was slightly hunched.

"Belle, your grandpa's here." Sissy hollered over her shoulder, then sauntered into the room.

Dayton came to the door instead. "I told you she doesn't want to talk to you."

"You're not Belle. Belle can speak for herself." Grandpa Ernie dismissed Belle's friend with the two gruff sentences.

"You're not children, and this isn't a game." Taylor crossed her arms and stepped across the threshold even though it knocked Dayton to the side.

Dayton grabbed her sleeve. "Listen, I wish it weren't like this, but Belle is pissed and won't tell us why. She doesn't want to talk to you."

"It doesn't really matter what she wants." Taylor shook her arm free and stared across the room. It was a large house, fancy in that new way where every surface is a faux something or other and clean and shiny for the moment. Her feet echoed on the laminate wood floors. "Belle! Come down here!" Taylor stood at the base of a fairly grand staircase and hollered up.

Cooper came running. "Ms. Quinn, I'm sorry. I've been trying to get her to come downstairs. She's really not in a good place."

"I'd agree. The place she's supposed to be right now is home."

"It's just something happened today that really upset her, and she needs time."

Taylor was too mad to go soft now, but that didn't stop the worry from pinching at her heart. "What happened?"

"It's stupid, I don't think you'll get it." Dayton's voice came from behind Taylor.

"Try me."

"It's just the senior projects.... It's hard to explain." Dayton came around to the banister of the staircase.

"Belle, I don't have time for this!" Taylor hollered again, knowing that in a house with this kind of floor, her voice was bound to carry.

"Let me try to explain." Cooper cleared his throat. "Seniors have these big projects to do before they graduate, and Belle had to do one this year as well, even though she's not a senior. There was kind of a thing about it, your mom was really mad that Belle had to do it. She tried to fight it."

"Why?" Taylor cringed, thinking about all the times she wished her mom had fought the school for her.

"Because it was a lot of work. The seniors have a class period for it, but Belle had to do it on her own time. So she did, and it's amazing. It's almost done."

"Get to the point or I'm going upstairs."

"It's just this other student did the same project. And turned in their final already."

Taylor rolled her eyes.

"She copied Belle's work. It's good, because this student is really talented. She saw Belle's work in progress and decided to do the same thing."

"And so now Belle won't go home? Ridiculous."

"That's not all." Cooper held out a hand, though Taylor hadn't tried to storm the stairs yet. "They had to have pre-approval for their projects, they had to turn in plans along the way, there were a million steps to take to do this thing, but since Belle isn't in the class, she didn't remember to get all of her phases of the project approved."

"Still no reason to be disrespectful to me."

Cooper took a deep breath, even his practiced politeness was beginning to suffer. "There are only like forty-five kids graduating, so the school requires that each project be completely unique."

Taylor was beginning to be equal parts annoyed with Cooper and the school. "So now Belle has to start over. It sucks but it can't be helped, and she still needs to come home."

"No, it's too late to start over. She's failing the class and they won't graduate her."

"Belle! Get down here."

A door slammed upstairs.

"Listen, this sounds like life and death to you all because you're basically children, but it's not the end of the world. I'll take care of it."

"But she can't go into her early admittance college program if she doesn't get her diploma."

"I said I'd take care of it." Before Taylor could elbow him out of the way, a loud thump came from behind her.

Taylor spun on her heel.

Grandpa Ernie had collapsed, falling into a decorative side table covered in framed photos.

Taylor rushed to help him up, but he was too heavy and unstable.

"Someone call 911!" This time Taylor knew her voice had carried. She'd never screamed anything so loud before in all her life.

More footsteps thundered above her, and in an instant, Belle was at her side.

Sissy was slower, but when Taylor spotted her, she noted Sissy had her phone to her ear giving her address.

When Sissy was finished, she looked at Belle with the stern look of an angry mother. "Get your things."

"Yes, Ma'am." Belle floated next to Taylor, her hands gently touching Grandpa Ernie's head, and then his shoulder and then Taylor's shoulder.

In a moment Dayton came with Belle's backpack.

Then the sirens.

Then Hudson, through the door, "What happened?"

His voice was there, in the midst of Sissy giving her kids directions, and Belle murmuring soft, worried nothings, and all of the alarms going off in Taylor's head at once.

And then the paramedics, and Grandpa Ernie in an oxygen mask and on a cot, and then they were following him to the hospital in McMinnville.

Taylor didn't breathe again till she was sitting in the waiting room of the ER.

Hudson was holding her hand.

Cooper was holding Belle's, though Taylor didn't remember him coming with them.

Sissy was at the desk demanding answers.

And Maddie was there too.

She was with someone else, but she caught Taylor's eye and blushed. She shuffled over, apologetically. "I don't want to get too close. I think Memphis has strep." Memphis was one of Maddie's kids, but Taylor couldn't recall which.

"It's Grandpa Ernie." Taylor could hear her own lifeless voice, but didn't associate it with herself talking.

"I thought maybe." There was no place for Maddie to sit, so she didn't. "Please call me tomorrow. We should talk."

Taylor nodded, but she couldn't picture tomorrow.

Maddie went back to her child across the room.

At the hospital.

In the other town.

How had she gotten here?

Why?

Taylor's head was spinning. It would make sense tomorrow.

Eventually she went back with a doctor who explained that Grandpa Ernie's oxygen was very low. The doctor said it wasn't a heart attack, don't fear. And that they were going to keep him overnight to monitor him and make sure his levels went back up, and that they could all go home and rest and not worry.

"Not worry?" Taylor stared at the doctor like he was speaking Swedish.

"There's no reason to worry tonight. Go home, get some rest. It's not very late. Have you eaten?" the doctor gave her a once over, full of concern. "Why don't you and your family head down to the café and have something to eat before you drive home."

The last thing Taylor wanted was to be all the way back home while Grandpa Ernie was here alone. She made her way to the waiting room, feeling like she was carrying everyone who was waiting for her on her back.

"Low oxygen. Not a heart attack."

Hudson stood and with a gentle hand on her back, led her to a chair.

"They're keeping him over night. They told us to go home." Taylor didn't sit.

"We can't just leave him here." Belle crossed her arms and tightened her jaw.

"I agree."

"You can very much just leave him here, Belly-boo." Sissy patted her shoulder. "You have school tomorrow and a confrontation with your senior project advisor awaits you."

"I said I'd take care of it." Taylor's words were firm, but it was all a show. She was hollow at the moment and the senior project advisor would destroy her with a look.

"I heard you say that, but if Belle is going to college next year, she's got to learn how to handle these things on her own. So, she's handling it tomorrow."

Belle shifted away from Sissy's touch.

"Taylor, may I have your permission to bring Belle home with me and Cooper so she can make it to school in the morning and handle her business?" Sissy changed her tone.

Taylor nodded, then added a thank you as an afterthought.

"You have a lot on your plate right now. Whatever you do, don't forget to eat. Come on, kids, let's get out of their hair." Sissy held out a hand to her son.

Belle stood, but only at Cooper's urging.

Taylor hugged her fast before Belle could realize she was doing it.

Belle's response left a lot to be desired, but at least she didn't push her away.

When they were through the doors to the ER waiting room, Hudson spoke. "I'll feed you, unless you don't want to eat."

"No, we should." They wandered around the labyrinth that was the medium sized town hospital till they found the café, which had closed for the night. It was almost one too many for Taylor, and she had to bite her lip to keep from crying.

They had a long slog back out to the car, and it seemed like it would be an even longer slog to find a restaurant and then a place to sleep.

"Oh, let's just go home." Taylor gave up. "We're less than an hour away. He's safer at the hospital than he is in his own bedroom at home."

"Whatever you want." Hudson was rolling with the punches, and Taylor was glad that he had been around tonight, but at the moment, all she wanted was to go home, close her eyes, and wake up to find everything was better.

It was her car, so Taylor drove.

She ignored speed limits and made it home a lot faster than she ought to have.

"Now can I feed you?" Hudson asked, as Taylor pulled into her driveway.

"Your truck...." Taylor rested her head on the steering wheel. "It's still up at Flour Sax."

"The shop's close. That's not a problem. If we go in your house will I find any food I can serve you? A can of soup? A pb and j?"

"Probably." Taylor wanted to smile so he could see she appreciated his thoughtfulness, but she just couldn't.

They went inside. He found a can of tomato soup and fixed them each a bowl. He did not serve peanut butter and jelly on the side.

About halfway through the bowl Taylor began to feel more herself. "In addition to helping Belle fix this problem at her school," she said between careful spoonfuls, "I need to find a way to make up to her for the horrible things I said the other night."

"I assume you've apologized."

"Yes."

"Then, from my expert opinion, and remember, I do fix things for a living, I think consistently caring for her over time so that she realizes you meant your apology, is your best bet." Hudson gave himself seconds of the Campbell's tomato.

"So I should not fly her to Disneyland next weekend?"

"Definitely not."

"Colleen and Dave want to take her to their beach house for a family weekend."

"Ouch." He looked at her with huge eyes full of sympathy. Taylor could have drowned in those eyes, and kind of wanted to. "Yup."

"But you'll let her go, right?"

"They invited me as well, but I need to stay with Grandpa Ernie."

"And he, as much as you love him, is another problem you have to fix."

"Exactly."

"No wonder your mom needed a weekend away."

"No wonder she was such a wreck, she fell into the river and died." Taylor glanced at the clock. It was almost nine now, much earlier than it felt. "I need to call Roxy and tell her I won't be in tomorrow."

"I'm on a job all day tomorrow out in Sheridan."

"It's okay." Taylor stood and began to walk to the kitchen door, her subtle way of telling him to go home now. "It was extremely gracious of you to stick with me all evening."

"I'm sorry we missed our chance to talk to Nancy Reese, but if another one comes up, let me know."

"Thanks. Funny how playing detective seems to fall off the priority list when a real crisis comes up."

He took his bowl to the sink and rinsed it, then gave her a big bear hug.

Taylor had the feeling he wanted her to tip her face up so he could kiss her, but she wasn't in the mood, so she didn't.

All she wanted was to drop into bed and escape the world, but she forced herself to do her skin care routine, and brush and floss, and comb her hair out before bed.

It was almost eleven when there was a knock at the door.

Her first thought was that Belle had snuck out of the Dorney house, but it wasn't likely. Taylor was irritated with the knocker. Who visits at this hour? It wouldn't take all five fingers of one hand to name the folks in this town who would come see her at a reasonable hour, much less eleven.

She stomped down the stairs, hitting each wooden tread like it was the person on the other side of the door.

She peeked through the little spy-hole.

Nancy Reese?

Taylor considered not opening it, but Nancy banged with the side of a fist, like you do when you're agitated. If she needed help, like her car had broken down, Taylor supposed she'd come here for help as well as anywhere else.

With an overly dramatic sigh Taylor unlocked the door and opened it. "Nancy?"

"Oh, thank goodness, can I come in?"

Taylor pulled the door open further.

She'd spoken with both Gina and Nancy now, and if she had to pick, she'd say Gina was the crazy one, not this perfectly reasonable seeming older woman hanging her coat on the coat rack.

"I'm so sorry that Gina bothered you this afternoon."

"It was no bother."

Taylor stood next to the door, leaving it open, arms crossed while Nancy made herself comfortable on the couch.

"It's late. What do you need?"

Nancy froze, maybe Taylor's forthright statement had been unexpected, or even rude, but she didn't care.

"There's something you need to know about Gina."

Taylor closed her eyes and counted to three. "She's crazy. Yes. I noticed."

"She means well."

"Nancy, it's too late for this. Call me tomorrow if you need to talk." Taylor pulled the door open as far as it could go.

"But you can't trust anything she says." Nancy picked at the fabric of her slacks, a tweed that was wearing thin at the knees.

"I'll keep that in mind. You should head home now. It's late."

Taylor wracked her brain trying to think of another way to say "get out" that wasn't actually "get out".

"I don't mean to disturb your family." Nancy glanced at Grandpa Ernie's door which was open.

Taylor wondered if Nancy could tell the room was empty. "Everyone needs to get their sleep, school tomorrow."

"But your sister is with her friend." Nancy smiled. "And your grandfather is at the hospital."

"You need to get out." Taylor wrapped her hand around the doorknob, anger and fear fighting with each other.

How had Nancy known where Taylor lived?

How had she known Taylor was alone?

How did she know where everybody was?

Taylor's phone was by the sink in the bathroom upstairs, and she deeply wished it wasn't.

Nancy stood and laced her fingers together in front of her. "Listen, Taylor Rae Quinn, we're all alone. We have privacy. I just need you to tell me what Gina said to you. That's all. After that I'll leave."

"She told me she was very sorry my mom was dead. She said she liked Mom and missed her." Taylor scanned the room for any potential tools of self-defense. In her bathrobe and slipper clad state she felt particularly vulnerable. She slipped out of the slippers as subtly as possible. Her bare feet had better traction than those fuzzy comfortable things did.

"Nothing else?"

Nancy's coat was hanging on the coat rack inches away, so Taylor grabbed it for her and held it out.

A mood shift flashed across Nancy's features, fear maybe.

"What else could she say?"

Nancy faced off with Taylor, close enough to take the coat, but not doing it.

The coat was heavy. Something weighty was in the pocket.

"I think you know what she said."

Panic gripped Taylor's throat. She wanted to swing the coat

at Nancy, hoping whatever the heavy thing in the pocket was would knock her out, but somehow she knew that was an overreaction. Nancy hadn't done anything. She just wanted to talk.

Taylor gripped the coat in her fist and walked backwards out her front door. Her foot hung over the step of the front stoop. She didn't want to fall, but she didn't like turning her back on Nancy either.

Nancy's car was blocking Taylor's, but that didn't matter. Taylor didn't even have a bra on, much less her car keys.

She shifted the coat and felt the outside of the pocket. If the heavy thing in there was a gun, Taylor didn't want her fingerprints on it.

It didn't feel like a gun. She relaxed a little and gave it one more feel.

It was just a flashlight.

She walked to Nancy's car and set the coat on the hood. "This has been a stressful day for all of us. Go back to Andrea's, have a good sleep, and then call me. We can talk tomorrow, I promise."

Nancy had followed Taylor out and was coming down the stairs.

Taylor exhaled.

Nancy was nuts.

Gina was nuts.

That can run in families. Didn't mean either of them were dangerous.

Nancy walked slowly to the car. The look on her face disagreed with Taylor's assessment. Her eyes were cold and her face was shockingly still. "I just need to know what she said. I *really* need to know."

Taylor was halfway across her lawn, not sure where to head next. None of the neighbors' lights were on, but someone had to be home.

"Don't run off," Nancy said. "Just give me a second to ask you something." She picked up her coat and folded it over her arms. "Can't we go back inside for a moment? I have a long drive and I'd like to use the bathroom."

Taylor kept her pace steady slowly inching into the neighbor's yard. "The Arco has a bathroom."

Nancy laughed. "Now you're being ridiculous. We're old friends, aren't we? I remember when you were born and when your daddy died."

"Go home, Nancy."

Nancy reached her hand into her pocket and pulled out the flashlight. "No, Taylor. We're going to go back inside now."

Nancy pointed the flashlight at Taylor, but no light shown from it.

Taylor was sure now that Gina was correct. Nancy was unbalanced.

But Taylor wasn't scared of a flashlight, no matter what Nancy thought it was.

"I'm going over here, to the Morgan house, and I'm going to use their phone to call the police. You're trespassing and harassing me right now. Go home."

A shot cracked the night air, louder than it had any right to sound. Taylor's heart leapt into her open mouth, choking her. She ducked to the ground, hands over her head.

"That was the warning shot," Nancy said. "Get inside now. If you'd just told me what Gina said…."

Taylor peeked through her arms, hoping to see lights going on up and down the street, but there was nothing. She was still alone.

Nancy strode towards her. "I'm not a great shot, but even I can hit a person in the head from this distance. Now come inside."

Taylor tried to think creatively, but had nothing, so she stood slowly, hands in front of her, and walked one barefooted step after another across the damp grass and back into the house.

She walked across the bare wood floors that needed sweeping and went straight into the kitchen without rushing.

The landline phone sat on the counter behind a stack of decorative chicken wire baskets. She stopped at the stack.

"If you think you can grab a kitchen knife and stab me before I can get a shot out of this fun little thing, you're delusional."

"What are you doing?" Taylor didn't dare grab for the phone. Sudden movements seemed like a terrible idea.

"If you tell the police I was here tonight shooting you with a flashlight, they won't believe you. Andrea and I had dinner in her cozy little room at the B and B and then I went upstairs to bed early at, nine-thirty."

"I don't want to tell anyone anything." Taylor tugged her bathrobe belt just to have something to do with her hands. It cinched around her waist and she wondered if it would be strong enough to tie Nancy up. "I don't want to tell anyone that Gina and Mom had been fighting about a quilt pattern."

Nancy nodded. "That's more like it."

"But sincerely, that's all she told me. They had been fighting, but then they made up."

"I don't believe you." Nancy pulled out a kitchen chair and sat with a heavy sigh. The flashlight-gun went every which direction as she sat, but it pointed back at Taylor before she could grab the phone. "She told you other things. Gina called me. She told me she was coming here to make sure I hadn't done anything crazy."

"I told her you hadn't. You've been perfectly nice."

"That's because I am perfectly nice." Except for those cold hard eyes, she was even perfectly "nice" right now. Calm, smooth. Collected. Not at all like her nervous, manic daughter.

Taylor leaned on the counter, feeling proximity to that old cordless phone resting just out of reach.

"What did she tell you?"

"She told me that you were a lot of work, to be honest. And she had worried you'd come down here and tell me things that made her look like she had killed Mom." This wasn't a word for word report, but it was close enough. "And she told me about

265

the quilt pattern and the fight. She told me about how sad she was that her friend was dead. That's all she told me." Taylor wracked her brain trying to think of anything else. "Oh! And she told me about Colleen and your son. That was the last thing she told me."

Nancy shook her head, her face creasing in a frown. "Are you sure? That's everything?"

"Yes, I swear it is."

"Now, how hard was that?" Nancy stood, pointing the flashlight-gun at the floor. "I shouldn't have had to use this."

Another shot rang out in the night, from far away. Maybe a local person shooting a pest animal on their property. Maybe someone just messing around. Either way, it explained why no one seemed to care about the shot that had been fired in her front yard. And it reminded her again that she really was all alone.

Rather than attempt to disarm Nancy, Taylor needed to get her in the car and on the road.

"I'm sorry." Taylor held out a hand for her to shake. "Can you forgive me?"

Nancy seemed to consider this. "It's easier to forgive you than it was to forgive your mother for bringing that horrible woman around my daughter, after what she had done to my son." She held the gun up again. Crap.

"It must have been just awful to see Colleen again."

"It was rude. Insult to injury. Your mother was a terrible person."

Taylor opened her mouth to tell Nancy to go to hell, but she remembered the flashlight was a deadly one and shut it again.

"Not only did she want to rub my face in the fancy life that horrible Colleen had managed to create for herself after she destroyed my Brick, your mother was also trying to destroy my baby. My only daughter."

"But how?" Taylor whispered. She stood there, one hand out to a woman facing her with a gun, and her only hope of help stuck behind that stupid stack of wire baskets on the counter.

She wanted to drag some kind of confession out of Nancy, but with no witnesses, what good would it do?

Panic fought with hysteria, or where they the same?

Her head spun and her breath was ragged.

Business school had not prepared her for this.

"My Brick made this for me." Nancy stroked the side of the gun. "What's nice about it is, it's not registered and totally untraceable." She looked down at the weapon kindly, lost for a moment in memory of the criminal she had born and loved. "Not that you always need a gun to get the job done." She admitted the gun, gazing at it lovingly.

Taylor lunged, knocking her to the ground. The gun went off again, but Nancy's hand had fallen to the side and the bullet hit the kitchen door.

Taylor held her on the ground, a knee to Nancy's neck. She twisted Nancy's wrist till it went limp. Then she grabbed the weapon and stared at Nancy's face.

Nancy showed no sign of fear.

Panting, Taylor crawled backward, sitting on her feet, gun behind her back. "I'm all alone." She panted for enough breath to speak. "No one is coming to rescue me. But then again, no one is coming for you either." She stood slowly, one hand tight on the gun, scared she'd lose control of herself and drop it.

She knocked the stack of metal wire baskets to the floor with a clatter and picked up the phone with her other hand. She pointed the gun at the fridge as she dialed 911. She didn't know how to shoot it, so it didn't matter what it was aimed at.

"Police, fire, or ambulance?" The voice answered

"Police," Taylor said. "I've disarmed an intruder in my home."

CHAPTER TWENTY-ONE

*T*aylor called Roxy first thing in the morning and let her know that due to a pile of life crisis she hadn't expected, she would not be in.

"Taylor…. oh, you poor thing. I've got the shop for you. Let's talk as soon as you can breathe, okay?"

"Sure." Taylor didn't have a single idea of when she'd be able to breathe again.

All of her goals before last night seemed so small and useless. Film more YouTube videos? Please. She needed to convince the sheriff that an old lady had killed her mom, and she had no evidence.

Keep Belle from suing for emancipation? Emancipation wasn't death, and Taylor needed to figure out how to keep her grandfather alive.

Keep the shop running so her one employee would not have to find a new job? You know what, that still mattered, but it didn't matter so much at this moment. Taylor didn't mean to be heartless, but it was a big country. There had to be a job some- where if she failed and Flour Sax closed up.

Taylor called Belle next but didn't get an answer, so she

texted. Just good luck with the advisor. What else was there to say? Sissy was better at mothering than Taylor was, anyway.

She ate some bread and peanut butter, not bothering to toast it, then drove to the hospital. Guilt burbled inside her because she hoped that they'd want to keep him all day so she wouldn't have to worry about him while she was with the sheriff.

Grandpa Ernie was asleep when she got there, and the doctor wasn't available either. She sat in his room, listening to his snores while reading the news on her phone. Hurry up and wait, hurry up and wait. There was a reason people said that with a groan of despair.

Eventually a very nice doctor about her age showed up. The doctor read the chart then offered Taylor a handshake. "You're the granddaughter?"

"Yes." Taylor stood and stretched a little. "How's he doing?"

The doctor smiled at Grandpa Ernie. "He had a rough night, I'll be honest. He only fell asleep around five this morning. Do you know if he usually sleeps well?"

"I'm sorry, I don't."

"No matter. I'd like to keep him another night. He's sleeping great now, but if he tends to sleep all day and not in the night we should know."

Taylor pictured him snoozing most of the day away in his recliner. "I think he might."

"I'd like to order oxygen for him for home. It's clear that he needs it. It can help quite a few of the symptoms associated with aging. For example, how is his memory?"

"It's not great."

"I'd like to see how that changes with oxygen. For today, let's let him sleep. We can monitor him overnight again, and then talk tomorrow. Will that work for you?"

"Definitely." Taylor agreed and tried not to think of Roxy alone at the store for another day.

The doctor glanced at the chart one more time. "See you tomorrow, okay? We can make a plan then."

Taylor thanked her. She didn't know if the doctor was an internist or a gerontologist or what. She didn't even remember her name. But that could wait for tomorrow. For today at least, Grandpa Ernie was safe and sleeping, and that was all she needed.

Her phone told her the sheriff's office was here in McMinnville just across the South Yamhill River from the hospital, so she headed there.

Last night Taylor had told the police far more than was useful. Her statement had begun with the death of her mother and ended with the fight in the kitchen. It had run the gamut from adoption to raccoon infestation. She was supposed to come in today to sign a formal statement. She didn't know what she could say that hadn't been said already, except that she was definitely pressing charges.

Once at the station she waited for her turn with the lady at the front desk. The deputy who had taken her late night rambling tell-all invited her to a private room to write a statement of exactly what happened last night, and last night alone. It took a while—it was harder to remember all of the specific details than she had anticipated. She passed it to him.

He glanced at it, then leaned back in his chair. "You were telling me last night that you had questions about the death of your mother."

Taylor sucked a breath in. Questions about her death didn't begin to describe what she was thinking. "It seems to be highly unlikely that a healthy woman would fall like she did."

"The record of her death indicates there was an autopsy and no sign of foul play was indicated."

"Maybe she had been drugged. Did you take samples for a lab?" Taylor asked.

"It seemed a cut and dried accident, to us and to the coroner. But we aren't perfect, and we know it."

"Something happened to make my mom fall. Something worse than a margarita and the heel of her shoe getting stuck. If not poison, then she was pushed. And if she was pushed, I think it was Nancy Reese." Before he could interrupt, Taylor continued. "Nancy was desperate to know what her daughter told me. Why did she need a gun if it wasn't a lethal case?"

"The good news, if there is any in all of this, is that we have Nancy here now, and we know your concerns. That may be cold comfort, but it's a big step considering we didn't know we had a case till last night." He stood up.

Taylor did as well. They shook hands and she headed out. But where to? Home to sit alone and worry? The hospital to sit with Grandpa Ernie and worry? The shop to sell fabric and worry?

She considered going to Maddie, like she had asked, but that didn't sound like it was right either. Taylor needed real support right now. Someone she could count on.

GRANDMA QUINNY WAS on her back porch giving directions to Grandpa Quinny as he worked the soil in the family strawberry patch.

"It's all fallen apart now." Taylor sat next to her grandmother on a wrought iron chair.

"It was bound to, darling. It's not your fault." Grandma Quinny patted her hand softly. "You've done the right thing in coming home, and the right thing in coming here today."

"Grandpa Ernie's going to go on oxygen. The doctor thinks that could help a lot of his symptoms."

"I'm glad to hear that. He's always been one of my favorite people. It was hard to see him growing so very old so fast." She lifted an eyebrow.

"I'm not ready to kick him out of his home." Taylor sipped her lemonade. It was sweet and tart. It refreshed and made things clearer in her mind. "I don't know if I could anyway. I don't have any kind of legal right to. But I can get a day nurse, or whatever they're called."

"That's awfully expensive, Taylor." Grandma Quinn turned back to her husband for a moment. "Don't forget over there by the dogwood!"

He waved acknowledgment of her directions.

"The finances are complicated, I'll admit it. But there's enough money. Especially if it is only part-time."

"Good."

Taylor was relieved Grandma Quinny didn't question her too closely. "You wouldn't happen to know where to start looking for someone, would you?"

Grandma Quinny's eyes lit up. "You know, your cousin Ellery really enjoyed herself the night she stayed with him. And she is a certified nursing assistant."

"But doesn't she have a job?" Taylor dragged her finger across the beads of condensation on her glass.

"She's been trying to get into nursing school but has to get her math scores up first. She could use a job that left room for night classes." Grandma Quinny said it without judgment. Taylor wondered if Ellery was the current favorite, or if Grandma Quinny was just giving her a good sales pitch. She didn't have to though, Taylor liked Ellery. A kind, strong girl about four years older than Belle. The kind of girl you'd trust with your aging grandparent.

"I'll call her. She could be a real help to me."

"If you have plenty of money, you need more help at the store too. But I think you know that."

"I dream of the day I can sit with the books and make a full-fledged business plan. I don't know that Mom ever had one, and the business has changed an awful lot in the last decade."

"You should get Reid to come and fix up your website."

Grandma Quinny was speaking of the cousin who had been at the house playing cards the other day. Taylor laughed. "I'm sure what he really wants to do is make a flashy site for a quilt shop."

"You're family. He'd help you."

"Another thing to add to the list."

"Every life has a list, Taylor." Grandma Quinny held her hand to her eyes like a visor to get a better look at Grandpa. "Your list is quite long right now, but you don't have to do it all alone. We're here for you."

Taylor set her lemonade on the table, glad that there were two people out there who she could lean on when everyone else was leaning on her.

TAYLOR WAS at the school at 2:55 ready to pick up Belle.

Belle agreed to get in the car, but as she said, it was only for Grandpa Ernie's sake. As they drove to the hospital, Taylor caught Belle up on what happened the night before.

Belle stared at her feet in silence. She wasn't wearing the vintage Doc Martens. Just a pair of black and white Vans.

Taylor parked, slamming her brakes.

Belle sighed, a sound that got more annoying every day that passed. "We need to talk to Gina."

"We need to go in and see about Grandpa Ernie and his oxygen levels."

"Gina knows something. She came to see you to find out if her mom told you the 'thing'. Then Nancy came back to see if Gina told you the 'thing'. Of the two, Gina is clearly the one who would be easiest to crack." Belle glanced at her phone. "We're what, two hours from Troutdale because of traffic?"

"Yeah…"

Belle ground her teeth and scrunched her mouth. "I guess we can call and see if we can lure her down here."

"Nancy would have called Gina from jail, right? So it's not like she's going to answer a phone call from one of us."

"Which is why storming her gates would be better." Belle's eyes were narrowed, her face flexed with intensity.

"Doesn't it seem like Gina would be here, with her mom?" Taylor drummed her fingers on her steering wheel. "I feel like she'd have come down here to make bail, at least."

"Then we're back to calling." Belle tapped around on her phone for a while, then held it to her ear. She waited but ended the call in frustration. "No voicemail."

"How did you get that number?"

"Research. It's not hard. I guess we go in and talk to Gramps, but we're not done with this. Nancy tried to kill you, Taylor. That's big."

Taylor unbuckled and popped her door open. She didn't like the tone Belle was taking, like she was the adult and Taylor was the foolish kid messing around with something serious and beyond her scope. "I know."

When they got to Grandpa Ernie's room he was arguing with the nurse. "No one sleeps well at a hospital at night."

The nurse smiled at him, but her eyes were hard. "Your oxygen has been great all day."

"Sure, they're pumping me full of it, like I'm some old sick guy who can't breathe."

The nurse lifted an eyebrow at him, then turned to the girls. "Here to see Ernie? He's full of beans today."

"I'm hardly full of anything. They feed me terrible." He looked wonderful, all things considered. The hospital gown with its light blue pattern on white background wasn't the most stylish piece of clothing the old tailor had ever worn, but he had color in his cheeks and a twinkle in his eye. His hair was mussed though, and Taylor wanted to find a comb to fix it.

"Has the doctor been in recently?" Taylor sat in the visitor's chair.

Belle took a rolling stool and pulled it up to him. "Bad night?"

"Terrible. Let's get out of here and get some burgers."

"Can't. I have some homework to make up. I got a little behind on a project."

Taylor's mom-stand-in antennae tingled. "Did you get to talk to your advisor?"

"Yeah. They're bending the rules for me. Just this time. Just because Mom is dead. They accepted that I would never have missed an appointment if Mom hadn't died, and even acknowledged that intellectual theft is real theft."

"Are they going to do anything about the girl stealing your project?"

"Nope. While they acknowledged it was real theft, they didn't care."

Grandpa Ernie coughed. "Idiots. We'll see what they say after I'm done talking to them."

Belle reached for his hand and held it. "Thanks Gramps, it's nice knowing you have my back."

"Grandpa, I have an errand to run, can I leave Belle with you?"

Belle shot her a look of great frustration.

"No, you can't. I'm exhausted and can't babysit." He huffed into his mustache.

"Okay then. I hate to leave you like this, but we do have to run." Taylor kissed his cheek and left.

A bug had bit her when Belle mentioned intellectual property theft, and more than ever, she needed to talk to Gina.

Belle was on her heels, and they were back at the car in seconds. "Call Gina. Keep calling her, and texting. She's got to pick up eventually."

While she was giving instructions, her own phone rang. Maddie.

Taylor stared at her name on the screen. She gave in and answered—using the blue tooth built into her mom's car. "Yes?"

"We need to start over." Maddie sounded sad. "An important part of being a counselor is seeking regular counseling, and I see how I screwed up. I messed up helping Belle in a few different ways."

"Can we talk later?" Taylor was about five short minutes from the sheriff's office and all she wanted to do was get there.

"We can, but if I could just say one more thing I need to confess."

"Make it quick."

"I wanted to publish an article about our experimental treatment. I was using Belle's grief for my gain and I am so sincerely sorry."

Taylor held her tongue. She had words for Maddie, and questions for her, but this was not the time. "Okay. I hear you. We'll talk later."

"Just…."

"No, not 'just' anything. Seriously Maddie, this is not your issue or your concern. I need to run."

"Okay. Later then."

Taylor ended the call and snarled at the phone.

"Still no answer." Belle had been steadily trying to get in touch with Gina.

"That's okay. We're here." Taylor pulled into the parking lot at the sheriff's office. "You know how the teachers didn't really care that the student stole your project?"

"Yes, I am painfully aware of that."

"Well, I care. I care so much I want to go punch the teachers."

"Hmm. Interesting."

"Because you don't want to punch them, right? I'm way angrier than you are."

"I wouldn't say angrier…."

"I would. Punching is very much angrier than not punching."

"Fine." Belle poked at her phone.

"Similarly, Nancy was far angrier than Gina was over that thing with Mom's quilt. I think Nancy was so angry that she got physical with Mom and caused her death. Probably manslaughter and not murder, but still."

"And that's what Gina knows, isn't it?" Belle was quick to pick up the trail Taylor was going down.

"Yes, that's what she knows."

Taylor had her hopes pinned on talking to Nancy one more time. She didn't know if they'd let her, but if she had the chance, she just knew she could egg her into some kind of dramatic confession. Especially if she played it like Father Brown and implied Nancy would get a much easier sentence if she admitted the fight she had engaged in with her mom.

But as she walked toward the building, a weeping Gina Croyden was walking out.

Belle and Taylor moved as a unit, flanking her.

"She wasn't there, was she?" Taylor asked, not giving any kind of room for subtlety. "When you went to check in on Nancy the night my mom died. Did you wait up for her till she got back? Or did you just go to sleep?"

Gina tried to push away, but she was a shaking, confused mess.

It was easy to guide her to a bench. "The next morning, when Mom was found, did you realize where your own mother had been? When you were talking to the police did you tell them what you suspected?"

"Mom could have been in the bathroom." Gina's words were shaky whispers. "She might have been in the bathroom. I told them I said good night to her. I did. She wasn't in bed, so I said goodnight anyway, because she was probably in the bathroom."

"What did your mother say when you asked her where she had been?" Taylor kept probing.

"Nothing, she said to forget it. She said whatever happened wasn't our problem."

"But you know your mom." Taylor was talking too fast, too aggressively. She needed to cool it down, find a way to make Gina feel safe. "Come inside, let's sit down."

Gina froze.

"Let's go back inside, you need to talk to the deputy."

"She might have just been in the bathroom," Gina's voice was a whisper.

"She was really mad about the quilt pattern though, wasn't she?" Taylor matched her whisper and held the door open.

Gina nodded.

"You forgave my mom, but Nancy didn't."

Gina nodded again.

Beside her, Belle was also agitated. She held her hand out to stop Taylor. "Gina, I'm sorry. This must be an awful kind of revelation."

"Nothing has been this bad since Brick passed…" Gina held her hand to her eyes as her shoulders shook with body wracking sobs.

"What happened to your brother?" Belle asked.

Taylor shuddered, remembering Belle did not know she was asking about her own biological father.

"It was a fight—they said it was a fight. He was stabbed in an alley not far from Mom's house. He'd been robbed."

"No drugs on him?"

"Plenty in his system. He'd promised Mom he would stay sober."

"Oh crap." It was an unsatisfying oath, but the picture came to Taylor so clearly that the words just escaped. "Your Mom was really mad about it, wasn't she?"

"If he had just stayed clean." Gina took one last wracking breath, and then her sobbing stopped. She found a seat in the waiting room and sunk into it.

"What made you think it was your mom?"

Gina looked up at Taylor, her eyes terrified. "It was her knife. I'd know it anywhere. The one she used to clean fish when we were camping as kids. Just a knife, and yet, the handle was this worn, red plastic. So familiar. How could he let someone kill him with a knife like that, if it was really a fight? He'd have snapped the handle. But if it was his own mom, and he didn't see it coming.? Didn't think she'd stab him?"

Belle leapt to her feet and began pacing. "They probably said he was high and that's why someone with a weak knife like that was able to kill him."

Gina nodded. "Just pot though. He was trying to stay clean. But it was enough for her. He'd promised Mom he'd stay off everything."

Belle raked her hand through her hair. "And then she got mad at Mom..." She caught Taylor's eye, and Taylor nodded. "And she tried to kill you, Taylor. Gina, you have got to go tell them what you know. Please. She's got to get off the streets. She will get mad again. You know that, right?"

Gina glanced at her forearm where Taylor saw the scar again. The jagged, round wound like a stab wound. Gina pushed her sweater sleeve over it.

"Come with us, please. If she's sick, she can get help in the system, somehow, and then she won't hurt anyone ever again."

Gina stood and they walked in together, but the deputy spoke with her alone.

CHAPTER TWENTY-TWO

On Gina Croyden's testimony, Nancy Reese was held without bail on charges of the attempted murder of Taylor Quinn, while investigations were opened into the deaths of Richard "Brick" O'Doyle, and Laura Quinn.

Taylor wouldn't be satisfied till she heard the final verdict. Or maybe she'd never be satisfied, since none of this would bring her mom back.

But Nancy being held without bail wasn't the end of her problems. Grandpa Ernie was home from the hospital, and though her cousin Ellery was a good babysitter, he was not thankful to be babysat.

Taylor also still had raccoons in her attic, Belle had snuck her weird genius boyfriend over and he had stayed the night, and they were behind schedule on the YouTube series.

These were the tales of woe and trial Taylor poured out for Hudson over dinner at Berry Noir.

He passed her his phone. The number for a local pest control was on the screen. "Call now and it's one thing off that list."

She smiled fondly at the phone. She could appreciate a problem solver. She used to think she was one, after all. She called and scheduled the raccoon removal for the beginning of the next week.

"When they're gone," Hudson said, "I'll come in and do the real repair work. It's a pretty great apartment, I have to say. Ever thought of renting it out? Could be a nice side income for you."

"I'd rather turn it into the operations base for Flour Sax. Mom was onto something with her show. This could get pretty big if I play it right."

"Everyone but Dutch Hex would be thrilled."

Taylor laughed. Having a set plan for the raccoon problem had lifted a weight. "You follow Comfort quilt gossip?"

"Just since you came back to town." He gave her a half grin, his eyes hooded and frankly sexy. Though he wore yet another plaid shirt, this wasn't flannel, and he had that cleaned up on a date look that never does a man wrong.

"Listen…" Her mood shifted like a cloud on a windy day.

"I know, you're not up for a rebound. I get it. No pressure. And look! A change of subject." He grinned broadly. "How about I swing by this weekend and build a ramp for Ernie? I know the oxygen has been helpful, but I'm thinking those steps to the door might not be his best friends."

Taylor considered the amount of anger and fighting she'd get back from Grandpa Ernie if she made permanent changes to "his" house. "How about to the kitchen door?"

"Can do."

"Having my cousin stay with Grandpa Ernie is a temporary fix. I can see that now. He's going to have to go to a home and I'm going to have to figure out how to make that happen."

"That won't be easy."

"Nope."

They ate in silence for a few minutes.

"Speaking of quilt gossip, Shara over at Dutch Hex is refusing to participate in the Christmas in July event."

"Why?" Whether he really cared about quilt shop gossip or not, he acted like he did, which was sweet.

"She said it's against the aesthetic of her store."

"But she's pseudo Amish, right? And they're some kind of Christians."

"They're the not-fussy ones. They don't decorate for the holidays, I guess. I wonder if it's really that she can't pony up for the coop ads we're running." Taylor dabbed at the sauce that was left over on her plate with a bite of dinner roll.

"Let me guess, you had to put all of that together."

"Far from it. It's a well-organized event and no one even called to ask for help. Much good my retail management and MBA are in this town." Not that Taylor minded right now. She couldn't imagine when she would have found time to create an ad campaign. "There was an emergency meeting of the Guild the other day. They texted Mom's old number to tell us about it." Taylor shrugged. "They did call the shop to apologize and updated my contact info after I was a no-show."

"Your raccoon problem is checked off the list now, what's next? Belle? Need me to knock some sense into that guy who stayed over?"

"Nah, I suspect when she hits the scene at her new college, he's going to have a lot of competition. He won't be a problem forever."

"Won't those college boys be a worse problem than the genius kid her own age is?"

"Probably, but I won't know about it because she'll be on campus."

"They grow up fast, don't they?"

Taylor closed her eyes briefly and pictured Belle as an eleven year old ballet dancer. The kid she'd been when Taylor moved to grad school. "Too fast. So fast that I can't even laugh about it."

He changed the subject again and they discussed the food, the weather, and ideal vacation spots. His involved places where he could kill delicious animals.

Hers involved places she could go barefoot and wear a bikini.

He said the bikini tipped the scales and he'd take her vacation after all.

Taylor said he could bring his meat by any time and she'd cook it.

He nodded in approval, and she blushed. It went on like that for a while, then they called it a night.

She drove herself home.

She wasn't ready for a fling, or a rebound, or even a healthy relationship with a nice guy. She just had too much on her plate for any of that right now.

They say after someone major in your life dies you should hold off on any decisions for a year. Her mom had waited a full year before she'd adopted Belle. Taylor now knew that hadn't been a planned decision on her part, but her big heart reaching out to a friend in need.

Belle was at the beach with the Kirby family at this very moment. She hadn't texted so Taylor didn't know how it was going from her perspective, but Dave had sent pictures, and Colleen had sent some messages.

Dave's eldest daughter had joined them too. There was a picture of Belle and Ashleigh sitting on a log that pinched Taylor's heart painfully. She should have been the one sitting with Belle. She was her real sister, after all.

BELLE AGREED to walk with the graduating class because Grandpa Ernie asked. Her exact words were, "Oh Gramps, it's dumb."

And he scowled at her and said, "Education is the exact opposite of that."

And she laughed and said, "I'll do it, but only for you."

The graduation was in the grand auditorium at the Comfort College of Art and Craft. The graduating class wore silver colored gowns for the ladies and black for the boys. It was an outdated tradition, but Taylor was excited to see what color Dayton would wear. Then she remembered Dayton was not graduating till next year.

They had plenty of seats, so Grandpa and Grandma Quinn sat with the family, as well as her cousin Ellery.

And Colleen and Dave.

Belle had invited them. She hadn't said she was going to, but Colleen had called and asked if it would be all right.

What could Taylor say to that?

She wanted to echo Belle and tell Colleen graduation was dumb so she wouldn't come. But like Grandpa Ernie, she knew that graduation was the opposite of dumb and that it was an event Belle needed everyone who loved her at, since she didn't have her mom.

Taylor took more pictures than was healthy.

Cooper's sister Pyper graduated as well, so they got pictures of Belle and Cooper and Pyper with Sissy and her husband, and Pyper and Belle and Cooper and Dayton. So many pictures. Taylor would cherish them. She considered photoshopping a partially translucent mom floating over them as a Victorian-ish symbol of how she was still with them, but she managed to refrain.

For now.

Sissy's family held a barbecue to celebrate the graduation.

Taylor had expected Grandma and Grandpa Quinny to offer to host one for Belle. Her own had been at their house. But she took their attendance at Sissy's party as a good sign. A sign they were investing in Belle in a new way. A sign they were seeing she had needed them all along, maybe.

But Taylor tried not to hope for too much from everyone.

She expected Belle to come home for the holidays, but toward the end of the party at the Dorney house Colleen, Dave, and Belle were huddled in a corner together comparing phones. She feared they were making holiday plans and didn't dare approach them.

But Dave spotted her staring at them and waved her over. "Belle was telling us there's a fall break. We were thinking it would be a good opportunity for another family beach trip. Do you think you might be free for it?"

Taylor sucked her bottom lip in thought.

Belle held out her phone. "That's the weekend."

It was early. Weeks before Thanksgiving. "Let me check with Ellery and Roxy. It depends a little on their schedules."

Dave nodded approval. "But if Ellery's not free, we'd be honored to have Grandpa Ernie join us. All of our parents are gone, and the boys could use a grandpa."

Taylor swallowed thickly. He was such an honestly nice guy, this Dave. "I'll get back to you about it." She wandered away, but Belle followed.

"Tay, I like Dave."

"I know." Taylor sat on the step to the back porch. Sissy lived in a new home, in the new development with a thick, green, new lawn rolled out over a perfectly flat and newly fenced yard. The party was dying down and she found all of the newness and freshness and greenness around her soothing.

Belle sat next to her. "I've never had a dad before. Mom never even had a boyfriend."

"And Grandpa Ernie wasn't young when you were growing up," Taylor offered.

"No…he wasn't."

Belle straightened up, as though she had to resolve to confess something. "I've always wanted a dad. You guys talked about your dad so much, the whole concept of 'dad' sounded magical. You did such a good job keeping his memory alive that it made me want one. Of my own."

"And now you have Dave."

Belle took Taylor's hand. "Exactly. I had a mom. The best mom ever. But I've never had a dad."

Taylor turned to her and wrapped her in her arms. "I'm sorry."

Belle gave her a quick kiss on the cheek. "Don't be. Dave is a good thing and I'm happy to know him."

"And Colleen?"

"It's funny...technically Dave would be like, my stepdad, but it feels backwards from that. Like Colleen is a stepmom. Not my actual mom, but someone who wants to know me and love me. And Dave feels like...."

"Like the first dad you've ever had."

Belle bit her lip like a little girl. "I don't know if this is what having a real dad feels like, but I like it." She peeked at her phone. It must have vibrated. Her faced turned pink.

"Levi?"

She nodded slightly and left.

Taylor sat up, stretching her arms out before her. Well, this was it. Her new normal. Mostly alone, but with a great deal of responsibility. Not mom to a teen finishing high school, but big sister to a young adult with more opportunity than seemed right for her age.

Taylor didn't know how she was going to do it, but as she looked around at Sissy laughing with Dayton and Cooper, Dave and Colleen pointing toward the sunset, his arm around her shoulders, and all of little Comfort enveloping them in its familiar arms, she realized a funny thing. Though her mom was gone and Clay had dumped her, she wasn't really alone. As far as the hard parts of life were concerned, she did not have to handle any of it by herself.

BOUND *and Deceased*

November rain battered the sides of the little house on Love Street. Taylor Quinn snuggled deep into her quilt. Her bedroom window was shut to the warring weather and her door was barred with the dresser she had dragged in front of it before turning out her light.

She'd managed to get her heart rate to settle down with the aid of her mother's soothing voice on the phone.

If there was one comfort left in life, it was that Laura Quinn had recorded so many episodes of her YouTube show before her death almost nine months ago.

Some nights were better than others.

Some nights Taylor didn't think of the murderer who had attacked her in the kitchen of her own home.

But most nights she did.

It was already midnight.

She needed to shut off her phone and go to sleep.

She missed sleeping.

She missed closing her eyes and the world turning off.

With her baby sister Belle living on campus now, Taylor's mind never turned off, and neither did her phone. What if Belle needed her? She was only sixteen and that school was full of older guys who liked to drink.

Taylor gave her phone screen a quick, embarrassed kiss and closed YouTube. It was a little painful to turn her mom's videos off, as though watching them would make up for all of the times she hadn't returned her calls or hadn't gone home for a visit.

The phone buzzed a text just as she was setting it on her side table.

Her heart twisted at the sound.

Had the worst happened? She grabbed it up and stared at the picture attached to the phone number.

It was a face she hadn't seen in months, though she still thought about him every day. A picture she didn't want to see. She froze, overwhelmed with anger and hope and dread all at once.

"*I drove all night. I'm here. Can I see you?*" Clay Seldon, the ex-boyfriend.

"*What?*" That single word response was all Taylor could

muster. She sat up and hunched forward, not really trusting her senses.

After the initial shock of her mom's death had passed, Taylor had been left to face everything else she had lost when she moved back to her hometown to finish raising her teenage sister: her home in the city, her career, and her boyfriend of four years.

"There aren't any hotels in this town and I'm in the cloth top Rabbit. Please let me in out of the cold."

It was a horribly wet night, but not all that cold, not hurts-you-cold. This was a mild November. Constantly damp, but not freezing. Clay could sleep in his car just fine or he could drive home again, the same way he had come. He could even warm up with a coffee from the twenty-four hour Arco to keep awake.

And yet, her heart nudged her to let him in, to help ease the fear and loneliness of this new life she lived, at least for a night.

She would have given anything for her mother's wisdom right now. She navigated away from the texts that stood there like little temptations and opened the Flour Sax Quilt Shop YouTube channel again.

The smiling, warm, and loving face of her mother was practically begging to be listened to. Not that she needed the video. Her mom's voice was in her head right now, telling her she needed to learn to be content with her own company.

Taylor turned to the video she had just watched.

Laura Quinn the famous quilter, teaching the audience how to pin the corners of their quilt blocks so they match.

Over and over she showed them dozens of wrong ways, and the one right way. As she worked, she said, "Spending time with practice squares will save you tons of heartache once you're working on a real quilt. It's soothing, too, in its own way. Contemplative, even. When my eldest daughter was little, I used to make her do this. She wasn't much for playing by herself and it drove her to distraction, but I made her do it. 'Taylor Rae Quinn...' I'd say..."

Taylor backed up the video and listened to her mom give this advice again. And again. Be comfortable with her own company.

Someday she'd be comfortable alone again.

She turned her phone off and set it on the bedside table.

She took a deep, cleansing breath and reached up to the ceiling, stretching the muscles of her shoulders and back.

Grandpa Ernie was just downstairs.

She wasn't alone.

The doorbell rang.

Taylor collapsed, shoulders curving forward, arms wrapping around her abdomen. She shivered.

It was just Clay.

It was just Clay.

It wasn't a maniac who had stolen his phone and used it to find her.

This wasn't a reasonable fear, but cold sweat broke out on her forehead.

She knew it was what they called traumatic stress response. Because of the fight she'd had with the woman who'd killed her mother, she panicked at unexpected midnight visitors. And loud noises. And people who popped by in the daytime, or who said "Hi!" too loudly when she didn't see them coming.

Her phone buzzed, rattling on the old wooden nightstand.

She picked it up with a shaking hand, turned it over, and swiped it open.

The text was a photo of Clay's face, pouting. He stood on her front doorstep, the streetlight casting a gray-green haze on the road behind him.

Visit your favorite online retailer to buy Bound and Deceased!

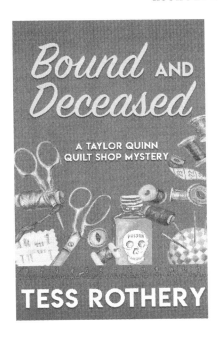

She had the pattern for a perfect life, but murder has her all to pieces.

Taylor is a fixer when it comes to quilts, cases, and her family. As she continues to mourn her mother, she hopes to turn her unintentional rival Sissy into her first friend in sleepy Comfort, Oregon. But when her new pal's favorite aunt suffers a poisonous fate, Taylor must switch her attention from cotton to killers.

As Taylor digs deeper, she finds a host of frustrated family members, all of whom could have done the deed. With her town in danger and her anxiety on the rise, she follows the victim's fortune to pin a top suspect as quickly as possible. But when her instincts are dead wrong, all she gets for her troubles is a massive target stitched to her back.

Can Taylor nab the killer before her new small town life ends up six-feet-under?

Bound and Deceased is the second book in the Taylor Quinn Quilt Shop series of cozy mysteries. If you like believable characters, surprising clues, and heartwarming relationships, then you'll love Tess Rothery's poignant, delightful story.

Buy *Bound and Deceased* to cozy up with your favorite quilter today!

FLOUR SAX ROW
2016 Home Sweet Home

GRANDMA'S CABIN
Grandma's Pride framed in a Log Cabin

Assault and Batting is Taylor Quinn's coming home story, so the Flour Sax Quilt Shop row for this book is 2016's theme, Home Sweet Home.

I suspect you can imagine why Grandma's Pride is integral to the Flour Sax's idea of home.

Pieces
For the Block

4 dark squares, 2"
4 medium squares 2"
4 medium light squares, 2"
4 light squares, 2"
4 very light squares, 2" cut into half triangles
1 very light square, 2" cut into quarter triangles

1 light strip, 1" wide by 6.5" long
1 light strip, 1" wide by 7" long
1 medium strip, 1" wide by 7" long
1 medium strip, 1" wide by 8" long
1 dark strip, 1" wide by 8" long
1 dark strip 1" wide by 8.5" long
1 very dark strip 1" wide by 8.5" long
1 very dark strip 1" wide by 9.5" long

The finished row fudges a bit on the 9"x 36" row size so cut the outside strips a little large to give you room to cut the row to size.

ABOUT THE AUTHOR

Tess Rothery is an avid quilter, knitter, writer and publishing teacher. She lives with her cozy little family in Washington State where the rainy days are best spent with a dog by her side, a mug of hot coffee, and something mysterious to read.

Sign up for her newsletter at TessRothery.com so you won't miss the next book in the Taylor Quinn Quilt Shop Mystery Series.